FIRST TO
KILL

Also by Andrew Peterson

Forced to Kill
Option to Kill

FIRST TO
KILL

ANDREW
PETERSON

TTHOMAS & MERCER

The characters and events portrayed in this book are fictitious. Any similarity to real persons, living or dead, is coincidental and not intended by the author.

Text copyright © 2012 Andrew Peterson

Published by Thomas & Mercer
P.O. Box 400818
Las Vegas, NV 89140

ISBN-13: 9781612187082
ISBN-10: 1612187080

Dedication

To my wife, Carla. You've been my best friend for twenty-four years.

PROLOGUE

The warm glow from the cabin's window told a lie. The scream from within told the truth. Bound to a chair with baling wire, the federal agent was thoroughly battered. Eyes swollen shut, fractured cheekbones, chipped teeth, and worse. Kicked aside, six severed fingers lay scattered on the plank floor. The air reeked of cigar smoke and charred flesh from dozens of burns that marched up the man's arms and across his chest like tiny cattle brands. Where he'd struggled against the wire, his wrists and ankles were torn and bleeding.

"He's out again." Ernie Bridgestone grabbed the man's hair and yanked his head back. Bridgestone, a trained drill instructor, was tall and lean with a thin mustache, cropped dark hair, and acne-cratered cheeks.

"Leave him be. He's had enough." Leonard Bridgestone towered over his younger brother and outweighed him by sixty pounds. Aside from their clothing, blood-spattered T-shirts, old woodland fatigues, and combat boots, they looked nothing alike except for their pale blue eyes—a gift from their mother's side. They never talked about their father's gifts.

Ernie released him. "I'll give the dumb son of a bitch credit, he lasted longer than I would've."

"Let's hope you never have to find out." Leonard was a trained Army Ranger, but unlike Ernie, he'd been decorated during the first Gulf War with a Silver Star, two Purple Hearts, and a Navy Cross for rescuing a downed Hornet driver. He grabbed a five-gallon can of gas and began sloshing its contents around the cabin's stark interior. He saved the last two gallons for human flesh and tipped the can just above the agent's head. The man shivered and moaned under the stinging fluid.

As the smell of gasoline fouled the air, the rain intensified. The windows flashed white. Once. Twice. Half a second later, thunder rattled the glass.

"Damn shame to torch this place," Ernie said.

Leonard parted the curtain and looked out the window, where morning twilight crept across the Sierra Nevada. "I figure we've got three days, max. He said his last check-in was five days ago and they expect to hear from him at least once a week."

"But Lester saw him in town yesterday. He could've reported in already."

"Naw, he would've told us. It only took two fingers to verify he was FBI. Nobody can take what we did to him, not for five hours. No way."

Ernie spat in the man's face. "I still can't believe this asshole set us up."

"Kinda evens the score a little."

Ernie grabbed the bloody pliers, wire cutters, and ice pick from the table.

"Leave those."

"They're perfectly good tools."

"Leave 'em. Don't let anger cloud your thinking. This isn't about revenge."

"The hell it isn't."

"Let it go, Ernie."

"Easy for *you* to say." He hurled the pliers across the room.

Leonard understood his brother's anger. In Ernie's third year in the US Disciplinary Barracks at Fort Leavenworth, several inmates had beaten him to the brink of death for stealing a pack of cigarettes. He'd spent fourteen weeks in the infirmary, the first two in a coma.

The fed stirred in his chair and moaned. Leonard approached and crouched down like a catcher. "You got something more to say?"

"Kill me...First..."

Leonard looked at his brother.

"Screw him. Let him feel it."

"He's been through enough." Leonard stepped back, pulled his .45, and took aim. But before he could shoot, Ernie shoved him aside and lit an entire book of matches.

"Then I'll do it."

"Ern, stop!"

But his brother tossed the matchbook as casually as dice at a craps table. The *whoosh* of ignition was chilling.

The burning man leaned his head back and howled.

Leonard raised his pistol again, but Ernie grabbed him and yanked him toward the door.

It was too late anyway. They retreated from the growing inferno out to the Bronco. Leonard got behind the wheel, but Ernie stood in the rain watching the fire until the heat forced him into the cab.

Leonard started to speak, but Ernie cut him off. "You're wrong," he said, his eyes glittering with flame. "It's always about revenge."

CHAPTER 1

Stretched out in a room of the Crowne Plaza Hotel in San Diego, Nathan Daniel McBride stared at the ceiling. With a sigh, he touched his face where three deep scars reminded him of another time, another world. The longest scar started at his left ear, ran down the side of his face, and ended at the tip of his chin. The next followed a diagonal path from the top of his forehead, across the bridge of his nose, and etched his left cheek. Visibly the worst, the third drew a deep arched line from temple to jaw. Nice touch, that one. At six foot five, 240 pounds, he kept himself in top physical condition. His forty-fifth birthday was right around the corner.

He rolled toward the woman beside him. In contrast, Mara had flawless skin. Her kind brown eyes and black hair perfectly complemented an athletic physique. In her midtwenties, she was nothing short of stunning. But perhaps what he appreciated the most about her was that she rarely broke their silent moments.

"Have I ever really thanked you?"

She slid a leg over his hips. "Thanked me? I should thank you. You're not like the others."

The others. It felt like slap in the face. Denial was so self-serving. Mara was a prostitute. He was a john. *One* of her johns, he reminded himself. Sure, they'd seen each other twice a week for the last eight months, but what kind of relationship was that? Empty. Going nowhere. She was so beautiful and he was...What? Did the scars make him ugly? Or something else. Like what he used to do for a living? He wondered how different his life would be if he hadn't become a marine. Would he have a wife and children? A home? Not just a roof over his head, but a real home with a sense of purpose and belonging? None of that mattered now. Fresh out of college, he'd joined the marines and discovered a natural aptitude he'd never known about. He could shoot and it didn't take the marines long to identify him. He spent seven years with the corps as an elite scout sniper before the CIA recruited him.

More than a decade ago, his career abruptly ended after a botched mission. He'd fallen into the hands of a sadistic interrogator and endured three weeks of pure torment. His Nicaraguan interrogator had carved him like Thanksgiving turkey. An inch apart, dozens of crisscrossing scars marred his torso, making him look like a human wicker basket. At the end, his interrogator crucified him in a tight vertical cage that forced him to stand. After four days and nights on his feet with no food or water, the pain in his legs had been literally blinding. He'd been hammered from infection and fever, drifting in and out of consciousness.

"Where are you?"

"Huh?"

"You were gone again."

"Sorry."

She traced one of the grooves on his chest with a forefinger.

"Are you happy, Mara?"

"You've never asked me that before." She smiled, but it didn't reach her eyes. "I can't meet you Friday."

He sat up. "What? Why not?"

"Shh...It's okay. I have another meeting. Some drug company bigwig. Karen set it up."

"Mara, if it's money…"

She touched his lips. "You're so generous to me. It's not the money."

"You could work at my security company. I can get you an apartment. You don't have to do this. It's dangerous."

"I'm glad you care. Will I see you next week?"

His cell interrupted them. He reached over to the nightstand.

"Nathan? It's Karen. That big guy's here again. He's got Cindy!"

"I'll be there in seven minutes. Can you make it out to the patio?"

"I think so."

"Do it. Turn off all the lights."

Two minutes later, he was striding through the hotel's lobby with Mara in tow. Once outside the automatic glass doors, he sprinted over to his Mustang. Mara's heels clicked on the concrete as she hurried to keep up.

After turning west onto Hotel Circle North, he accelerated to fifty. Mara fastened her seat belt as he swerved into the oncoming lane to pass an SUV.

"I thought it was over with that guy."

"Apparently he didn't understand my warning."

"What are you going to do?"

"Give him a stronger warning."

He ran the red light and smoked the tires merging onto I-8. Within ten seconds, he was doing eighty miles an hour as he screamed under the Morena Boulevard overpass. He followed a minivan down the I-5 north on-ramp before punching his Mustang up to 110 miles an hour.

Four minutes had passed since Karen's call. A lot could happen in four minutes. He forced the thought aside and concentrated on driving. His phone rang. Seeing his business partner's name on the screen, he answered it. A call this late at night raised concern. "Are you okay?"

"Me?" said Harvey. "Yeah."

"I can't talk right now."

"Are *you* okay?"

"Ten minutes."

"You got it."

Nathan felt additional pressure because Karen had called him, not the police. She could've dialed 911. He suspected the police knew about her escort service, but her women were high-class and low-key. Karen's women weren't hookers who trolled for twenty-dollar tricks to feed meth or heroin habits. They were escorts, sophisticated corporate types. Expensive. Besides, her operation was small and no one had blown the whistle. Karen had also called Nathan because of his relationship with Mara. He looked out for her and the other women. Several years ago, he'd personally installed a high-tech security system in Karen's house.

Nathan looked at his watch as he exited the freeway. Six minutes. Too damned long.

After slowing for a stop sign, he accelerated to sixty miles an hour.

"Nathan!"

He saw it.

An orange cat darted out from the left. It skidded to a stop in the middle of the street and froze. Shimmering in the headlights, its bluish-green eyes looked like tiny flashlights. Nathan executed a smooth adjustment of the wheel to the right and hugged the curb.

"Did we hit it?"

Mara whipped her head around. "No. It's still there."

Nathan eased away from the curb and braked hard for the next turn. Half a minute later, he parked fifty yards north of Karen's place and left the engine idling. It needed a cool down after being worked so hard.

"Stay here. Turn the engine off after a couple of minutes." He reached across Mara, popped the glove box, and grabbed his Sig Sauer P-226 9-millimeter. Climbing out, he jacked a hollow-point round into the chamber and lowered the hammer, using the pistol's de-cocking lever. He tucked the weapon into his blue jeans at the small of his back and sprinted up the sidewalk. Several houses distant, a dog barked three times, then went silent. Beneath orange cones of streetlight, chest-high recycle bins were stationed in the street like sentries.

An off-road pickup sat in Karen's driveway. It was hyped with oversized tires and augmented with floodlights mounted on a roll bar above the cab. Nathan shook his head. Everything oversized and out of control, just like its owner. He paused in Karen's yard and listened, then placed an ear against a dark window. No music. No sounds of a struggle. Nothing.

At the side yard, he reached over the top of the gate and unlatched the locking mechanism from its cradle. The gate swung silently. He advanced to the corner of the house and peered over a planter full of barrel cactus. Karen looked cold, hugging herself in the damp air. He issued a low, warbling whistle. She hurried over.

"What's the situation?"

"He's inside with Cindy."

"Where?"

"I don't know."

"Has he hurt her?"

"I don't know!"

"My Mustang's down the block."

"I can't leave Cindy."

"I'll handle this."

"Nathan—"

"Karen, please. Get going."

Anger began to stir as he pictured Cindy being brutalized by the guy. It tightened his body with adrenaline, threatening to overwhelm him. He closed his eyes, slowed his breathing, and relaxed his hands. When he'd calmed his mind, he removed his shirt and dropped it to the deck. He didn't want to give his opponent anything to grab.

He pulled his handgun and followed the rear wall of the house, his movements precise and silent. At each dark window, he paused and listened. All quiet. No sound at all. Working his way through the maze of potted plants and patio furniture, he approached the sliding glass door. Detecting no movement, he slipped inside.

He heard it right away. A man's voice. Muffled, from down the hall behind a closed door.

Another surge of adrenaline swept through him, this time under his command. A smile touched his lips. Nathan McBride, in his environment.

The next sound banished the smile, an unmistakable sound of a hand slapping flesh. Nathan kicked the door so violently it tore away from its hinges. Fully clothed, Cindy cowered on the floor in a corner, her legs tucked against her chest. The left side of her face showed a fresh impact.

The man leaning over her whipped around and squinted. "You."

"Yes, me."

Just as Nathan recalled, this guy was solid muscle and huge, taller by an inch or two. With his shaved head and hourglass torso, he looked like a bouncer. To anyone else, he might've looked intimidating. To Nathan, he was three hundred pounds of hamburger with an amphibian's brain attached.

Nathan stepped forward and slapped him with his free hand, a wet, meaty impact on the man's cheek. He moved back and waited for the reaction he knew was coming.

He looked Nathan in the eyes, looked at the gun, and then looked him in the eyes again.

"What, this?" Nathan tossed the Sig Sauer onto the carpet at the man's feet.

His expression confused, the bouncer looked down at the gun and unconsciously wiped his nostrils with his thumb and forefinger. Cocaine.

If this guy had any sense of reality, he would've surrendered right then and there, because he was now face-to-face with a shirtless opponent, covered in menacing scars, who looked like he belonged in a bare-knuckle cage-fighting match on an alien war planet. But this man wasn't thinking straight. No doubt he was accustomed to winning fights. Well, that was about to change.

Ignoring the gun at his feet, the bouncer lowered his head and charged.

Nathan saw it coming.

He sidestepped and shoved the man into the wall. The guy's head struck the drywall and left a cereal-bowl impression in its surface. Nathan kicked him in the ass, making the impression deeper. The man grunted, cursed, and yanked himself free.

Nathan stepped back. "It's a little cramped in here," he said. "Shall we finish this in the living room?"

"No problem."

Nathan gestured toward the door and moved aside, allowing the bouncer to exit the bedroom first. He pointed at Cindy. "Stay here." Following at a safe distance, he sensed his opponent disappear around the living-room corner more than he saw it. Then he heard a metallic sound and knew what it was.

The fireplace iron.

Nathan took loud, deliberate steps down the hall and stopped four feet short of the corner. The poker's black form *whooshed* and penetrated the wall where he would've been had he kept going. He kicked the bouncer's arm, pinning it to the wall, and had the satisfaction of feeling the mid-ulna and radius bones snap. The hand released the iron and fell away.

"That's gotta hurt," Nathan said. "Had enough?"

He stepped into the living room and the bouncer charged again, surprisingly fast, but not fast enough.

Nathan ducked low before thrusting upward with all his strength.

The man literally flew over Nathan's back and landed with a grunt. He rolled onto his belly, tried to get up, and seemed surprised when one of his arms didn't work.

"Broken," Nathan said.

"You're a dead man."

Nathan spread his arms and looked down at himself.

The bouncer struggled to his feet and lunged forward with a left jab zeroed at Nathan's jaw. Anticipating the punch, Nathan jerked his head to the right and snapped up with his left elbow, smashing the man's nose. That was a bingo. For 99.9 percent of Earth's population, that level of blunt-force trauma did the trick. Party over. Lights out. Send the babysitter home. But this man simply wiped his nose and squinted at the fresh blood on his fingers.

"It was cocked about thirteen degrees to the right," Nathan said. "It's straight now. No charge."

The bouncer grabbed a toppled chair with his good hand and hurled it. Nathan ducked. Behind him, the glass door shattered.

Roaring like a maniac, the bouncer charged a third time.

He never made it.

His foot caught on the corner of the coffee table. Had the fall not landed him squarely on an overturned chair, it would've been comical, but his left eye socket made solid contact with the bottom of the chair's leg. Three hundred pounds of momentum...With a little luck the eye could be saved, provided it wasn't dangling out of the socket.

The man rolled into the fetal position and cupped his eye with his good hand.

Nathan felt it, a tangible presence evaporating from the room. This fight was over.

An absurd memory flashed through his mind, something his mother used to say: *It's all fun and games until someone loses an eye.* He hoped that wouldn't be the case here. Spending the next fifty years with a glass eye and no depth perception wouldn't be a fair trade for slapping Cindy. A broken arm and pulverized nose should be punishment enough.

"Come on," Nathan said. "Let's have a look. It's over, okay?"

The big guy staggered to his knees, still holding his left hand over his eye.

"I'm gonna look at that eye. If you try anything, we'll start over."

No response.

Nathan flipped a wall switch and squinted at the sudden brightness. Clutching his eye, the bouncer looked broken and bloody, like a bully who'd finally met his match.

"Let me see your eye. Easy now. What's your name?"

He slowly removed his hand. "Toby."

Blood was streaming out of Toby's nose and running down his lips and chin. Nathan examined the eye from a safe distance. Fortunately, the impact hadn't been directly on the orbit itself. It had missed by half an inch, but the skin was laid open on the upper brow.

"Well, Toby, I've got good news. You aren't going to lose your eye, but you'll have one hell of a shiner. You had a close call here." He paused to make sure he had Toby's full attention. "You can blow this experience off, or you can use it to turn your life around, to walk a different path." Nathan watched him ponder the comment for a few seconds. Toby was a big man—huge, really—and people often associated his kind of size with stupidity. Nathan was also big, not like this guy, but he often felt people treated him as though he was all muscle and no brains.

"I lose my temper," Toby said.

"I noticed. Did you notice things I said were designed to make you lose your temper?"

"I can't help it."

"Yes, you can."

Toby said nothing.

Nathan crouched down. "Here's what I do. When I feel anger coming on, and I really want to hurt someone, I stop it by using a mental image. I call it a safety catch. You can call it anything you want. For me, it's a safety catch. With me so far?"

Toby nodded.

"Picture autumn-colored leaves falling from trees and gently settling on the ground all around you. Give it a try. Start by closing your eyes and imagining it."

To Nathan's surprise, Toby closed his eyes.

"You're standing under the trees with your head tilted up, your arms out, palms up. The leaves are falling all around you, brushing against your skin. Breathe in deep. Let it out slowly. See the leaves as they flutter past you. They're moving in perfect harmony. Each leaf picks up a small piece of anger and carries it away. Take another deep breath and let it out slowly."

Toby looked pretty calm for a moment, then winced. "Oh man, my arm hurts."

"You're just now noticing that?"

Toby nodded again.

"How high are you?"

"A couple of lines."

"Do yourself a favor and lay off the blow. You'll save a ton of money, and you'll enjoy life a whole lot more. Life is rich with detail. You need to see the world around you, be aware of its details. You may need some help to quit, but as soon as you realize you don't need drugs to have fun, you'll have the problem licked."

"I'll try. You fight well."

"Like I said, it's all about details. I knew you were on some sort of amphetamine high because your pupils were too small for the ambient light in the room. I knew you were right-handed because you used it to wipe your nose. You're right-footed because you took your first step toward the door with your right foot. I wanted that info in case you were a kickboxer. I knew when you were going to charge because your eyes gave you away. Stuff like that. It can save your life. It's all about the details."

"Those scars all over your body?"

"What do they tell you?"

"Somebody did that to you on purpose."

"Why did they cut my stomach and back?"

Toby thought about it a few seconds. "No major arteries."

"That's right."

"You were a soldier and got captured, they tortured you."

"Sit tight for now. You're going to need some stitches and that arm needs to be set. When you get to the emergency room, don't lie to them. Tell them you were in a fight. Observe the doctors and nurses closely. Learn from them. Ask them questions. Ask them what they're looking for when they examine your eyes and take your blood pressure. Ask them how broken bones heal."

Toby said nothing, just looked around the room as if he were already seeing things from a new perspective.

"Make sure the vision in your left eye doesn't become blurred or doubled over time. If it does, see a specialist right away. Your retina got jarred. Hopefully, not too badly. I want you to wait here while I bring the women back in. They're human beings, Toby, not just objects of entertainment. They have feelings. Like you and me."

"I should leave."

"Not yet. You need a few butterfly bandages to control the bleeding." Nathan retrieved a clean washcloth from the kitchen and folded it into a quarter of its original size. "Hold this over the cut with pressure. Is your truck an automatic or stick?"

"Automatic."

"Think you can drive?"

"Yeah, probably."

Nathan patted his shoulder. "Details. Start noticing them." He retrieved his 9-millimeter from the bedroom and told Cindy to follow him. They left the house through the front door and found Mara and Karen sitting in his Mustang.

"Party's over," Nathan said.

Karen climbed out and hugged Cindy. "Are you okay?" She looked at Nathan. "Is he gone?"

"No, but he will be soon. I think you'll find he's sorry for what he did."

She stared at him for several seconds. "We'll see about that."

He led the women back into the house. As Nathan hoped, Toby apologized and offered to pay for all the damage he'd caused. Karen said she'd forgo the money if he agreed to never come back, and they struck a deal. When Nathan was sure things had cooled down and Toby was no longer a threat, he motioned for Mara to follow him. Once outside, he removed his wallet and handed her a wad of hundred-dollar bills. "To cover the damage."

She was reluctant to take the money, but accepted it with thanks and a long hug.

"You could've hurt that guy a lot worse than you did."

Nathan didn't respond.

"Did you want to?"

"At first." He answered her unspoken question. "I saw something in him."

Mara stared for several seconds, hugging herself in the cool air. "If you ever want to talk, I mean, you know, just talk…"

He turned to leave.

"Nathan?"

"I'll call you soon. Thanks, Mara."

He retrieved his shirt from the rear deck and pulled it on. On his way back to his Mustang, he diverted over to Toby's truck, pulled a business card from his wallet, and set it against the Plexiglas cover of the speedometer where it wouldn't be overlooked. It was a dual message he was sure Toby would understand. He slid into his car and waited. Sitting there, he ran the whole encounter back through his mind. Mara was right. He could've hurt Toby, hurt him badly. He knew the consuming rage Toby felt. Knew it well. But over the years since his captivity, he'd learned to control it, to use it like a tool and make it work for him, not against him. Maybe Toby could too.

His cell rang. "Harv. Sorry about that."

"No worries. Everything okay?"

"Yeah. I'll call you right back."

"You got it."

Toby walked out the front door a few minutes later, his right arm hanging uselessly. Using compact field glasses he kept in the glove box, Nathan watched Toby grab the business card from the dashboard. The big man stared at it for several seconds before backing out of the driveway. Keeping his headlights off, Nathan followed Toby's truck until it was clear of the neighborhood.

He called Harvey back.

His partner answered after the first ring. "All right, tell me what happened."

"One of Karen's girls got slapped around by that big guy I told you about last week."

"And..."

"I put a reprimand in his personnel file."

A pause. "Did you kill him?"

"Now would I do something like that?"

"Yes."

"I'm deeply hurt by that comment."

Silence on the other end.

"I didn't kill him," Nathan said. "The circumstances didn't warrant it."

"I would've helped."

"There wasn't time. I broke a few traffic laws getting there and a few bones after I arrived."

"How many?"

"Bones or laws?"

"Is there a difference?"

"Radius, ulna, and a nose. Nothing serious."

"I'm proud of you."

"Thank you. Now, is everything okay with you?"

"I'm fine. But Frank Ortega's not. He's worried about his grandson."

"Frank Ortega? The former FBI director?"

"The same."

"Who's his grandson?"

"Third-generation FBI. He's currently undercover inside some kind of arms-smuggling racket."

"What kind of arms?"

"I don't know yet."

"Where?"

"Up north. Lassen County. Nate, he's missing. Ortega wants our help. I didn't promise anything, but I said we'd meet with him."

"What, tonight?" Nathan heard his partner sigh.

"Yeah, tonight. Hold tight. I'm already on my way."

CHAPTER 2

Nathan's Clairemont home was similar to every other on the block, meticulously landscaped with a pastel stucco exterior and tile roof. What set Nathan's apart was its state-of-the-art security system. Some would call it overkill, but Nathan called it an indulgence. He and Harvey Fontana owned a company that installed such systems. Why shouldn't he own the best?

A metallic-blue Mercedes pulled into Nathan's driveway and its driver climbed out. Harvey, the same age as Nathan, stood six inches shorter. His light hazel eyes were an extreme contrast to his tanned Latino complexion. Gray hair was definitely winning the battle. Nathan thought Harv had the classic look of a politician, but wouldn't hold that against him.

"You know I'm here," Harv muttered. He sounded like James Earl Jones with a Spanish accent. "The least you could do is meet me outside."

"I am outside," Nathan said.

Harv whipped around. "Damn it, Nate. I hate it when you do that."

"Why do you drive that big thing?"

"I'm a big man, I need a big ride. What's it to you?"

"You're an average-sized man…Everywhere."

"It's good to see you too, Nate."

"How's the family?"

"If you'd visit once in a while, you wouldn't have to ask."

"You know how it is."

"Yeah, I know."

Nathan's tone changed. "From one to ten, what's the urgency of tonight's meeting with Ortega?"

"Ten."

* * *

They drove south on I-5, enjoying a comfortable silence. After a few miles, Harv merged east onto I-8.

"You get a chance to look at the financials I sent last week?"

Nathan grunted.

"Our net worth went up another eight hundred grand this quarter."

"Just paper."

"I know money bores you, but honestly. You own a helicopter, for cryin' out loud, and your home in La Jolla is to kill for." Harvey shook his head. "If you ever get truly bored with your share of our company, you can always sell it to me."

"Don't worry, it's yours for free when I kick the bucket."

"I wish you wouldn't talk that way. My world is much more interesting with you in it."

"So"—Nathan's tone signaled a change of subject—"you and Ortega go pretty far back."

"I know his son, Greg, better. He was doing Middle East satellite intel for the CIA at the same time we were in Nicaragua. He transferred to counterterrorism work in the FBI eight years ago."

Nathan said nothing. He already knew all of this. Harv was setting a stage.

"He's a good guy," said Harvey.

Nathan didn't respond. He fully planned to help Frank Ortega, but had some nonnegotiable conditions.

"I couldn't have rescued you without Greg's help," Harvey continued. "I know you know that. But Greg knows it too. We spent long nights studying satellite imagery together. He volunteered his time freely, without strings. I owe him, Nate. Big-time. *We* owe him."

They rode in silence for the rest of the trip. Everything Harv said was true, and Nathan didn't resent it being said. Harv had saved his life. He wouldn't have lasted another day in that damned cage. In fact, he had no memory of being carried three miles through the jungle. Mercifully, he'd been in and out of consciousness, mostly out.

During their botched mission, Nathan had sacrificed himself to ensure Harv's escape. They'd been surrounded by guerilla soldiers hell-bent on capturing them alive. They separated to give themselves the best chance of making it out, but Nathan had doubled back to cover Harv's exit. He'd purposely given his position away by firing shots to draw the mercenaries away from Harv.

Bottom line? He and Harv were closer than family and either of them would give his life for the other—no questions asked. If helping the Ortegas was that important to Harv, Nathan would be there for him.

They pulled into Frank Ortega's driveway at 11:50 PM. It was a steep climb, snaking up to a Spanish-style home with a terra-cotta roof. Lit with spots, mature palms lined both sides of the driveway, creating an impressive colonnade. A dark Ford Taurus was parked in front of a detached three-car garage. Nathan figured it for an FBI vehicle, probably Greg Ortega's ride. The white stucco house was big, but not overly so, and the classic symmetry of design was pleasing to the eye. A wheelchair ramp had been constructed to one side of the entrance, bypassing the steps up to the front door.

As their Mercedes rolled to a stop, a Rottweiler bounded out from the side yard and challenged their intrusion.

Nathan opened his door.

Harv put a hand on his shoulder. "Maybe you should wait until Frank comes out."

Nathan slid out and took a step forward, addressing the dog in a near whisper. "Easy now. You're not in charge here. I am."

"Come on, Nate, get back in. That dog's going to tear you to pieces."

He took another step forward. "I'm not afraid of you. Settle down. Now." The dog backed up a step, unsure of its standing with this new arrival. Hearing something Nathan couldn't, it raised its ears and turned toward the house. Nathan looked up just as two men appeared at the front door, the older of the two in a wheelchair: former FBI director Frank Ortega.

Its docked tail wagging, the dog trotted up the driveway, turned up the wheelchair ramp, and sat by its owner's side. The man patted the dog's back.

Nathan had met Frank Ortega once before, but couldn't remember where. Maybe a political event. They walked over as the two men came down the ramp, one rolling, one walking.

Harvey spoke first. "Hello, Frank." They shook hands. "This is Nathan McBride."

"It's an honor to meet you again," Nathan said.

"The honor is mine. You're an unsung hero, Major McBride."

"I appreciate that, sir, but I'm retired now."

"You've earned the title, and please call me Frank."

The man issued a firm handshake, overly so. Nathan figured it was a gesture saying *I may be in a wheelchair, but I'm still a force to be reckoned with.* Frank Ortega had kind brown eyes behind a pronounced brow line. The former director was thin, but not slack. There wasn't the slightest hint of a belly under his white buttoned shirt. He wore tan slacks with penny loafers that looked brand-new. Although he did his best to hide it, his face looked taut with tension.

Frank's son, Greg, strongly resembled his father. He had the same eyes and brow line, just twenty-five years younger. Nathan guessed his age at fifty, plus or minus. Greg wore a dark jogging outfit and running shoes.

Harvey gave Greg a hug. "Greg, this is Nathan McBride."

"Pleasure," Greg said, shaking hands without a smile.

"The same," Nathan answered. Greg's handshake wasn't as firm and he spent a fraction too long looking at Nathan's face. Nathan didn't resent the staring. He'd gotten used to that over the years. It was just a natural reaction to seeing the damage.

"Tell me something, McBride," said Frank. "How did you know about Scout? Most people are intimidated by Rottweilers."

Nathan didn't mind being called McBride. Frank Ortega would be in the habit of speaking that way. He'd been the FBI's top man under two presidents.

"Body language," Nathan said. "When a dog's going to attack, it lowers its head, crouches down, and curls its lips back. Scout was barking, but he wasn't singularly focused on me. He knew you'd be coming out the door, so he was dividing his attention. By approaching him, I established dominance."

Frank nodded a silent compliment.

"I like dogs a lot. They're amazing animals. They freely give affection and loyalty."

Frank Ortega looked at Harvey, but said nothing.

Nathan hadn't intended the comment to be suggestive of their current situation, but he wasn't going to backpedal from it.

"Let's go inside," Frank said.

Nathan watched as Frank easily maneuvered up the ramp and through the front door. He was also acutely aware of being studied by Greg. The surveillance was subtle, but steady. Understandable. From what he knew about Greg, the man rode a desk. Nathan hated offices and avoided his own as much as possible. First Security Incorporated was Harv's deal, and he gave his partner complete freedom to manage everything. Although an equal owner, he had neither the desire nor the temperament to be actively involved in a complex business.

Inside Frank's home on the left, Nathan saw a small library. On the right, a sitting room with a beige leather sofa and matching love seat. Straight ahead, the kitchen. But what impressed Nathan the most was the stone floor. Staring in amazement, he stopped short of a fifteen-foot reproduction of the official FBI seal. Every aspect of the insignia was intricately recreated in a mosaic of colored stone. Inscribed within the seal were the words *Fidelity Bravery Integrity.*

A small elderly woman approached from the kitchen. "Frank spent a fortune on it."

Mrs. Ortega had shoulder-length silvery-gray hair and a kind, matronly face. Like her husband, she was thin, but not frail. With those oval glasses, she could've come directly from baking cookies or reading the *Wall Street Journal.*

Nathan winced as she strode across the symbol.

"We walk on it all the time," she said, reading his expression. "It's the floor, after all. I'm Diane. It's nice to meet you, Mr. McBride."

She offered her hand. It felt like warm bones in a velvet glove. "Please call me Nathan. This should be in a museum." In the corner of his eye, he caught Greg shifting his weight. The man was strung tight and could be a problem. Probably would be a problem.

"Harvey," Diane said.

Harvey bent and kissed her cheek. "It's good to see you, Diane."

"Would anyone like tea or coffee?"

"No, thank you," Nathan said.

Harvey also said no.

"Greg?"

Her son shook his head.

"Let's talk in the library," Frank said. He wheeled himself in that direction. His ride had no bells or whistles. It was a seat on wheels, as basic as they come. Nathan reevaluated his earlier assessment of Frank's grip during their handshake. The man had a powerful grip out of necessity, and the firm handshake hadn't been phony or intended to show off at all. The man simply had strong hands.

Despite Diane's comment, Nathan avoided stepping on the FBI seal as he followed. It didn't feel right walking on it. Frank maneuvered himself behind his desk while Nathan, Harvey, and Greg sat in tan leather chairs arranged in a semicircle. Nathan studied the photos behind Frank's desk. They displayed him shaking hands with five presidents: Carter, Reagan, Bush, Clinton, and George W. Bush. Frank stood in the Carter, Reagan, and first Bush photographs and was in a wheelchair for the other two. Portrait-type pictures of his two adult children were hung on the wall to his right: Greg and presumably a daughter. Nathan waited through an uneasy silence while Frank reached into a side drawer and pulled out a thick file. Nathan looked at it, then back to Frank.

"I know your father well. We go back a long way."

Nathan said nothing.

"He's a good man," Frank said quietly.

Nathan locked eyes. "We aren't here to talk about him."

Out of Frank's line of sight, Nathan felt Harv nudge his foot. If Greg had noticed the gesture, he didn't react.

"No, that's true. We're here to talk about my grandson. He's MIA. Has been for several days now. He was undercover inside an arms-smuggling operation up in Lassen County. An outfit called Freedom's Echo." Frank paused for a moment. "How much do you know about Semtex?"

"It's Czech-made plastic explosive."

"That's right. Extremely potent stuff. And we know for a fact that this group got their hands on some of it, a lot of it, actually. Around a ton. It was the last thing my grandson reported before he disappeared. It's likely he blew his cover relaying the information."

"That's a bad situation," Nathan said.

"And not just for him. Seizing the Semtex is critical. In the wrong hands, it could mean several more World Trade Center–type incidents. A few well-placed car bombs in the underground parking structures of skyscrapers could bring them down. Unlike the World Trade Center, there wouldn't be time for an evacuation. The buildings would collapse with everyone inside."

Nathan had seen footage of buildings being demolished with explosives. Implosion, he believed they called it. But if you changed the pattern and timing of the charges, the buildings could fall more like trees, taking out other buildings like dominoes. If the Trade Center towers had fallen sideways, it would've been worse.

"What exactly do you want us to do?"

Frank leaned back in his wheelchair and stared out the window like a man looking back on his life and wondering about all the things he could've done differently. "The FBI is about to send SWAT teams under the command of the Sacramento Joint Terrorism Task Force to raid the compound. They have two objectives. The first is to recover the Semtex if it's still there and the second is to determine the fate of my grandson. But the main plan is to put Freedom's Echo out of business before that Semtex disappears." Frank locked eyes with Nathan. "You two were the best covert ops team this country's ever had. I'm not patronizing you. I mean it. You guys were the best. What I need is for you to be my eyes and ears up there. I have a personal stake in this. It's my grandson, my own flesh and blood. I no longer have the access I used to. I could make a call and get boilerplate information, but it wouldn't be firsthand visual intelligence coming from a source I trust. I want you to back up the FBI raid. Things could go badly, there could be a firefight. You guys were the best damned sniper team in the world. The FBI could use—"

"With all due respect," Nathan cut in, "we don't do that anymore. We aren't hired guns. We run a security business. The FBI has its own sniper teams."

Harv moved uncomfortably in his chair, but remained silent.

"I'm not asking you to be hired guns. I'm asking you to serve as a safety net for the SWAT teams in case things go south. These smugglers are hard-core guys. Elite-trained military. Now they've got Semtex. You could save lives. I cashed in a major favor with Director Lansing to involve you in this operation. He gave me the okay, but he's considering it a don't-ask, don't-tell situation. I personally vouched for your integrity. I'm putting my reputation on the line here. If you're willing to do this, then the trust will have to work both ways. You need to trust me, I need to trust you."

"Then you must know the potential ramifications of what you're asking us to do."

Frank Ortega looked at Harv with a troubled, almost annoyed expression, and Greg was gripping the armrests of his chair too tightly.

"I understand the ramifications, McBride. Do you?"

Nathan said nothing.

Ortega raised his voice a little. "There's more at stake than just my grandson. That amount of loose Semtex on American soil makes this a national security issue as dangerous as any al-Qaeda threat. More dangerous. These guys are Americans, they look, act, and talk like us. They blend in. They're invisible."

Over the ticking of the regulator clock, no one spoke for several seconds.

"We have some conditions," Nathan said.

"Conditions."

"That's right. Conditions. We'll find your grandson and back up the SWAT teams, but we don't want to be left standing when the music stops. Understood?"

"Clearly."

"And we'll need complete background and intelligence information on the targets and their compound."

"Not a problem."

"One more thing. No armchair quarterbacking. Once you turn us loose, that's it. No second-guessing our moves. We do this our way, without interference, or we don't do it at all."

"Like I said, it's an issue of trust in both directions."

Frank pushed the file across the desk.

Nathan didn't touch it. He knew what it was, what it represented.

"This is everything we have on Freedom's Echo. Everything," Frank said. "It's an exact duplicate."

Frank kept saying *we*. Understandable, the man had spent over forty years with the bureau.

"I'm coming with you," Greg said.

"Out of the question."

"He's my son."

"Out of the question."

Greg stood and squared off with Nathan. "Listen, you son of a bitch, I don't care who or what you used to be. He's *my son*."

Nathan got up and pivoted toward the door.

"Damn it, Greg," Frank said. "McBride, wait. Please."

Nathan stopped but didn't turn around.

"We're all under a lot of stress. Please, sit back down."

Nathan didn't move.

Please," Frank said again.

"I need some air," Nathan said and left the room.

* * *

Harvey stood and lowered his voice. "Damn it, Greg. What the hell was that all about?"

"McBride's a smug asshole, that's what."

"Hey, I've known the man through life and death. He has a lot of faults, but being smug isn't one of them."

"Sounded like it to me."

"Well, you heard him wrong. He's not smug. He's confident. You can't see it because you're too close to this. You're asking us to risk our lives, and if the situation warrants it, you're asking us to kill. And we've said yes. But we can't have the father of the missing agent involved, much less someone who's never worked in the field. You've never killed anyone, Greg. Trust me, there's nothing glamorous or exciting about it. This isn't some half-baked Hollywood movie. We're talking real bullets and real death. There's no place for you in this mission."

Greg looked down but didn't respond.

"Now when he comes back," Harvey continued, "don't apologize. It won't be necessary. Nathan doesn't hold grudges and he knows you're wound up tight. We all are. When he offers to shake your hand, you take it, understood?"

No response.

"Am I getting through?"

"Yes."

* * *

Nathan found Diane Ortega in the kitchen, emptying the dishwasher. "May I trouble you for a glass of water, please?"

"It's no trouble at all." She retrieved a glass from the cabinet and pressed it into a small alcove in the refrigerator. She had a kind face that reminded him of his own mother. "I heard that last exchange, it was hard to miss. Will you sit with me a minute?"

Nathan pulled a bar stool out from the island for her.

"Thank you." As they sat facing each other, Diane placed her hands in her lap. "It's been difficult for Greg, his father being the former director of the FBI and all."

"I can imagine."

"You've seen the pictures in Frank's office?"

"They're impressive."

"The bureau was Frank's life, still is, I'm afraid. He's always known it took a heavy toll on his family. I think if Frank had it to do over again, he would've spent more time with his family." Diane's face clouded for an instant. She looked like she was about to cry, but made a recovery. "Greg is our oldest, so he took it the hardest. I think he understands the sacrifice now, but some wounds never fully heal." She reached out and held his hand. "Your father's a lot like Frank, and you're a lot like Greg."

"I'm...not sure what to say."

"Our time on Earth is limited. I'm understanding that now. We can't change our pasts, but we can guide our futures."

"I've killed fifty-seven people, Mrs. Ortega. It's taken a long time, but I've come to terms with it. Finding your grandson might increase that number. Are you okay with that?"

She held his hand tighter. "I don't see the world through rose-colored glasses. Being an FBI director's wife has taught me that much. There are genuinely evil people out there. I'm sure you're not indiscriminate. I trust your judgment."

"Thank you for saying so, it means a lot."

"Frank and Greg know it too, but men have a harder time expressing their feelings. It's a genetic flaw of the gender."

"Amen to that."

"Guide your future, Nathan." She released his hand.

Nathan reentered the library, approached Greg, and extended his hand. "Can we start over?"

They shook hands.

Everyone sat back down. "Your mother's a remarkable woman."

"Yes, she is," Greg said.

"May I explain my reasoning to you?"

He held up a hand. "There's no need. I understand why I can't be involved. We have the same policy in the bureau, and for good reason."

"We'll keep you informed every step of the way."

"I appreciate it."

"We'll find your son."

"All right then," Frank said. "There's one more vital piece of information you need to know." He lowered his voice. "I can't guarantee the FBI SWAT teams will know you're there. As you can imagine, it's a delicate situation with outsiders being involved in bureau business. I'll do everything within my power to make contact up there, but you should assume they won't know you're there."

Nathan just stared at the man.

"That means anyone not wearing SWAT uniforms will be fair game."

Nathan nodded. "When is the raid?"

"Tomorrow at fourteen thirty hours."

"A daylight raid. One more question. Does my father know of our involvement?"

Frank answered without hesitation. "Yes."

CHAPTER 3

It was a windy evening in the nation's capital. The horizon's last remnant of violet was fading to black. Four miles high, lit by the amber glow of the city, thin clouds drifted toward the east. Fall colors had come early. Red and orange cherry leaves lined the sidewalks and gutters.

The office of the Committee on Domestic Terrorism, or CDT, was located in the Russell Senate Office Building. Its members met in a lavish conference room furnished with high-backed leather chairs surrounding an oval mahogany table. Oil portraits of every president adorned the walls. A corner table hosted a pitcher of ice water. In the opposite corner, a matching table supported an elegant flower arrangement that perfumed the air with the scent of Stargazer lilies. It was an impressive room, appropriate for the purpose it served: protecting the nation's security from home-grown threats.

The moment CDT chairman Stone McBride strode into the room, all conversation ended. At six-four, the senator had a commanding presence. Like the trained marine he was, Stone kept his gray hair short and formal. Deep blue eyes complemented a square jawline. The man looked like a career politician because he *was* a career politician. He offered a friendly smile when he wanted something and an unfriendly smile when he didn't get it.

Now seventy-eight, the senior senator from New Mexico had earned the nickname "Stonewall" during the Korean War. It happened in March 1951 during the advance to Line Boston on the south bank of the Han River south of Seoul. His marine platoon had been reassigned to shore up I Corps. They'd been pinned down by machine-gun and mortar fire for half an hour. In an act of rage more than anything else, he'd climbed to the edge of his foxhole, stood up, leveled his M1 at the hip, and emptied five clips at the enemy position. Bullets had thumped the ground in front of him, not one of them finding its mark. Inspired, the platoon to his left added their bullets, giving the platoon on his right the chance to advance and overrun the enemy's mortar position. Stone had been decorated for that reckless bit of bravery, receiving his nickname in the process.

"Thank you all for coming on such short notice," Stone said. "I apologize for the late hour, but the subject matter demands it." He made eye contact with everyone seated around the table. "I've called for this meeting because of a critical new development. I've already been briefed, but everyone here needs to know about the new threat."

The CDT consisted of a hardworking group of five men and four women, all handpicked by the senator. Each of them represented a federal law-enforcement agency. It was the first group of its kind. A prototype. In theory, having a representative of each agency encouraged cooperation and sharing of information. In reality, tension often filled the room. But despite their many differences, they all shared one thing in common: loyalty to the United States of America. Without exception, everyone seated around the table shared a strong resolve to defend and protect the security of the nation.

Stone turned his radar toward his right-hand man, the FBI's member, Special Agent Leaf Watson. Watson was a career fed who'd entered the FBI academy after spending seven years in the Air Force as a herky bird driver. He was a no-nonsense guy who didn't mince words. In his midforties, he walked with a slight limp from a helicopter accident dating back to his Air Force years.

Watson shuffled some papers and cleared his throat. "The FBI has had an undercover agent on the inside of an arms-smuggling group called Freedom's Echo for several months now. Until now, Freedom's Echo has dealt in small weapons. Many of the guns aren't even illegal until they're modified to fire on full auto, which this group does. The group's located in Lassen County in Northern California and operated by two brothers, Leonard and Ernie Bridgestone. You can read about this pair in your briefing packet, if you haven't already. To summarize, they're both in their midforties and the older brother, Leonard, is a trained Army Ranger, retired. Ernie Bridgestone was a marine drill instructor and got himself court-martialed for killing a pedestrian while driving drunk. He spent five years in Fort Leavenworth. Both brothers had plenty of disciplinary citations in their files, and both left the military without looking back. Neither they nor their younger brother, Sammy, who works for them, got much attention from law enforcement until they came into possession of a large quantity of Semtex."

Stone McBride nodded for Watson to continue.

"Semtex was originally manufactured in Communist Czechoslovakia. As some of you might recall, when that regime toppled, the new government gave the world some very bad news. The old Communist regime had exported at least nine hundred tons of Semtex to Qaddafi's Libya and similar amounts to rogue states such as Syria, North Korea, Iran, and Iraq. Worldwide, there could be as many as forty thousand tons of Semtex out there."

While Watson let that sink in, Stone got up, walked over to the corner table, and poured himself a glass of water. Even though he'd been briefed on all of this earlier, the number still seemed outrageous. Forty thousand tons translated into eighty million pounds. Eighty million pounds. How could that be? Who besides the military or mining companies needed even ten tons of the stuff, let alone a thousand tons? But forty thousand tons? Where was all of it? How much had terrorists already stockpiled?

Watson resumed. "We think Leonard Bridgestone made a connection with a Syrian official when he was stationed on the northern border of Iraq. He and his brother appear to have obtained around one ton. As you know, Semtex is extremely potent. In 1988, less than a pound was molded into a Toshiba cassette recorder and used to bring down Pan Am Flight One-Oh-Three over Lockerbie, Scotland, and an undetermined amount was used to bomb the USS *Cole* when she was moored in Yemen. Semtex was also used to bomb our embassy in Nairobi."

"Now," Stone McBride said, "we come to the point of this meeting. Our missing man is Special Agent James Ortega. All of you recognize his last name because his grandfather is former FBI director Frank Ortega, who served in that capacity under two of the portraits on these walls. Among other things, Frank Ortega is a lifelong friend of mine. We were in the same unit in Korea. James Ortega is the third generation to serve with the bureau."

"He volunteered for the job," Watson added. "When he failed to make a scheduled check-in and officially became MIA, the FBI had to assume the worst. In his last report, he saw several pallets of Semtex being unloaded from a rental truck and stacked inside the compound's main building. We've had the compound under constant surveillance since his report. As far as we know, the Semtex is still there."

The chairman leaned on the table with both hands. "I called this meeting to give everyone a heads-up on what's about to happen. The FBI will be raiding the compound tomorrow at fourteen thirty hours, local time. The FBI's Joint Terrorism Task Force will conduct the raid, so we can count on a certain degree of media fallout. Something of this magnitude can't be kept from the press for long. We're hitting that compound at full force tomorrow. I'll brief you afterward on the status of James Ortega, the Semtex, and the teams that conduct the raid. Until then, thank you all again for coming on such short notice."

The committee members stood, gathered their belongings, and silently filed out of the room.

Watson started to leave. Stone stopped him. "Not you, Leaf."

Watson faced the senator.

Nathan McBride's father gestured toward a chair. "Have a seat. I've been in touch with the president. We have a few things to discuss."

* * *

Nathan and Harv's flight helmets crackled to life with the approach controller's voice. *"Helicopter Five-November-Charlie, contact Sacramento Executive tower on one-one-nine point five. Frequency change approved. Good night."*

From the left seat, Harv pressed a preset button containing the tower's frequency and pulled the transmit trigger. "Sacramento Exec, Helicopter Five-November-Charlie is with you with information, sierra."

The tower's response came back immediately. *"Helicopter Five-November-Charlie, radar contact confirmed. Maintain heading and speed for landing on Taxiway Hotel. Advise upon two-mile final."*

Nathan made a slight course correction and eased the collective down a hair. Harv acknowledged the tower's instructions. Although they could speak to each other any time they liked through the intercom system, Nathan hadn't felt like talking much. He knew Harv was aware of his mood. There was little he could hide from his friend. He appreciated the distance given at times like this, but sooner or later, Harv would mention it, saying something like, *You've been a little quiet lately, is something bugging you?* Nathan planned to tell his friend what was bothering him, he just didn't feel like doing it now.

As if on cue, Harv spoke. "You've been awfully quiet since we left San Diego. Want to talk about it?"

Well, there it was, out in the open where it belonged. No avoiding it now. "I don't know. I can't stop thinking about Ortega's grandson, how much time's passed since his last check-in."

"You figure he's been compromised and interrogated."

"It pisses me off thinking about it. They probably tortured the shit out of the poor kid. Maybe still are."

"That's not the only thing bugging you."

Nathan didn't respond, didn't have to.

"It's how far Greg and Frank are willing to go to save James. You're wondering why your father didn't go to the same lengths to find you."

Harv had hit pay dirt. That's exactly what he'd been wondering. For many, many years. During his four-day crucifixion, he'd had lots of time to think about it. Hour after hour, then day after day, he kept waiting for the cavalry to arrive, hoping for the cavalry to arrive, *praying* for it to arrive. Toward the end, his prayers changed and death had been welcome.

"You okay?"

Nathan nodded. "I just don't like my father knowing of our involvement. It makes this whole thing...I don't know, seem dirty."

"Come on, that's not fair. The CDT is a vital part of the nation's security. It's an important job, being the chairman. Of course he's involved."

Nathan said nothing.

"Despite how you feel about him, Ortega was right. He is a good man."

"He's a politician. It's all about money. The size of his damned war chest. Kissing babies is total BS. It's all about campaign contributions. Television and radio time. Mass mailings. What's the biggest issue facing a career politician? The economy? Crime? Unemployment? Illegal immigration? It's none of those things. It's getting reelected to another term. Can you believe he has the balls to send me campaign contribution letters?"

"Come on, that's not fair either. Your dad cares about all those issues."

"I suppose you're right. Sorry, I'm just venting."

"Your father, he really does that?"

"Does what?"

"The fund-raising thing? He sends you letters?"

"Yeah, he does."

"I'd call it reaching out."

"I call it reaching for my wallet."

"Do you send him money?"

He knew he couldn't lie to Harv and get away with it. "Yeah, I do. The maximum amount allowed for an individual. Every year."

"No wonder he keeps sending them."

Nathan grunted.

"It's no different than any other profession," Harv continued. "People want to keep their jobs. It's hard work being a politician, especially on the federal level. They make a lot of personal sacrifices."

Nathan knew all too well about the great Stonewall McBride's personal sacrifices because he was one of them. He had an absentee dad during his childhood. Deep down, he'd come to terms with it, but there was still a sliver of resentment left over, like the smell of an extinguished candle. He didn't hate his father, he just didn't feel any kind of familial bond with him. How could he? He hardly knew the man. Diane Ortega's comment was still fresh in his mind. *Your father's a lot like Frank, and you're a lot like Greg.*

"You should cut him some slack," Harv said, "maybe try to patch things up."

"You know, you're the only person in the world I'd let say that to me, besides my mother."

"Why do you think I said it? You need to hear it. He's getting up there."

Nathan said nothing.

"For your mother's sake."

They flew in silence for several minutes.

"Harv?"

"Yeah?"

"Thanks." He turned on the Bell's landing light a little early as a courtesy to the tower. They were now a bright spot in the sky, easy to see. "You did a great job on the radio through LA's bravo airspace. You want to make the landing?"

"I do, but stay close to the controls."

"Will do." Nathan spotted the airport's beacon and made a tiny course change to put them on a straight-in final. Even as experienced and seasoned as he was, the green-and-white flashing beacon of their destination airport at night was always a welcome sight. "She's yours. You've got the controls."

"I've got the controls," Harv echoed.

"I'm on the radio," Nathan said.

In the distance, Sacramento looked like a million multicolored jewels laid out on black velvet. Visibility was good at fifty miles plus, a positive aftermath of rain. At two miles, Nathan keyed the transmit trigger. "Helicopter Five-November-Charlie's on a two-mile final."

The tower gave them clearance to land on Taxiway Hotel.

Harv made a near-flawless approach, handling the two-and-a-half-ton Bell 407 with precision and confidence. His only hitch was slowing the helicopter down a little early. It wasn't dangerous, but on a busy day with multiple aircraft in the pattern, the tower would probably ask for an expedited landing, meaning *get your butt in gear and land*. Harv set the ship down near the large white *H* painted on the tarmac just west of Taxiway Hotel, as instructed. Two other helicopters were parked in the transient area, one of them a California Highway Patrol bird, the other a Department of Forestry firefighter. Nathan went through the shutdown procedure, cooling the engine and flipping avionic switches. The four seventeen-foot rotors slowly wound down.

"Nice job," Nathan said, taking off his helmet.

"Thanks."

While Nathan went through the shutdown procedure, Harv got out and checked the baggage compartment. He knew his friend was making sure everything was secure. Their duffel bags contained everything they'd need for tomorrow's operation. Nathan's Remington 700 was in a separate aluminum case. The duffels held their ammunition, binoculars, spotter's scope, transmitter detector, woodland MARPAT uniforms, backpacks, bottled water, and perhaps the two most important items, their ghillie suits. A sniper's ghillie suit was an amazing piece of gear. Once donned, it broke up the sharp-edged outline of a human body by employing thousands of shaggy, tattered pieces of fabric that hung in random disarray from every square inch of its surface. The wearer ended up looking like the Swamp Thing from the classic comic book series. Harv returned with their overnight bags.

"Did you know Frank Ortega had a daughter?" Nathan asked. "I'd always thought Greg was an only child."

"What brings that up?"

"I saw a picture in Frank's office."

"It's a sore subject. She was killed fifteen or twenty years ago. She'd just passed the bar exam when it happened, the very same day, as I recall. Some kind of traffic accident."

"That's a bad deal. Sorry to hear it."

"It was really bad for a while. Greg never talked about it. It was too painful. I think he was pretty close to his sister. He took her death really badly. We didn't talk for over a year. I didn't push and he didn't need any pressure from me."

"I can imagine."

When the main rotor stopped, Nathan made a final shutdown check of all the systems and switches before climbing out to join Harv. It was a cool evening with a light wind. In an unbroken tradition, he gave the Bell an affectionate pat on the fuselage after locking her up. They walked in silence toward the terminal.

It took the taxi twenty minutes to arrive, and twenty minutes after that, they were checked into the Hyatt Regency in downtown Sacramento for the night.

* * *

The following morning Nathan met Harv in the lobby of the hotel just after sunrise. Over breakfast, they talked briefly about their expectations regarding the raid, in particular about what Frank Ortega had said about not being able to guarantee that their presence at the raid would be known. Nathan wasn't concerned, in fact, he preferred it that way. They were used to working alone.

After breakfast, they returned to Nathan's room, where they took a closer look at the file Frank had provided. They reviewed every little detail, from topographic maps and aerial photos to the military personnel files on the Bridgestone brothers. They also studied internal FBI memos, along with James Ortega's transcribed reports. It was a lot to absorb, but when they were finished, they had a pretty good picture of things. They retired to their rooms to catch some last-minute shut-eye before the afternoon raid.

Unfortunately, sleep didn't come for Nathan. Staring at the ceiling, he couldn't get his mind off James Ortega and what the poor kid could be going through at this very moment. In agony. Alone. Frightened. Hopeless. It really burned him, picturing the Bridgestones doing anything they wanted. Was James tied to a chair, wired with electrodes? Screaming until his throat bled? Nathan closed his eyes and tried to clear his thoughts. There was nothing he could do for James right now. They had to find him first. Deep down, he hoped the kid was dead, not still being tortured. He made a promise to himself: If the Bridgestones had tortured James Ortega, they were both dead men.

Later that morning, Harv drove the rented Tahoe over to the airport, where they retrieved their gear from the helicopter. Within ten minutes, they left Sacramento behind. Once they'd cleared the city, it was an easy cruise north on Highway 70 through Marysville and Oroville until it turned northeast into the Sierra Nevada and became a designated scenic highway. The road gradually climbed into one of California's greatest natural treasures. Oaks and grassland gave way to hundreds of thousands of acres of pine forest. An hour later, Harv found their turn onto the logging road they'd identified in the aerial photos. Using his handheld GPS device to find the exact spot they wanted, Harv followed the gravel track for eight miles before he pulled the Tahoe off the road and parked it deep within the trees, where it wouldn't be seen by a passing vehicle.

They quickly changed from civilian clothes into their woodland MARPAT combat utility uniforms, which would merge them into the native colors of the forest. They exchanged their shoes for combat boots. Nathan had cut one of the cleats away from his right boot, while Harv's left boot had the same missing cleat. Their footprints would be distinct and recognizable in the event they had to separate for any reason.

Harv secured his Kowa spotting scope along with twenty-five stripper clips, each clip holding five rounds of hand-loaded .308 ammo, into his backpack while Nathan inspected his cloth-wrapped Remington 700 sniper rifle from end to end. Each of them made one final check of all their gear, making sure nothing was left behind. Harv removed two Sig Sauer P-226 pistol belts from a duffel and handed one to Nathan. Next, they tied their ghillie suits onto their backpacks. The last thing they did was apply green, brown, and black body paint to their exposed areas of skin.

Nathan didn't talk during this part of the operation—it wasn't necessary—but still he noticed the occasional glances Harv was giving him. They were both thinking the same thing. It didn't need to be vocalized. They'd come to terms with it over a decade ago. Harv patted his shoulder. It felt good. Reassuring. He couldn't imagine his life without Harv. He nodded a silent approval to his partner.

Harv locked the Tahoe and put the keys atop the right front tire. They didn't want an untimely jingling in a pocket. Although the sound was inaudible to humans, it wasn't to dogs, and dogs were always a concern. Shooting an attacking dog was a surefire way to give away your presence. Besides, Nathan really liked dogs, more than most people.

All set to go, they started up the mountain, keeping fifty feet of lateral separation between them. Although getting footholds was easier because of the damp earth from last night's storm, it was still a difficult climb over decomposed granite, sand, and loose rock. After several hundred yards, they took a breather. Nathan motioned Harv over to his position.

"Time?" he asked.

Harv slid his sleeve up and looked at his watch, where he'd smeared soap over the dial to prevent a glint of light from the sun. "Thirty-seven minutes."

"Let's do an RF check." Nathan pulled the DAR-3 radio frequency detector from Harv's pack and handed it to him. With a price tag over four thousand dollars, it was a high-tech device and very reliable. About the size of a shoebox, it employed half a dozen dials, various jacks for input and output, and a small six-inch antenna. The DAR-3 could pick up signals from 50 kilohertz all the way up to 12 gigahertz.

Harv turned it on and after a minute or so said, "We're good."

Nathan secured the detector back into Harv's pack, and they resumed their hike up the canyon's wall. High overhead, a red-tailed hawk rode a thermal. The lonely whisper of wind through the pines was the only sound present. They diverted two hundred feet to the east to avoid a granite face they couldn't negotiate without climbing gear. Near the summit, Nathan slowed their pace. He turned toward Harv, pointed to his own eyes with two fingers, then pointed to the left. Harv went in that direction while he swept around to the right. He wanted to be certain there weren't any sentries overlooking the compound. There were countless places to hide up here. The summit's ridgeline was dense with pines, some reaching over one hundred feet high.

After making sure the ridgeline was clear, they began scanning for a shooting position that would give them a clear view of the compound below. Although he was more than capable of hitting targets at longer distances, he didn't want to be any farther than six hundred yards. Six hundred yards was a good distance because the bullet arrived before the report of the rifle. From their current location, they needed to advance another seven hundred yards closer. Using field glasses, they took a few minutes to study the layout of the compound. Just as the aerial photos had shown, Freedom's Echo was situated in a grass valley interspersed with mature pines. Twenty or so small cabins surrounded a larger central lodge along with several other metal outbuildings, presumably used for storage. The cabins were constructed in the classic log-cabin style with steep metal roofs. Several camouflage-painted pickups were parked next to the largest outbuilding.

Harv secured their field glasses into his pack before they started down.

Nathan kept his head up, always scanning the area. Wind, about ten miles an hour from the west. Temperature, about sixty degrees. Humidity was low, probably 20 to 30 percent. The scent of pines hung in the air and triggered a memory of his early camping experiences. He issued a warble-type whistle. Harv stopped and faced him. Nathan pointed to a small outcropping of rocks flanked by mature pines several hundred yards closer to the compound. Harv nodded his understanding. The approach to that location was going to be a little risky. The trees were sparse near the rock outcropping, so they'd be out in the open for the traverse. They'd crawl the last fifteen yards on their bellies, camouflaged by their ghillie suits. Anyone looking in their direction wouldn't see a human outline, and if they crawled slowly, an observer wouldn't see any discernible movement, and movement is what usually caught the eye.

The valley below sloped gently to the west, where the forest was much thicker. Most of the pine trees surrounding the compound had been cleared, creating a firebreak nearly two hundred feet wide, but more importantly, it forced any approach to be out in the open. Nathan gestured for his field glasses and Harv pulled them from his pack. He scanned the compound again. All quiet. No movement at all. He handed them back to Harv.

"What do you think?" Nathan asked. "Those rock spires over there."

"Low crawl."

They freed their ghillie suits, put them on, and dropped to their bellies. With Nathan in the lead, they started their crawl across the sandy surface covered with pine-straw fallout. The 30-degree slope made the trek awkward. To keep from rolling down the hillside, they had to align their bodies at 45 degrees to their actual path. Crawling on your belly over sloped terrain wasn't easy, even at a snail's pace, but the damp earth made it tolerable. Nathan hated being out in the open, even for brief periods. If an enemy sniper spotted them, they'd be dead. It took five minutes to crawl the fifty-foot distance. One foot every six seconds. They made it to the outcropping without incident. So far, so good. It turned out to be an ideal shooting position. Shaped like a European cathedral, two large spires of granite, each reaching twenty feet over their heads, were leaning slightly to the east. The larger of the two gave them shade from the sun and put them securely in depth of shadow. Between the spires was a flat area of sandy soil that offered a full view of the compound below and the dirt road leading into it. Staying below the compound's line of sight, they quickly unpacked their gear.

Harv handed Nathan a stripper clip containing five rounds of .308 NATO ammunition. Harv had used a black felt marker on the stripper clips, inside and out, to prevent an untimely glint of sunlight. Each hand-loaded round produced a muzzle velocity of 2,350 feet per second. Nathan preferred a lighter than normal load. Bullet time to the target at six hundred yards was just under a second. He removed the bullets from the stripper clip, drove them individually into the rifle, and closed the bolt.

He handed the empty clip back to Harv.

"Time?" Nathan asked.

"Eleven minutes."

A gust of wind dropped a few pine needles past their position from right to left.

Harv spoke without being prompted. "Maybe ten miles an hour. Four clicks right."

He made the adjustment to the external windage knob on his Nikon scope, while Harv set up his 10-to-50 spotter scope. Once in final position, they would be lying side by side with three feet of separation between them. He shouldered his weapon and began a slow visual sweep of the compound below through the rifle's optic. "We'll call the main building zero and vector from there."

"Copy."

"Elevation?" Nathan asked.

"Nine clicks."

"Copy, nine clicks to zero. Plus three to the far side of the compound, minus two to the near side. Concur?" Nathan asked.

"Concur."

Because his rifle was currently zeroed for a three-hundred-yard shot, he knew an elevation adjustment for a six-hundred-yard shot was twelve additional clicks, but since they were shooting downhill, a negative adjustment of three clicks was needed.

"Here we go," Nathan said. Moving in classic leapfrog progression from tree to tree, six men in woodland SWAT gear approached the compound from the south, their movements crisp and rehearsed. "Six o'clock low," he whispered.

Harv adjusted his scope. "Got them. I count six, with two more in flanking positions. I've got eight more moving in from the west."

Nathan tracked the second team. Six agents were advancing with two more flanking for support. Both teams were advancing at right angles, staying out of each other's line of fire. Tactically sound. As the two teams approached the compound, he admired their precision and stealth. As they moved through the sunlight filtering through the trees, not a glint of reflection bounced off anything they wore. Their helmets were matte green and even their boots had a dull finish. These guys were damned good.

"Something's wrong," Nathan whispered.

"Talk to me."

"It's too quiet down there. We haven't seen a damned thing. Nothing. No movement at all. Start searching the trees. I'll take the west end."

Harv adjusted his scope and began a slow pivot around the east end of the compound. Halfway through his sweep he stopped. "Shit."

"What've you got?"

"Spotter's nest at one-five-zero east, elevation, three-zero feet."

Nathan swung his rifle 150 yards east of the center of the compound and began looking in the trees thirty feet high. He saw it instantly. A sentry posted in a tree platform, the type deer hunters used. He was speaking into a radio and looking through a pair of field glasses in the direction of the advancing FBI SWAT team to the south. "They've been made."

Harv stayed in his eyepiece and cranked the scope to maximum zoom. "Nate, he just put the radio down. He's got something else. He's pulling an antenna on a remote."

Nathan swung his rifle back to the south and began sweeping the ground out in front of the SWAT teams. Through an opening in the trees, he saw a mound of pine needles at the base of a large sugar pine. The pile of needles was on the side of the tree facing away from the compound. Nathan searched for other piles. There. Two more piles, also facing away from the compound.

"Son of a bitch. I think they've got IEDs or M-eighteens on the perimeter. Those piles of pine straw."

"Claymores," Harv whispered.

"They're walking into a shredder."

"How close are they?" Harv asked.

"Thirty yards."

"Shit, they're in range. We have to warn them. Put one in the dirt out in front of the lead man. Elevation minus two. Clear to shoot."

CHAPTER 4

Sammy Bridgestone's voice sounded metallic through the small radio speaker. "*We've got company.*"

Ernie stood up and looked at his older brother.

"What's happening out there?" Leonard asked.

"*SWAT team moving in from the south. At least a half dozen, probably more!*"

"Calm down, Sammy. Are they at the perimeter minefield?"

"*Not yet. Almost.*"

"Blow the southern perimeter when they reach twenty yards. Wait a few seconds, then blow the rest. Hustle back here. Don't wait. Understood?"

The radio clicked once in reply.

Ernie grabbed an M-4 and ran to the rear door. "He shouldn't be out there alone. I'll go get him."

"Wait!" Leonard yelled, but his brother was already outside.

* * *

Nathan took two clicks off the elevation knob, aimed for a spot twenty feet in front of the lead SWAT man, and squeezed the trigger.

His rifle jumped.

Nearly two thousand feet distant, the ground erupted in front of the lead SWAT member. Both teams instantly dropped to the ground. Four seconds later, at least eight claymore antipersonnel mines detonated simultaneously.

From high above, the effect was horrifying to watch. As if coming alive, the forest shuddered as though a giant shiver had raked across its body. The concussive thump of the blasts reached their position a full second later. An area the size of a football field had been turned into a maelstrom of flying dirt, rocks, and splintered tree branches. An angry cloud of dust began drifting down the valley toward the west. Nathan swung his rifle in the same direction of the wind and saw the other SWAT team on the ground. If there were more claymores, they hadn't been detonated yet. The answer came five seconds later. Another giant concussion shook the forest to the west, followed by a third to the east and a fourth to the north. The compound now looked like a huge doughnut, untouched in the middle, total mayhem on the outside.

As Nathan tapped his memory for what he knew about the devices, a curved block of C4 explosive blew hundreds of steel balls outward in a 60-degree pattern. Like its Scottish broadsword namesake, the claymore could literally cut a swath through the ranks. If those guys hadn't been on the ground...

"I want that shit bird in the tree," Nathan said. "He just tried to frag a dozen federal agents."

"We can't see him until the dust clears."

"Break out your RF detector, let's see if the good guys are talking."

Harv reached to his right and grabbed the detector out of his pack and turned it on. "I'd say so, we've got a spike in the fifteen-megahertz range, signal's close by. It wasn't there before."

"Can we listen?" But Nathan already knew the answer.

"No way, encrypted for sure."

"There might be a second ring of claymores down there."

"Probably is. At least the feds are aware of them now. We saved a bunch of lives with that warning shot."

Nathan grunted. He wanted that spotter in the tree.

The firecracker sound of sporadic bursts of automatic gunfire reached their position. "Here we go," Nathan said. "Windage."

Harv had already given him four clicks right. From the speed of the dust cloud moving toward the west, Harv gave him one more click right.

"Corrections to the tree stand," Nathan said.

"Give me the two clicks back on elevation plus one more and give me a final click right. A few more seconds, I can almost see him...Got him. Nate, he's got a rifle. He's lining up on the SWAT teams."

Nathan swung his weapon back to the tree and saw the man bench-resting his rifle on the rail of the tree platform, taking careful aim. He was dressed in cheap catalog camo with shiny black boots. His ball cap masked his facial features, but Nathan had the impression he was young, maybe midtwenties. He moved the crosshairs onto the man's chest, took a deep breath, and blew half of it out.

* * *

Ernie had made it halfway to Sammy's tree stand when the first salvo of claymores detonated to his right. For a split second, the air seemed to shimmer as if suspended in time. Then the concussive shock wave vibrated his body like a bowstring. Knowing more blasts were coming, Ernie crouched down and covered his ears. The ground shuddered and shook with each progressive detonation surrounding him. The perimeter of Freedom's Echo disappeared into a choking cloud of dust and flying debris.

Ernie called, "Get down, Sammy. Come on."

"I can nail some of those bastards when the dust clears."

"Sammy, get your dumb ass down from that tree. We're buggin' out."

* * *

"Clear to shoot," Harv whispered.

Nathan began a controlled squeeze of the trigger.

His rifle bucked against his shoulder.

"That's a bingo," Harv said. "Solid impact. Center mass."

* * *

Ernie Bridgestone recognized the sound. The bullet's supersonic arrival sounded like a giant bullwhip crack. He watched in horror as his little brother shuddered from the impact. From thirty feet high, Sammy fell like a rag doll into a pile of crumpled arms and legs.

"Sammy!" Ernie sprinted to the base of the tree and slung his brother's limp form over his shoulder.

* * *

"I see him," Nathan said as he ejected the spent shell and closed the bolt on another. He placed the crosshairs on the running man's hip. Then something twitched on his spine and caused a shiver. It was the kind of premonition he couldn't ignore. He'd felt it before and had never been wrong. He swung his rifle back toward the lodge. A man was standing in the open doorway using the jamb to steady his stance. Nathan found himself looking directly into the business end of a sniper rifle.

"Get down!"

The air cracked as the supersonic bullet arrived.

Behind him, the rock wall exploded in a barrage of hot copper, molten lead, and pulverized granite. Something stung his face. A second later, the thump of the discharge reached his position.

Nathan pointed his rifle at the ground and fired. A burst of earth blew upward, giving himself and Harv a few seconds of cover.

"Harv!"

"I'm okay."

They scrambled backward as another deafening crack tore the air. Son of a bitch! That shot hadn't missed by more than six inches. Three more shots smashed the stone above their heads. Nathan protected his face with his forearms, but the rest of his body didn't fare as well. Blood began oozing from a dozen minor wounds on his back and legs.

* * *

Ernie burst through the door and laid Sammy down. If the bullet hadn't killed his brother, the fall would have. Sammy's blue eyes stared blankly into space.

"Those fuckers," Ernie said. "Those lousy motherfuckers."

Leonard grabbed his brother's shirt and yanked him closer. "I nearly lost both of you out there. There's a sniper team on Eagle Rock. I just saved your fuckin' life. You were two seconds from getting nailed."

"I don't give a shit. I'm gonna kill every one of those fucks."

"Damn it, Ernie, I'm pissed too. But there's nothing we can do for him now. He's dead. If we go out there, we'll die too. I promise we'll get some payback, but not now."

"I can't believe this."

"Ernie, we have to go."

"Those motherfuckers."

"Ernie, now."

* * *

Harv was crouched down, looking at his partner. "How'd you know?"

"Can't explain it, I just did."

"That guy's a good shot. He nearly lit us up."

"Probably the older Bridgestone brother. I doubt he's still there, but we need to relocate. Can you sneak a look without getting your head blown off?"

"I think so." Harv inched his way forward, crawling on his elbows until he could just barely see over the sand. He peered through his spotter scope.

"He was standing in the doorway of the main building." Nathan saw that Harv was also bleeding from half a dozen spots on his back and legs.

"Nobody's there now."

"Let's bug out. Sprint to tree cover. Ready?"

"Yep."

The two men grabbed their gear and took off, dashing across the sloped open ground. Within seconds, they were deep within the safety of mature sugar pines. They looked at each other in unspoken relief.

"I know we're not here officially, but I think we should head down there," Nathan said.

"I'm betting there are more claymores, and we need to let them know about the sniper in the main building, I doubt they saw him through all the dust."

"We need to let the SWAT teams know we're coming," Harv said. "Any ideas?"

"Yeah, we can yell."

"Any other ideas?"

"Sorry, fresh out. As far as they're concerned, we just took a shot at them."

"Why do I get the feeling I'm going to regret this?"

"Relax, Harv, I've got things under control."

His partner snorted. "I was afraid you'd say that. Hell, I guess it's a good day to die. Let's go."

They took off their bulky ghillie suits and started down the mountain. Two minutes later, they reached the bottom of the incline. Not wanting to appear threatening in case they were spotted, Nathan had slung his rifle over his shoulder. There wasn't much he could do about his Sig Sauer secured in his waist holster, because he wasn't willing to approach an FBI SWAT team who had just been trashed by several dozen antipersonnel mines without being armed. Without a doubt, they were thoroughly pissed off.

Harv took out his scope and scanned the area ahead. "I've got a spotter at one o'clock, two hundred yards. Are you sure about this? Those are high-strung guys. They'll shoot first and ask questions later."

"Wait here." Nathan handed Harv the rifle and shucked off his backpack. "I'll make the approach. Just don't let anyone shoot me."

"I've got your six."

Nathan worked his way through the trees, covering the two hundred yards in just under a minute. Twenty-five yards from the SWAT spotter, he ducked behind the thick trunk of a ponderosa and looked back toward Harv. He had to lean several feet to his left to get a clear view. Harv gave him the okay sign. Now came the tricky part. He was pretty sure how he'd handle it. The SWAT spotter had positioned himself behind a fallen tree branch, which gave him solid chest-high cover from the front and broken cover to his right. This was a small man, he could see that right away. An old adage flashed through his head. How did it go? *God made men different sizes, but Sam Colt made them all equal,* something like that. Well, this guy was a little more equal. Nathan's pistol was no match for a fully automatic MP5 in the right hands, and he figured this guy knew how to handle one. Hell, the guy was a damned expert with the thing. Of course he knew how to handle it.

The downed branch where the spotter was crouched was thick, nearly two feet in diameter. Its structure fanned out to the spotter's left, while the meaty part of its splintered end faced Nathan.

He judged the distance between them again: twenty-five yards, give or take. The spotter was down on one knee, sweeping the area in a back-and-forth motion with his upper body, gun at the ready. Every fourth or fifth sweep, he'd keep the arc of his motion going and look behind him. Nathan studied him for about thirty seconds and formulated a plan. Precious seconds were passing, and he didn't have the luxury of conducting a prolonged surveillance. And he sure as hell didn't want to get sprayed with MP5 fire, so it was all about timing. He needed to make his presence known at the exact moment the man was lined up on his position. If he timed his move too early or too late, it would be interpreted as unintentional. The most likely result would be a horizontal maelstrom of copper and lead traveling at eight hundred miles an hour. Not a pretty picture, especially if you're on the business end of those slugs.

Here goes.

Nathan timed it perfectly. When the man swung toward his position, he leaned out from behind the tree and said, "Don't shoot." He said it loudly and forcefully, somewhere between a command and a request. A tense movement of shock and surprise raked the spotter's body with a predictable result.

He ducked behind the ponderosa a split second before the MP5 erupted. With his back to the trunk, he felt a continuous vibration as dozens of bullets slammed home. Pulverized chunks of bark shot out from either side of the tree as if sprayed with a fire hose. When the gunfire stopped, he knew he had two or three seconds while the shooter ejected the spent magazine, slammed another home, and cycled the bolt.

"Hold your fire. I'm on your side."

"Bullshit." The unmistakable voice of a woman. He knew she'd already communicated with the rest of her team, and he figured he had less than thirty seconds to get control of the situation before being surrounded by angry FBI SWAT agents who were—

as Harv suggested—going to shoot first and ask questions later. What he said next was perfect for the situation he faced.

"My name is Nathan McBride," he shouted. "I'm not one of the bad guys. I fired that warning shot before the claymores went off."

"Bullshit."

"It's not bullshit."

"How do I know you're telling the truth?"

"You've got a pair of field glasses?"

No response.

"Take a look at your five o'clock position, two hundred yards. My partner has a rifle trained on you. If we'd wanted you dead, we wouldn't be talking right now." He figured it would take about five seconds for the spotter to verify his claim. It happened faster than that. What the agent saw must have caused her some concern. Nathan knew what seeing a sniper lined up on you felt like. He'd just seen it a few minutes ago.

"Very slowly, I want you to step out from behind that tree."

"You aren't going to shoot, are you?"

"That depends entirely on you."

"I'm coming out. I'm wearing a sidearm. Don't shoot or we both die." He slowly pivoted from behind the trunk and faced the spotter, holding his arms out to his sides. Nathan watched her whisper something into the boom mike of her combat helmet. He knew she was strung tight from the claymore detonations. He also knew she was now facing a large, menacing man in a woodland combat uniform with his exposed skin painted in black, green, and brown. Nathan's sidearm closed the deal. In essence, she was face-to-face with a Special Forces soldier whose colleague had a sniper rifle trained on her. Harv wouldn't hesitate to shoot if she made a wrong move. He hoped she'd be delicate with her actions. Nothing sudden. Nothing threatening.

"Place your hands on the top of your head and lace your fingers together. Please do it now."

She'd said *please*. A good sign. Nathan complied.

She whispered something into her boom mike again, probably responding to the other team members who were on their way. Nathan glanced to the right and saw three camouflaged figures advancing in leapfrog progression again. He figured he had twenty seconds before being surrounded. "I need to give my partner an all-clear sign."

"Please don't move," she said, her tone more relaxed.

Nathan saw her backup was seconds away, and security came with numbers. He kept his hands atop his head and turned to face the first SWAT member to arrive. Under his olive-colored helmet and clear protective goggles was a four-part expression of pure intensity: one part curiosity, three parts anger. His woodland combat uniform had turned tannish gray from being blasted with dust and debris. Charred pine needles clung to his backpack. He'd been up front when the mines detonated. Had to be hell on earth. His MP5 aimed from the hip, the SWAT member stopped ten feet short. With a bloodstained hand, he issued a crisp signal for the others to advance. Two more SWAT figures appeared in front of Nathan, seemingly out of nowhere. They too were covered with dust and burned pine needles. A hand signal was given to the woman near the fallen tree branch and she assumed a sentry's demeanor again.

"Are you McBride?" the man asked.

That question spoke volumes. Ortega had gotten the word out. This man knew he would be here, but the woman who shot the hell out of the ponderosa hadn't.

Nathan nodded.

"All right. Let's do this delicately. I want you to ask Mr. Fontana to stand down."

"I need to give him a hand signal."

"Please."

Nathan unlocked his fingers from the top of his head and turned to face Harv's position. He slowly took his right hand, formed a fist, and placed it across his chest with the knuckles touching his right shoulder. He interlocked his fingers atop his head again.

"Thank you," the man said.

"No problem. Your teams are top-notch," Nathan added.

The slightest hint of a smile touched the man's lips, but vanished instantly. "You fire that warning shot?"

"Yes."

"At ease."

Nathan brought his hands down from his head.

"We've got three down, one dead."

"I'm sorry."

"Took a fragment down through his shoulder close to his neck. Clipped his carotid. The toll could've been a lot worse."

Nathan looked at the man's bloody hands again. "There's probably another ring of claymores closer to the buildings."

"We're on hold for now. I'm Assistant Special Agent in Charge Larry Gifford with the Sacramento Joint Terrorism Task Force." He closed the distance and held out his right hand.

Nathan shook it, ignoring the sticky feel of drying blood. "I'm sorry about your man."

"Me too."

"How are the other two?"

"One has a concussion from a tree branch. Clocked him pretty good, but he'll be okay. His bucket saved his life. The other has a separated shoulder. At least his vest worked. I heard a shot about a minute after the mines detonated, followed by several shots coming from the compound."

"I killed the man who detonated the mines. He was in a tree platform sighting in on your team with a scoped rifle when I nailed him. I'm damned sorry I didn't get him sooner."

"This isn't your fault. If our teams hadn't been on the ground when those claymores went off..." Gifford looked at Nathan's fatigues. "You're bleeding."

"Those shots you heard," Nathan offered. "The rock face above our heads took a few impacts. The shooter was hoping for a cornering shot. Nearly got one."

"Do you need medical attention?"

He shook his head. "Fragments."

"I'll have our medic look at them anyway. Please bring Mr. Fontana forward."

He turned toward Harv's invisible position and signaled him with a slight nod. Two hundred yards distant, Harv stood and began jogging toward them, weaving his way through the trees.

Harv arrived thirty seconds later. Introductions were made.

"Nobody else knew we were here but you," Nathan said.

"That's right." There was no apology in his voice.

"Understood. If you had told your team there were friendlies in the area, they might hesitate at the moment of truth, which could get them killed. They needed to know anyone not in a SWAT uniform was fair game. I would've played it the same way. Risky, to us."

"The price of admission, Mr. McBride. I wouldn't agree to your involvement any other way. I've also got a sniper team on the north rim of the canyon. They couldn't see the tree stand where you nailed the shooter, but they followed your movements the entire way, reporting only to me on a different frequency. You want to talk about top-notch, they said you guys looked like part of the landscape."

"What now?" Nathan asked.

Gifford looked back in the direction of the compound. "We've got an explosives unit being flown in from Sierra Army Depot. Two Black Hawks are on their way from Amedee Field as we speak. Should be here within the hour. We run an explosive investigation unit out of there."

"The FBI does?" he asked.

Gifford nodded and looked at his agents, then pointed at Nathan and Harvey. "Collins, Dowdy, these two were never here. I want the compound's perimeter secured out to a distance of two miles. Keep everyone well behind the first detonation ring. I want all the doors and windows of the main building constantly watched. I don't want anyone firing a shoulder-launched weapon at the approaching choppers."

The two agents hustled back toward the compound, the lead man talking into his mike as he ran.

"I only saw three guys," Nathan said. "I got one of them, but the other two are still in the main building. One of them has a rifle and he's a shooter."

Gifford turned away and spoke quietly into his mike. He turned back toward Nathan and Harvey. "I'll be honest. I was resentful you two were going to be here, but now I'm glad you were. We would've made this a night raid otherwise. It's no secret who's missing." Gifford issued a hand signal to the woman SWAT member, and she hustled over to their position. "Cover us." He addressed Nathan and Harvey. "You two, you're with me." Gifford began walking deeper into the forest.

Nathan exchanged a glance with Harv before following. When they were fifty yards away, Gifford stopped and faced them. He reached into his pocket and gave Nathan a slip of paper with a handwritten phone number on it.

"Call me in six hours. If you're willing, I've got a special job for you guys tomorrow night."

CHAPTER 5

"A tunnel?" Senator Stone McBride's irritation couldn't be concealed. Gripping the telephone too tightly, he continued. "And nobody knew about it?"

Leaf Watson hesitated before answering. "I'm afraid not, sir. I think it's fair to assume if Special Agent Ortega had seen it, he would've reported it."

Stone had sent Watson out to California on a red-eye for a firsthand report. Now he couldn't help but wish he'd gone along with him.

"I have FBI Assistant Special Agent in Charge Larry Gifford with me. We're on speaker, Senator."

"Nice to meet you, ASAC Gifford, even under the circumstances."

"Thank you, Senator," Gifford said.

"Any sign of James Ortega?"

"No," Watson said.

"I want the entire property searched. Bring in whatever resources you need. I want that compound torn apart. Dogs, whatever it takes. I want James Ortega found."

"Yes, Senator. I'll see to it personally."

Stone rubbed his eyes. "What about the Semtex?"

"I'm looking at several pallets of wooden crates stacked head high."

"How much?"

"Just over sixteen hundred pounds."

"Did we get all of it?"

"We're pretty sure ten crates are missing. About four hundred pounds."

"So, let me get this straight," Stone said. "The raid nets us over three-quarters of a ton of Semtex and the youngest Bridgestone brother, but in the process we lose one of your men, four hundred pounds of Semtex, and the operation's two ringleaders. Not a great trade-off, I'm afraid."

An uneasy silence hung on the other end.

Larry Gifford broke it. "It could've been a lot worse."

Waiting for Gifford to continue, Stone said nothing.

"We had a sniper team on the south rim of the canyon. They saw a compound member with a radio remote, put two and two together, and fired a shot out in front of my SWAT team. Fortunately, when the claymores blew, we were on the ground. We could've lost a dozen more agents."

"Is that the official story?" Stone asked.

"Yes."

"Good, let's keep it that way." Stone knew the truth and knew that both Gifford and Watson also knew the truth. His son had fired that warning shot. Chalk up another victory for cold-blooded snipers.

"Tell me about this damned tunnel."

Gifford continued. "Before storming the main building, we fired flash bangs and tear gas, but they were long gone. On the inside west wall of the main building, the concrete had been saw cut, then removed with a jackhammer. We found a small room below the slab reinforced with railroad ties. It connects to nearly a mile of thirty inch-diameter concrete pipe. Must have cost a small fortune. They attached skateboard wheels to the undersides of water skis and used them like toboggans to traverse the tunnel."

"They didn't haul four hundred pounds of Semtex through that tunnel yesterday."

"We think it was moved several days ago, just after Special Agent James Ortega went silent. The tunnel ended in the tree line to the west of the compound nearly a mile away. We followed their footprints another half mile and found camouflaged netting they'd used to cover off-road quad-runners. The tire tracks extended to the west down the valley. We think someone met them on a logging road about fifteen miles away. The quad-runner tracks ended there. They probably loaded them onto a trailer or hauled them into the bed of a truck. We're checking that angle, asking at every gas station and convenience store in the area if anyone remembers seeing them, but it's a fairly common sight— quads in trailers, I mean. We're doing our best to piece together the chain of events."

"Keep after it." Stone paused a moment before asking, "Did you see my son during the raid?"

"Yes, he approached our teams after the claymores went off."

"What did you think of him?"

"I'm...not sure what you're asking me," Gifford said.

"What was your impression of him?"

"He was definitely in his environment. He seemed comfortable in a high-stress situation. I'm glad he was on our side, that's for sure."

"That sounds like Nathan."

"He's an incredible soldier. *Was* an incredible soldier. He's given a lot for his country, more than I'll ever know."

"That's true, he has."

"I offered him another job."

"Oh?"

"I need someone to talk to the Bridgestones' cousins living on the outskirts of Sacramento. They've been in and out of jail most of their lives. A week before the raid, we put their farmhouse under surveillance. They might know something, or the Bridgestones might call them or show up there. It's a long shot, but it's worth pursuing."

"So Nathan's to *talk* to them?"

"Yes, a friendly fireside chat."

"Uh-huh. And I suppose he can *talk* to these Bridgestone cousins in a way your people can't? Is that about the long and short of it?" Stone knew Gifford wouldn't respond, so he continued. "I see. Then this conversation we're having never took place."

"I think that would be best, Senator."

"Nathan's your man, then. Anything you need, Special Agent Gifford, you talk to Special Agent Watson directly."

"Thank you, Senator, I will."

Stone had one last question for Gifford. "Do you believe James Ortega is dead?" He waited through a brief silence.

"I want to believe he's still alive, but it's unlikely. The Bridgestones tried to frag my entire SWAT team. If James Ortega were discovered, they would've interrogated him and killed him outright. I can't see any reason they'd keep him alive. My people have searched every building within a five-mile radius of the compound, but he's nowhere. We've also set up roadblocks on every road leading in and out of here. We're bringing in cadaver dog teams tomorrow in case he's buried up here. Later today, I'll have two FBI helicopters searching the area out to a twenty-mile radius coordinating with CDF and Lassen County Sheriffs' horseback teams on the ground. We're doing everything possible to find him with the limited resources we have available."

"I'll call Sierra Army Depot's commander, see if he can muster a couple of platoons for you. Maybe a Black Hawk or two."

"That would really help. The more people we have up here searching, the better chance we have of finding him."

"If it's any consolation, Special Agent Gifford, I'm going to nail those Bridgestone brothers to a cross."

"Thank you, Senator," said Gifford. "I'll be there with the hammer."

* * *

It promised to be another long day for Nathan and Harv. Yesterday, after speaking with ASAC Gifford, they'd received some stitches and small field dressings on their legs. Sitting on their wounds hadn't been especially pleasant during the flight back to San Diego, but other than that, the flight had been uneventful. They'd arrived well after dark. Then, early this morning, they'd met with the Ortegas at a coffee shop in Mission Valley and given them a complete update on the Freedom's Echo raid, including their latest phone updates from Gifford. Although disappointment was evident in their voices and body language, they seemed encouraged by the new assignment Nathan and Harv had accepted.

After the Ortegas, they again went their separate ways and agreed to meet back at Montgomery Field at 1800 hours for the return flight to Sacramento. Harv told Nathan he needed to make a brief stop at the office to follow up on some potential contracts before heading home to say happy birthday to his oldest son, Lucas.

Nathan needed sleep. He could barely concentrate. One rule he'd taken to heart while in the marines: Sleep when you can. He'd had less than six hours of shut-eye in the last two days and he faced another long night of flying. He needed to call Mara and find out if Toby had caused any additional problems. He dialed her cell number from memory.

"Any sign of our problem child?"

"No, nothing at all. I really think he's gone for good this time. Karen said to say thank you for the money. A handyman's there now, fixing the walls and replacing the sliding glass door. Karen said she wants you to upgrade the security system with that new mobile link stuff."

"That's a good idea. Tell Karen we'll hook her up."

"You're a gem."

"Take care, Mara."

"Bye, Nathan."

Maybe he'd read Toby right after all. A few miles later, his phone rang. It was Harv. "What's up?"

"I just had the damnedest conversation with the office."

"And?"

"Gavin said a big guy came in and applied for a job yesterday. I believe she used the word *gorilla*. She said his right arm was in a cast, and he looked like he'd gone ten rounds with George Foreman. You know anything about him?"

"I might."

"You didn't..."

"I did." Nathan listened to the sigh on the other end.

"Think he can pass a background check?"

"I have no idea, probably not."

"You must really hate me."

"Consider it a personal challenge."

"I'll run the check myself. You could've told me."

"Must have slipped my mind."

"Do me a favor and get some sleep. I don't want you nodding off at the stick tonight. Waking your ass up is hazardous business, especially in a helicopter."

"It's called a cyclic, not a stick."

"Whatever."

"How was your son's birthday party?"

"I missed it. I was tied up with a national security issue up north in Lassen County."

"You know what I mean."

"Well, let's see. You want the long or short version?"

"Short."

"No surprise there," Harv muttered. "I spent an hour removing toilet paper from my trees in the front yard. After that, I drained the pool. The water had mysteriously turned pink. But you know what the worst thing was?"

"Do tell."

"His friends wrote *Happy Birthday Lucas* with gasoline on the front lawn and lit it on fire. Can you believe that? It wasn't dangerous, but honestly. Today's youth."

"Well, he *is* a teenager."

"Don't remind me. I'm making him replace all the burned grass. A pallet of sod's coming tomorrow morning. Should keep him busy for most of the day. Candace grounded him for a month."

Nathan chuckled.

"Oh that's right, laugh it up. This is what happens when I turn my back for a few days."

"If that's worst thing he ever does, consider yourself lucky."

"That's not very reassuring."

"What, you never did anything like that during your formative years?"

"Point taken."

"See you at eighteen hundred."

* * *

At close to midnight, Nathan set the helicopter down at Sacramento Executive Airport in the exact spot where they'd landed before. They were both suffering from major cases of flight fatigue and needed head call. A plain four-door sedan was parked near the hangars to the south. It looked dark blue or black, Nathan couldn't tell which under the bland sodium light. Its headlights flashed once.

"Our FBI friends," Harv said, removing his flight helmet.

"Yep."

"You ready for this?"

"Not really."

"Come on, it'll be just like old times."

"That's what worries me."

While Nathan went through the shutdown procedure, Harv retrieved a duffel and two overnight bags from the baggage compartment. The duffel held their gun belts, spare ammunition, night-vision visors, two Fox USMC Predator knives in ankle sheaths, a roll of duct tape, and two LED flashlights.

They climbed out, and Nathan gave the helicopter an obligatory pat on her fuselage before locking her up. A man and a woman slid out of the sedan and walked toward them. The male agent was perfectly tailored in a dark polo shirt, pressed slacks, and expensive-looking shoes. The woman wore new blue jeans, hiking boots, and a white-buttoned shirt. They both wore Glocks on their right sides, secured in waist holsters. The woman looked like the real deal, but her partner looked a little forced—like the picture of a fast-food burger on a menu board.

"Mr. McBride, Mr. Fontana? I'm Special Agent in Charge Holly Simpson of the Sacramento field office. This is Special Agent Bruce Henning." Handshakes were made all around, and it was agreed to use first names. As they walked toward the sedan, Nathan evaluated his escorts. SAC Simpson was small and compact, but her demeanor said otherwise. She had a firm handshake and an aura of confidence surrounding her. Her black hair was shoulder length, not too long, not too short. It was…just right. And she hadn't reacted to the scars on his face. Henning had stared way too long, and Nathan got the distinct impression he resented outsiders being involved in bureau business. An understandable attitude, but too damned bad. The guy was medium height and build with perfect, blow-dried hair. There was intensity in his dark eyes and something else harder to pinpoint. Nathan didn't like him.

"I'm very sorry about your man up at the compound," Nathan offered to Holly.

"I appreciate that," she said.

"What exactly are you authorized to do with the Bridgestones' cousins?" Henning asked.

Nathan stopped walking and faced the man. Henning's statement and tone were clearly designed to put him on the defensive. *Not on my watch and not from the likes of you.*

Nathan leaned forward and locked eyes. "We're authorized to torture them, Bruce. Do you have a problem with that?"

Henning stared for a few seconds. "There's no evidence they had anything to do with Freedom's Echo. They're just a couple of hayseeds."

"Well, that's what we're here to find out."

"Look," Holly said, "the bureau's in debt to you for firing that warning shot at the compound. You saved a dozen lives, but you need to understand we're uncomfortable with this kind of thing. The FBI doesn't condone it. It's a serious breach of ethics for us."

"That was you?" Henning asked. "You were the sniper at Freedom's Echo?"

"*We* were," Nathan said, nodding toward Harv.

Harvey jumped in. "We're retired. We don't do this anymore. It's a personal favor for an old friend."

"Frank Ortega," Holly Simpson said.

Harv nodded.

She issued Henning a glance. "Let's get going."

"Nice helicopter," Henning said. "Yours?"

Nathan ignored the question and tucked himself into the back of the sedan.

Henning muttered something and opened the sedan's trunk with a key. Harv placed their bags inside and let Henning close the lid before getting in next to Nathan.

"Can we stop somewhere for a head call and coffee?" Nathan asked.

From the driver's seat, Henning looked at Holly Simpson as if the request was a royal pain in the ass.

We just spent four hours in a helicopter, you dumb ass. Nathan was sorely tempted to smack the guy in the back of the head.

"We passed a Denny's about a mile from here," she said.

"That's fine."

Henning drove through the automatic gate of the airport's transient aircraft parking area and waited for the gate to close before pulling away. Holly Simpson began briefing them on the Bridgestones' cousins' background and the layout of their farmhouse. Basically, these guys were your garden-variety, petty-criminal losers. Most of their adult lives had been spent in jail on a variety of offenses against society. Drunk driving. Drug possession. Larceny. Vagrancy. Poaching. Spitting on the sidewalk. You name it. Both of them were currently on parole and probably would be for the rest of their lives. *A matched set*, Nathan thought. *Give 'em a six-pack and a TV and they're happy as clams in mud.* They lived together on the outskirts of Sacramento and took odd jobs when they could, mostly as auto mechanics for mom-and-pop garages. Their father, Ben Bridgestone, was currently serving a life sentence in Pelican Bay for his third strike.

Henning pulled into the Denny's parking lot and killed the engine. No one spoke. Nathan exchanged a glance with Harv.

"Do you guys want anything?" Harv asked.

"No, thank you," she said.

Henning stared straight ahead.

They got out and walked the short distance to the Denny's entrance.

"Henning's an asshole," Nathan said.

"Don't bust his balls."

"Keep him out of my hair."

"I don't think he'll be a major problem. He just doesn't like outsiders being involved in bureau business. If the situation were reversed, we'd feel the same way."

Nathan grunted. One of the fluorescent tubes over the entry was flickering with an annoying electronic buzz, a result of absent management. He caught the nasty smell of a Dumpster nearby. Once inside, Nathan used the head while Harv ordered two black coffees to go. Then Harv used the head while Nathan paid for the coffee with a twenty-dollar bill. He told the server to keep the change. Graveyard shifts could be lean and he, like Harv, had a generous nature, even when in a foul mood.

Four minutes after stopping they were on the road again, heading east on Highway 50. The drive took just over thirty minutes, the last ten in silence. The geography gradually transformed into dark country roads lined with barbed-wire fencing. The foothills of the Sierra Nevada were mostly horse and cattle country. To the west, Nathan could see barns and small houses backlit by the orange glow of Sacramento. As the sedan slowed, Henning flashed his high beams twice, pulled behind a plain gray van parked on the shoulder of the road, and killed the engine.

"Please wait here," Holly said. She climbed out and approached the surveillance van. The rear doors opened, and she disappeared inside. Nathan had a brief look at the wall-to-wall black boxes and video monitors.

"The bureau doesn't condone this sort of operation," Henning said.

"Actually, it just did." Nathan yawned. "And we aren't with the bureau." He stared out the window, bored with the conversation. "You're following orders. Can't we just leave it at that?"

"So that makes it okay? Just following orders? Sounds like Nuremberg to me."

Nathan ignored the comment.

"Who are you, McBride, some kind of has-been CIA interrogator? Some burned-out spook for hire?"

"You're in the FBI, check me out for yourself."

"Your service record is classified top-secret by the Department of Defense."

"And?"

"And I don't like not knowing who you are."

He leaned forward and whispered, "We're legitimate businessmen with a successful security services firm. We can provide you with customer references if you feel you really need them."

"That's cute, McBride."

Nathan nudged Harv's leg.

"What exactly do you want to know about us?" Harv asked. "And what would that information mean to you? Suppose we gave you our colorful background, then what? How are you better off by knowing it?"

"For one, I'd like to know who I'm getting in bed with. I need to know I can trust you if the shit hits the fan out here."

"Did it occur to you we might be wondering the same thing about you?" Harvey asked. "We're on the same side here."

"The hell we are."

Nathan sighed. The man lived in a fishbowl. If you weren't FBI, you weren't jack. In Nathan's limited experience with the bureau, he hadn't found that a common attitude. Every FBI agent he'd ever met before—granted, there hadn't been that many—had been reserved and professional. He supposed every law enforcement agency had its share of gung-ho types. But deep down, he respected the FBI and what it stood for or he wouldn't be here, debt or no debt to the Ortega family.

"Aren't you forgetting something?" Nathan asked.

"And that would be?" Henning asked.

"Four hundred pounds of missing Semtex. Don't you want to recover it?"

Holly Simpson emerged from the back of the van and walked over to Nathan's window.

He rolled it down.

"You're on," she said. "We haven't heard anything but snoring for the last two hours. We have bugs in every room. They're both crashed out in the living room just inside the front door."

As Nathan and Harv climbed out, Henning opened the trunk and stepped back. Harv grabbed their duffel bag, set it on the asphalt, and unzipped it. He removed two pistol belts and handed one to Nathan. Harv strapped on a small black waist pack containing their LED flashlights and two rolls of duct tape.

"Dogs?" Nathan asked.

"None," Holly answered. "I doubt they could handle the responsibility."

"I only have one condition," Nathan said. He retrieved two sets of night-vision visors from the duffel bag.

"It's a little late for conditions," she said.

"None of it gets recorded. I don't care if you listen in, but the black boxes aren't running. Deal?" He strapped his Predator knife to his ankle.

Harv did the same.

Nathan placed his NV visor on his head. "I mean it. We'll have...unresolved issues otherwise."

"Are you threatening us?" Henning asked.

He ignored Henning and stared at Holly, his eyes unwavering. "Do we have a deal?"

Henning took a step forward. "Nobody threatens us."

Without taking his eyes from Holly, Nathan pointed at Henning's face.

"Get your finger out of my face."

"Holly? Do we have a deal?"

She looked at Henning, then back to Nathan. "Yes."

He turned toward Harv. "Let's go."

After they left, Holly faced Henning. "You're out of line, mister. I'm in charge of this operation. Are we crystal clear on that?"

"I just—"

"You just nothing. Don't ever test me again."

CHAPTER 6

As Nathan and Harv walked toward the farmhouse, they lowered their night-vision scopes and turned them on. Their EX PVS14-D devices were state-of-the-art, third-generation design, the same model used by the US military. Their compact size allowed them to be mounted on a visor-type headgear that gave the user the option to pivot the monocular down to his eye, or up out of the way. Once activated, the device literally transformed night into day in the form of a tiny television screen. Internal lenses brought the miniature green image into focus. Both of them preferred to use their right eye for night vision while leaving their left eye uncovered. The world around them materialized. Although it was nearly pitch-black, they could plainly see the road's dividing stripes against the dark asphalt. On both sides of the road, five strands of barbed wire paralleled their path, defining the sixty-foot-wide easement. Cattle were lying down in the field off to their left, watching them. High in the stratosphere, wispy-thin clouds reflected the glow of the city, which was all the light the devices needed.

"We go in fast," Nathan said. "Shock attack. I'll cover the left side of the room, you take the right."

"How rough do we get?"

"We'll have to see. My best guess is light to moderate. Like Henning said, they're just a couple of hayseeds who've drifted through life doing the minimum to survive. I'm not expecting anything different tonight. If they hold out, there'll be a damned good reason. We'll just have to wring it out of them."

Twenty yards ahead, Nathan saw the entrance to the property on the right side of the road, a makeshift gate with empty beer cans littering the landscape—probably tossed every time the Bridgestone cousins left. Two tire-worn impressions across the weedy ground pointed directly at the farmhouse. Nathan nodded to Harv, and they drew their pistols. Invisible against the black backdrop behind them, both men transitioned into stealth mode and entered the property. From Holly Simpson's description, he knew the house was located in the middle of the four-acre parcel, with unused ranchland surrounding it. A detached one-car garage was situated thirty yards to the north, its door facing the house. When they got closer, two old pickup trucks took shape. Both had numerous rust spots, dents and dings, broken taillights, and bald tires. Neither had current registration tags. Several hundred yards distant at the far corner of the property, some sort of big pipe extended a few feet above the ground. An old windmill sat atop its cylindrical form, and Nathan could see the outlines of a well pump and pressure tank. Its paint peeling, the house was on the small side, maybe seven hundred square feet. The grimy front door was flanked by two windows with bedsheets for curtains. Several wooden steps led up to a covered porch.

Nathan stopped and held his left hand up in a closed fist.

A string was stretched across the planks of the top step, its left side tied to the handrail's post. The other end wrapped around the opposite post and turned the corner toward the front door. The string terminated at a platoon of empty beer bottles, their Miller labels clearly readable through his NV scope. If the trip wire had been triggered, it would've pulled the rear bottle through the others, knocking them all down, making a boatload of noise. It was a dirt-cheap and yet fairly reliable security mechanism, but it worked only against an unknowing intruder.

Nathan turned toward Harv, simulated pulling a string between his fingers, and pointed to the top step. Harv acknowledged with a nod. Nathan pulled his knife from its ankle sheath, carefully cut the string, and tossed the loose line over the side of the steps. He tested the first step with a few pounds of pressure under his boot. No creaking. He slowly transferred his weight until he was completely standing on the first step. Nothing. No sound at all. So far, so good. While Harv watched the windows, he repeated the same procedure for the next two steps. No creaking. Once atop the landing, he flattened himself against the wall between the left window and front door. The stack of bottles was on the opposite side of the door. He nodded to Harv, who navigated the steps with equal stealth.

Nathan pivoted and faced the front door. "Infrared on," he whispered.

They reached up and turned knobs on their scopes. Small red dots could now be seen in the lower corners of their images, indicating the infrared spots were activated. The front door instantly brightened, and Nathan's device automatically lowered the image's intensity to compensate.

Harv tucked in close behind him.

A smile touched his lips. Here he was again, Nathan McBride in his environment.

He reared up with his right foot and stomped. ·

The door burst open in a crash of splintered wood and dust.

In the green images of their night vision, they could see everything.

Two men were present, caught in midsnore. The first lay back in an easy chair, the second in a fetal position on the couch. Simultaneously, both pairs of eyes snapped open. Nathan stepped forward to the easy chair and clubbed its occupant with the butt of his gun. It wasn't hard enough to knock him unconscious, but it *was* hard enough to render him dazed and groggy.

Harv jammed the muzzle of his gun against the couch potato's forehead and said, "Don't move."

The guy tried to sit up. "What the fu—"

Harv clocked him. With a grunt of pain, he slumped back into the stained fabric. With his free hand, Harv unzipped his waist pack and grabbed a roll of duct tape.

Nathan yanked his mark to the floor and rolled him onto his stomach. He grabbed the tape from Harv, set his gun down, and secured the guy's hands behind his back with several loops of tape. He covered the man's mouth with a six-inch strip and tossed the roll to Harv, who did the same to his man.

Within eight seconds of bursting through the door, they had overwhelmed and immobilized both targets. *Just like old times,* Nathan thought. "Check the rest of the house," he whispered.

Harv disappeared down the hall and returned twenty seconds later. "Clear."

"Let's get them situated."

Harv grabbed a couple of chairs from the eating area. Nathan was hesitant to think of it as a dining room because these two didn't dine, they merely ate, and from the look of things, didn't get all of it into their mouths. He removed his night vision, turned it off, and reached into his pocket for the lens cap.

"NV off?" he asked.

Harv reached up, turned his unit off, and capped the lens. Harv took both NV visors outside and placed them on the front porch. Nathan flipped a switch on the wall and a bare bulb on the ceiling came to life.

"Oh, man," Nathan said. He hadn't expected to see Wayne Manor, but this place belonged in a hall of shame museum. He'd seen the mess in shades of green through the scope, but in Technicolor the true nature of this pigsty took on a whole new dimension. The family-room table consisted of three bald tires stacked atop one another, capped off by half a sheet of painted plywood. Household trash was strewn everywhere. Beer bottles. Empty soup and chili cans. Milk cartons. Wadded paper towels. Apple cores. Peanut shells. Candy-bar wrappers. Half-eaten hot dogs and hamburgers. Microwave popcorn bags. Dirty dishes. Crusty silverware and girlie magazines. Clothes were thrown on every available surface. Shoes. Work boots. Socks. Soiled T-shirts. Old blue jeans. Mechanic's overalls. Several cases of motor oil were sitting under the living-room window. Cleared paths through the clutter and filth connected the various rooms like worn trails on college campus lawns. And the smell: it was like a landfill in here. Nathan shook his head.

"You should see the bathroom," Harv said. "I don't know how people can live like this."

"That's just it, they don't live. They survive."

"I've never seen anything this disgusting before."

"Ever watch the show *Cops*? Let's clear an opening on the floor and set them up right here." Nathan kept his gun up while Harv went to work. After a minute or so, he'd kicked enough crap out of the way to place two chairs about three feet apart. Harv hauled the two men into sitting positions and wrapped several layers of duct tape around their chests and the backs of the chairs to keep them from slumping over. The guy on Nathan's left was thin and lanky and might weigh one-fifty with his clothes on. Blood was seeping through a gauze bandage taped on the triceps portion of his arm. That bandage looked uncharacteristically clean, Nathan thought. It didn't track with this environment. Beneath the guy's shaved head was a narrow, pointed face with a mustache shaped like a horizontal butter knife. His brother was compact and fit. He had a square face with strong cheekbones and short dishwater-blond hair that looked like he'd combed it straight up with bacon lard. This guy weighed two hundred, and looked somewhat formidable.

"Knife and Fork," Nathan said, nodding toward them.

Harv stepped back, stared for a few seconds, and smiled.

The Bridgestone cousins were dressed in dirty blue jeans, white tank tops, and scuffed work boots. Their hands, arms, and faces were smudged with motor oil and grease. The bigger guy had a tattoo on his arm that looked like it had been etched with copper wire and a blowtorch. It was impossible to tell who was older—they both looked twenty years past their actual age.

"Let's bring them around," Nathan said. He reached down, grabbed an empty beer can, and crumpled it in his palms. As if shooting a free throw in basketball, he tossed it at Fork. It bounced off Fork's forehead with a metallic *clink*. A few drops of stale beer splattered the man's nose and cheeks. His eyes fluttered open, then grew wide with terror.

"Nothin' but net," Harv said and gave Knife a firm shake. Knife's eyes registered fear, then changed to rage. He whipped his head back and forth, trying to dislodge the tape covering his mouth.

Nathan dragged a chair over and sat down. Without taking his eyes off Knife, he pulled a thin pair of black gloves from his front pocket and slowly pulled them on. Harv did the same.

"Here's the deal," Nathan began. "We aren't going to play good cop, bad cop with you two miscreants. For one, we aren't cops, and the other, we're both bad. We don't work for the FBI, CIA, NRA, PTA, or the ASPCA. We're…" He looked up at Harv. "What are we?"

"Independent contractors."

"We're independent contractors, so your Miranda rights are not in play here. In fact, this is an anti-Miranda situation. You absolutely do not have the right to remain silent. Oh, and the Eighth Amendment of our beloved Constitution is hereby suspended until further notice. If you're curious, it has to do with cruel and unusual punishment being inflicted. Now, before we get started, is there anything you'd like to say?"

Knife began nodding furiously, but Fork stared straight ahead, refusing to make eye contact. Nathan leaned forward and yanked the tape from Knife's mouth. It came off with a sound like tearing fabric. Knife's poor mustache didn't fare so well. It had been reduced by a good 20 percent. With an expression of revulsion, Nathan held the strip with his thumb and forefinger and tossed it aside like a plague bandage.

"You stupid motherfuckers," Knife hissed, "I want my phone call."

He looked at Harv. "He wants his phone call. Would you bring me the phone, please?"

Harv walked into the kitchen and yanked the phone off the wall, cradle and all. Its cord dangling uselessly, he handed it to Nathan.

Without warning, Nathan swung the phone like an oversized palm sap.

"Oh, man," Harv said. "That's gonna leave a mark."

Blood began streaming from Knife's nose.

* * *

Out in the surveillance van, Holly Simpson and the two techs looked at each other in the glow of the black boxes. They'd heard the impact. As promised, nothing was being recorded.

* * *

"Would you like to make another call?" Nathan asked.

"You son of a bitch. You broke my fuckin' nose!"

"In about ninety seconds, the mucus membrane of that pointed beak you call a 'nose' is going to swell to twice its current volume. Breathing through it will become quite labored. If I have to tape your mouth again, you'll start choking on your own blood."

"Fuck you."

Nathan sighed. "I am truly disappointed." He peeled another six-inch length of tape from the roll.

Cursing like a madman, Knife began whipping his head back and forth.

Harv maneuvered behind Knife while Nathan retrieved a filthy washcloth from the kitchen counter. Harv grabbed Knife by the ears and held his head still while Nathan wiped the blood from Knife's mouth before jamming the strip of tape into place. He held his wrist up in an exaggerated manner, looking at his watch.

Knife's face turned a bright shade of crimson and his chest began heaving for air. Nathan raised an eyebrow, silently saying *I told you so*. Knife coughed behind the tape and was forced to inhale his own blood. His body wrenched in a violent spasm.

"It's only going to get worse. Soon, you'll be aspirating blood and vomit into your lungs. That's a bad situation. You could get pneumonia, and after I've broken all your ribs, coughing is going to be a tad uncomfortable."

Fork's bladder quit. The liquid ran down the legs of his chair and soaked into the carpet. The pungent smell of urine drifted.

Knife's desperate wrenching reached a peak and Nathan knew the guy was close to passing out. He yanked the tape free, reducing Knife's mustache to 60 percent. Vomit spewed.

"That's disgusting." Nathan looked at Harv. "Garden hose, please."

Harv walked out the front door and returned a few seconds later, dragging a green hose with him. He handed the business end to Nathan and stepped back out outside. "Say when."

Nathan removed the glove from his right hand. "When," he called.

There was a faint squeak from outside.

Knife wrenched in his seat. "What the fuck you doing?"

Nathan used his thumb to form a jet of water and summarily hosed the two men down like dogs. Water flew in every direction. As if washing off a driveway, he used the hose to spray the vomit in front of Knife's chair aside, then soaked the carpet under Fork's chair, diluting the urine. Knife shook his head back and forth, trying to clear his vision.

"Okay," he yelled to Harv. Another squeak.

Harv returned from outside.

"Once again, here's the deal," Nathan said, keeping his tone even. "We have all night and there are all kinds of things in an everyday household that are perfectly suitable for inflicting pain. Almost anything works. Take your pick. Scissors, screwdrivers, pliers, lamp cords. I once beat a guy senseless with a twelve-inch salami and then made myself a sandwich. Ever had your fingers inserted into a toaster? A frying pan is effective too. You know, those heavy-duty cast-iron jobs? What we do is heat it up several hundred degrees and then lovingly place it in your lap for safekeeping. Let's see, what else works?"

"A grinder," Harv said.

"Go take a look in the garage. I'll bet they've got one."

Harv took a step toward the door.

"What the fuck do you want from me? I don't know where they are. My cousins are crazy. I don't have nothing to do with them. I swear."

Without looking, Nathan reached over and yanked the tape from Fork's mouth. "Is there anything you'd like to add?"

"Tell him about the cabin!"

Nathan squinted at Knife. "What cabin?"

Knife twisted toward his brother. "You dumb shit."

Nathan asked again, slower. "What...cabin?"

"There's no cabin," Knife said.

Nathan picked up the phone and held it an inch from Fork's nose. "Would you like to make a call?"

"I don't know where it is. I swear I ain't been there."

There was fury in Knife's voice. "Shut the fuck up, Billy."

Nathan nodded to Knife. "He's been there?"

"Lots of times. He goes hunting up there. It belongs to our dad's sister, but she don't want nobody knowin' about it."

Nathan tore another piece of tape from the roll and secured Fork's mouth. Avoiding the empty soup cans and milk jugs on the floor, he strolled into the kitchen and started rummaging around. He opened cabinet doors, tossed pots and pans aside, and purposely made all kinds of noise. He found what he was looking for, set it on the front burner with an audible *clang*, and twisted the knob. The rapid clicking of the stove's igniter was followed by the distinctive *whoosh* of the gas catching.

Harv said, "Uh-oh."

He returned to the living room and winked at Knife.

"My cousins will kill me."

"He'll do it," Harv said. "I've seen this before. It's pretty bad. It fuses the denim to your skin."

"They'll kill me!"

"Your concern should be more immediate," Harv said.

After a minute or so, the odor of burned cooking oil drifted into the room.

Knife jerked against the chair. "Son of a bitch. You motherfuckers."

"Warming up nicely," Nathan said.

"Son of a bitch, son of a bitch!"

"I'm going to tape your mouth. I just can't stand the sound of a grown man screaming." Harvey jammed the tape over Knife's mouth and pulled his Predator from its ankle sheath.

Knife's eyes grew.

"Hold still," Harv said, and cut a slit in the tape.

The tape hissed with each breath Knife took.

Nathan returned into the kitchen. With the frying pan's handle protected with a dish towel in one hand and a small cup of water in the other, he approached the bound men. Blue-gray smoke belched from the pan's black surface.

Knife began whipping back and forth, nearly toppling his chair.

Nathan stood in front of Knife and held the pan six inches above his lap. He poured an ounce of water onto its flat surface. The liquid burst to life in a macabre dance of boiling rivulets that hissed and sizzled like tortured snakes.

* * *

Out in the van, Holly Simpson held her breath.

CHAPTER 7

"Last chance," Nathan said. "Are your cousins really worth it? Do you think they'd take this kind of pain for you?"

Knife shook his head.

"Are you ready to talk about the cabin?"

He closed his eyes and nodded.

Nathan tossed the pan aside. It simmered on the wet carpet, belching steam. He tore the tape from Knife's mouth. "Well?"

"It's three hours from here. Up Highway Seventy near Quincy."

"What's the address?"

"It don't have an address."

"You're going to show us where it is. Is there anything else we should know about?"

"That's it, man, I swear. I don't know nothing else."

Nathan knew when someone was lying to him. It was hard to describe. Maybe it was in the eyes, or micro changes in body language, but whatever it was, it didn't matter. This guy was holding something back, something he was willing to risk a great deal of pain over.

"This isn't personal," Nathan said. "You understand that, right? I'm just doing my job." He walked behind Knife's chair and began cutting the duct tape. He sensed the man relax a little. Good. Now take it away. He stopped cutting the tape and grunted as though something wasn't quite right. "What about the cash?" he whispered in Knife's ear.

Knife stiffened a little.

"The cash," Nathan said, watching Knife's reaction. A bull's-eye. A direct hit. Knife gave it away as clearly as a kid who looks down after peeing his pants. Cash. Emergency money. Probably lots of it, and without a doubt, it was hands-off as far as these two mutts were concerned. It made perfect sense. The Bridgestones probably had stashes all over the place. The Bridgestones were many things, but stupid wasn't one of them. They hadn't been able to come here because the FBI stakeout had started before the raid on the compound.

"There's no cash," Knife said, but it sounded weak, unconvincing.

Nathan shook his head and looked at Fork, who was nodding furiously. "I think your brother has something to tell us."

Nathan yanked the tape from Fork's mouth.

"It's buried near the garage. Leonard told us if we ever touched it, he'd kill us."

Knife glared at his brother with pure hatred in his eyes.

"Your bro here sounds upset," Nathan said. "I'm a little disappointed you didn't mention it earlier, Billy."

"Look, man, I'm sorry, I wanted to, I really did. You don't understand, they said they'd kill us. Our cousins are crazy."

Nathan faced Knife. "It's simple, really. If anything happens to your beloved cousins, like life imprisonment or death, the cash would be yours, right? They'd be out of the picture, so it's easy money. There's no need to ask where your cousins are, because if you knew, you'd give them up. Then the money would be yours. Right?"

Knife didn't respond.

Nathan looked at Billy. "Right?"

"I guess."

"You mean you hadn't thought of that? Your brother sure had."

"You're so fuckin' stupid, Billy."

"Easy now," Nathan said. "He saved you a ton of pain. I would've wrung it out of you eventually. You might need a wheelchair and a colostomy bag for the rest of your life, but you would've told me. In fact, I think you owe your brother a thank-you for sparing you all that discomfort."

Knife wouldn't look at his brother. "Thanks."

"That wasn't so bad, was it? Don't you feel better now?"

"Yeah right, whatever."

"Billy is going to show me where the money's buried. You stay put."

Knife just stared. There was more than hatred in his eyes. Something else, something harder to pinpoint. Fear? Anxiety?

Nathan winked at his partner. "If he even looks at you funny, give him another phone call."

Harv answered in his best gangster voice, "You got it, boss."

"Cover us for a second."

Harv pulled his Sig, triggered the laser, and pointed it at Billy's chest.

Billy looked down at the tiny rose of death. "Hey, man, take it easy, okay?"

Nathan cut the tape from Billy's torso. "Hands behind your back, Billy. Do it now." Nathan was all business again. Although he doubted Billy's blabbering cowardice was an act, he wasn't willing to take any chances. He secured Billy's wrists behind his back with several layers of duct tape. "Outside. Let's go."

Holly Simpson was standing just outside the door when they stepped through. She had her Glock 22 in her right hand and a flashlight in the other hand. "We need to get up to that cabin right away," she said.

"They aren't there," Nathan said.

"How can you be sure? You really think there's money buried out here?"

"I seen it," Billy said. "They got it stashed in ammo cans right over there. Three of 'em."

"And you believe him?" Simpson asked.

Nathan shrugged.

"You better be right about this." She turned on her flashlight. "Show us."

They followed Billy through a maze of junked cars, rusted farm equipment, and fifty-gallon drums. Coming from every direction, the symphony of ten thousand crickets filled the night. Gun held at the ready, Holly swept her flashlight back and forth through the jungle of Americana crap. Nathan knew she was looking for threats. This was a good place to get ambushed. Lots of hiding places.

Billy stopped at the corner of the single garage. The bottom of its stucco walls were stained with reddish-brown mud from rain splatter dripping off the eaves. "Right here," Billy said. "I'm standing on them."

"How deep?" Holly asked.

"I don't know. Maybe a foot."

"Shovel."

"In there." He nodded toward the garage.

SAC Simpson tucked her flashlight under her arm, pulled her radio, and thumbed the button. "Copy?"

"*Copy,*" came the response.

"Hustle up here. We're at the garage north of the farmhouse."

Henning acknowledged with a click. Thirty seconds later he arrived, but stopped about one hundred feet short. He flashed his light twice. Holly pointed her flashlight in his direction and issued three flashes in response. Henning's beam bounced as he closed the distance.

Nathan was impressed. They'd used a predetermined signal in case Simpson was being held hostage and forced to use her radio. If Henning hadn't received the three flashes in return, he'd instantly know Simpson was in trouble. Breathing a little heavy from his run, he closed the distance and focused on Billy.

Holly looked at Nathan, then back to Henning. "We're going to open the garage door. You two okay?"

They both nodded.

Henning crouched down at the opposite corner of the garage.

Holly did the same on her corner. "On the deck, Billy," she said, "right here in front of me."

"In the dirt? I'm soakin' wet."

"Do it now."

"It's just a garage," he muttered. Because Billy's hands were secured behind his back, he had to drop to his knees first, then slide his legs out from under him. He plopped over with a grunt and lay still.

Holly nodded to Nathan. "Lift it slowly."

Nathan pulled his gun and stepped to the middle of the garage door. He grabbed its galvanized handle and began lifting. "Watch for trip wires," he said.

Henning crouched lower and swept his flashlight in an arc across the garage floor, his gun tracking the beam.

"Clear," he said.

"Clear," Holly echoed.

"Check the rafters," Nathan said.

They both swept the ceiling area.

Nathan raised the door the rest of the way. The garage was mostly empty. Its concrete slab was cracked in random lines, like a black widow's web. A red Suzuki Enduro occupied one corner and looked like it had rarely been ridden. A small storage rack was mounted above the Enduro's rear wheel. In the opposite corner, several shovels, hoes, and rakes were secured in a linear bracket screwed into the wall. A workbench occupied the left side. Various household tools were hung on hooks: Saws. Hammers. Pliers. Screwdrivers. Wrenches. Everything was arranged by type and function and nothing was out of place. The opposite wall hosted all kinds of power tools. They looked new or well maintained. And yes, there was a grinder. Most of the empty power-tool boxes were neatly stacked against the rear wall of the garage. Nathan frowned. This didn't look right.

Henning stepped into the garage and was about to flip a light switch.

"Wait!" Nathan yelled. He looked at Holly.

She nodded her understanding. "It could be rigged."

Henning stared at the switch for several seconds before backing away from it.

Holly returned her attention to Billy. "Stay put."

"Better let Billy dig up the ammo cans," Nathan offered. "They could be booby-trapped."

"Good thought."

"They aren't," Billy said.

"Your cousins tried to frag a dozen federal employees yesterday," Holly said. "We're a little short on trust."

Henning stepped forward and cut the tape binding Billy's hands. "On your feet. If you run, I'll shoot you in the back. Clear?"

"I ain't gonna run," Billy said, tearing the tape from his wrists.

She and Henning tracked him with their pistols across the garage floor and back.

"I'm going to check the perimeter," Henning said. "Two minutes."

"Two minutes," Holly acknowledged.

Henning disappeared into the darkness.

Tight and professional, Nathan thought.

Holly refocused on Billy. "Start digging."

Nathan and Holly backed away to a safe distance. It was close enough to plug Billy if he tried to bolt and hopefully far enough away from any sort of IED the Bridgestones might have rigged. He looked at Holly again. She was really quite striking, even in the reflective glow of their flashlights. She had well-defined Slavic cheekbones and a small compact figure. She stood five-three or four. She acted confident and self-assured.

Holly kept her voice low. "I'm sorry about Henning's attitude."

"Already forgotten," he said.

"I reviewed your classified file."

Nathan said nothing.

"I wouldn't agree to your involvement unless I knew exactly who you two were."

"Understood," Nathan said. "I would've played it the same way."

"Not many would've survived what you went through."

"I did the best I could under the circumstances."

They were silent for a few seconds. Billy's shovel clanked on metal.

"You don't have many friends," she said.

He kept his voice low so Billy couldn't hear him. "Just Harv."

"I don't either. You didn't seriously hurt them in there, did you?"

"Not really."

"Did you want to?"

"No."

"We should get up to that cabin."

"Let's play this out. A few more minutes won't make or break things. James Ortega's been missing for over a week."

Henning retuned and joined them. "What have we got?"

"We're about to find out," she said.

Billy was just finishing the dig. On his knees, he cleared the last of the dirt away with his hands. He looked up.

Holly told him to pull the first one out slowly.

"Could be a gun in one or more of them," Nathan said.

"Agreed."

Billy did as he was told. He reached into the hole, tore the plastic garbage bag away, and tugged one of the handles. He hefted the ammo can out and set it on the ground. It was matte-green and about the size of a large shoe box. Nathan read the five lines of yellow stenciled lettering and knew the can used to hold a disintegrating link of one hundred armor-piercing incendiary fifty-caliber rounds, with every fifth round being a tracer.

Billy looked up and squinted against the flashlight beams.

"Pull the others out," Holly said, "and place them five feet apart with their latches facing us. Stand behind the one on your left, reach over the top, and pull its lid open. Do it slowly."

Nathan knew that wasn't going to work, but didn't say anything. To open an ammo can like that, especially one that had been buried, you had to hold the carrying handle below its latch with one hand and yank the latch cover with the other hand. Unless it was filled with ammunition weighing it down, it would take two hands. He also saw dried sealant, probably silicon, under the rims of the lids. As predicted, Billy struggled with the can. Every attempt he made to lift the hinged cover didn't work. The entire can lifted into the air. He wasn't getting the necessary leverage.

"May I?" Nathan asked.

She nodded.

"Step away, Billy," Nathan said as he holstered his gun. He walked forward and showed Billy the exact technique needed to open the can. "It takes two hands, like this." He grabbed the carrying handle with his left hand and grabbed the latch cover mechanism with his other. "You have to give it a quick tug in opposite directions." He stepped back and crouched down.

Holly and Henning followed suit. Billy grabbed the ammo can like he'd been shown and gave the latch a yank. The lip popped open. Billy stared straight down into its contents. "Oh, man."

"Open the others," Holly said.

Five seconds later all three ammo can were open. Billy couldn't take his eyes off the contents.

"Move away, Billy. On the ground again."

Billy didn't comply. He just stood there, licking his lips.

"Back away, Billy, on the ground. Do it right now," she said more forcefully.

The three of them walked forward and looked down. Staring up at them were bundles of used bills. Lots of them. Stacked upright in two rows along each can's long axis, the bundles were a near-perfect fit. The distinctive smell of greenbacks scented the air.

Henning let out a low whistle.

Nathan crouched down and pulled a bundle from each can. The middle can held stacks of one-hundred-dollar bills and the other two cans held stacks of twenties. Each stack was about half an inch thick and secured with a rubber band. Probably one hundred bills. Nathan counted the bundles. There were twenty-two stacks of one-hundred-dollar bills and forty-four stacks of twenties. Nathan ran the calculation. "Two hundred twenty plus eighty-eight. That's…three hundred and eight grand, assuming that each of those bundles contains one hundred notes of the same denomination."

"Incredible," Holly whispered. "You think they have stashes like this in other locations?"

"Count on it," Nathan said. "I'm going to check on my partner." Ten feet from the front door, Nathan stopped and issued a whistle. He received the same whistle from inside. He found Harv sitting on the chair, facing Knife. "Billy wasn't lying about the money."

"How much?"

"Just over three hundred grand."

"Nice little stash."

"Yep."

"What now?"

Nathan looked at Knife. "After you and your brother change into dry clothes, you're taking us up to that cabin."

* * *

CHAPTER 10

"Nathan?"

He looked around. Holly's living room. She stood a few feet away.

"How long?" he asked.

"Fifteen minutes."

"Fifteen minutes, not too deep. I guess I didn't realize how tired I was. Sorry."

"No need to apologize. I checked on you ten minutes ago and saw you'd dozed off. I didn't want to wake you. I have a spare bedroom if you want a bed."

He waved a hand at the floor. "Do you care if I stretch out in here?"

"On the floor?"

He shrugged.

"Are you sure? It's no trouble setting you up in the spare bedroom."

"I'm good right here, thanks."

"At least let me put some blankets down, that wood is like concrete." She returned half a minute later with an armful of blankets and a quilt.

Nathan picked up the coffee table and moved it aside. He didn't want to drag it across the oak floor. Then he helped her spread the blankets out.

"Do you sleep on the floor very often?"

"I usually end up there by morning, so I may as well start there."

"Bad dreams."

He nodded. "It's just something I've gotten used to over the years. It's no big deal."

"I know I keep saying this, but I've never met anyone like you before."

"I'm just a guy."

"No, you aren't just a guy. Trust me on that."

"We had a hell of a day."

She took a step forward and took his hand. "Yes, we did. It doesn't have to end just yet."

"No, it doesn't."

* * *

An hour later, after Nathan had fallen asleep, Holly gathered her strewn clothes. Her body still tingling, she padded down the hall, being careful not to make any noise. He looked at peace. She wondered if he was truly asleep. The screams of her surveillance techs still fresh in her mind, she couldn't begin to imagine the horrors he'd endured at the hands of his sadistic captor in Nicaragua. When he'd removed his shirt, her mind couldn't register it. She'd betrayed outright shock and it had nearly ruined the moment. The crisscrossing network of scars on his chest and back looked vicious and brutal. He'd endured so much. And yet he had a positive outlook on the world. He still cared. Despite how he thought of himself, Nathan McBride was a truly remarkable man. He'd been so aware of her needs during their lovemaking. Granted, there hadn't been many: she could count them on one hand. But hands down, he'd been the most unselfish lover she'd ever been with. She hoped there might be a future for them. But given their situations and their professions, and given the distance separating them, she doubted it could work long-term. One or the other would have to relocate, and possibly give up the life he or she had built. She toyed with the idea of transferring to San Diego, but she liked being a special agent in charge of a major field office and was sure the same opportunity wouldn't be available in San Diego for some time. Such openings were extremely rare, and she felt fortunate to have been promoted to Sacramento's top position. *At least we'll always have something special between us*, she thought, tucking herself into bed. Nathan was right, it had been one hell of a day.

* * *

Holly awoke with a start. What was that sound? Had an animal somehow gotten into the house? She reached for her gun, but her hand froze an inch from its cold form. She heard a muffled moan followed by a hiss and spitting sound. No, not animal. Human. She tore the sheets away and hurried down the hall. In the living room, she dimmed the overhead light before flipping the switch. Oh dear Lord, Nathan. His hair plastered to his head, he was covered in sweat, moaning and waving his hands in front of his face at invisible demons. He issued a howl that sent a shiver through her body. He was there, in Nicaragua, being tortured. She remembered what he'd said on the ride up to the cabin, how he'd put a girlfriend in the hospital for waking him up, but how could she let this go on? Would he wake up on his own? She took several steps back and called his name from the opposite side of the couch.

No response.

She said it louder. Again, nothing. What should she do? Steeling herself, she yelled his name. His eyes snapped open, wild with anger. He jumped to his feet and assumed a low fighting stance, his hand clutching an invisible knife.

"Nathan, it's me."

His eyes darted around the room and returned to hers. Her instincts told her to back away, but she held perfectly still. His expression changed to recognition. She rushed around the sofa and wrapped him up in her arms, ignoring the sticky feel of his skin. They held each other without speaking for several moments.

His voice cracked. "What time is it?"

"Just after four in the morning. You okay?"

"I'm really thirsty."

"I'll get you some water." She returned a few seconds later and handed it to him.

He downed it in a single pull. "The moths came for me again."

They settled onto the floor, facing each other.

"Moths?"

"In Nicaragua, my interrogator put a bright light in my face at night. The moths were attracted to it. My hands were tied. I couldn't bat them away."

"That's horrible."

"Thanks for the water."

She could see he was still trembling.

"I'm okay."

But he wasn't okay. An echo of terror still etched his face. She reached over and held his hand.

He half chuckled. "I wasn't kidding when I said my picture was next to *baggage*. I'm sorry you had to see that. I was hoping for the night off."

"Hey, there's no need to apologize about anything."

He looked down at himself. "I think I need a shower."

"Come on." She led him down the hall to the guest bathroom. "You want some company in there?"

"Is there a mustache in Mexico?"

"I'll tell you what, Mr. McBride, because of who your father is, and because he's also a friend of mine, I'll agree to keep this conversation off the record. Hold the line, please."

Once again Nathan found himself listening to complete silence. Coming through the hotel room's window, he heard the muffled whine of a siren, followed by the staccato blast of a fire truck's air horn. A few seconds later, Lansing was back.

"Now that we're off the record, I'll agree to keep this conversation private because you and Mr. Fontana saved a dozen lives the other day. You're owed a debt of gratitude for that. I'll also thank both of you for your military service to our country."

Nathan felt the director's gratitude was genuine. "I appreciate you saying that. May I ask how much you know of our past?"

"All of it."

"I know you're a busy man, so I'll get to the point. We want a green light to pursue the Bridgestone brothers."

"I see. As private citizens, you're entitled to do that provided you conduct yourselves within the confines of the law."

"Director Lansing, may I speak freely?"

"You may."

Nathan frowned at a second siren outside. From the window, Harv shrugged. "Circumstances may dictate a certain amount of flexibility," Nathan said. "You're aware of how we found Frank Ortega's grandson?"

"Yes, I've had a complete briefing."

"I'm asking for a temporary extension of that flexibility."

"If I understand what you're asking for, then you must know that as a sworn law-enforcement officer, I can't agree to it. I did not approve the interrogation of those individuals at the farmhouse outside Sacramento, and I'm disappointed it took place."

"Director Lansing, I'm not recording this call either, you have my word. No one was seriously hurt at the farmhouse."

"That's beside the point, Mr. McBride. This isn't Nicaragua, or the former Soviet Union, and you aren't a CIA operations officer anymore. You're a civilian now, governed by the laws of our land. The Constitution isn't just a piece of paper, it's a fundamental building block of who we are as a society. It defines us."

The man's a politician, Nathan thought. *Of course he is, he has to be, it goes with the territory.* Forcing himself to relax his grip on the phone, he continued. "Frank Ortega's wife said something to me, and I agreed with it. She told me life is never as simple as a book of rules."

"Diane is a fine woman, and I don't disagree with her from a philosophical perspective. But what you're talking about is a very slippery slope. One digression could be regarded as a mistake, two is a pattern. I want containment at this point. Involving you further has considerable risks. Can you imagine the fallout if this ever leaked? The FBI can't afford that kind of coverage from the media. We're already under the microscope with the presidential-powers issue of wiretapping suspected al-Qaeda operatives."

"Based on everything you know about my past, I'm asking you to trust me, to trust my judgment. I'm not indiscriminate."

"For what it's worth, I do trust you, but I can't agree to what you're asking. I cannot, and will not, sanction your continued involvement. Don't get me wrong, I'm grateful for your help to this point, but that's as far as it goes. You're a smart man, you know why I've taken this position." There was a pause on the other end. "Hold the line, Mr. McBride."

Nathan looked at Harv. "What's going on out there?"

"Something big. I just saw another fire truck speed through an intersection, followed by two police cruisers."

Lansing came back on the line. "I've got to go, Mr. McBride. We've got an emergency situation."

"What's happening?"

"There's been a bombing at our Sacramento field office." The line went dead.

The sonic boom. Oh please, dear Lord, no. Not the missing Semtex. Holly! A horrible image flashed through his mind. Was she dead? Worse than dead? He imagined her burned, broken, and bleeding. He grabbed the note with Holly's phone number from the nightstand and dialed. It was ringing. More than once. That gave him hope she hadn't been there.

Come on. Come on. Answer. Answer the phone!

The line connected and a man's voice spoke. "Hello?"

Nathan used an alias. "This is Special Agent Robertson from DC. I'm calling for Special Agent in Charge Holly Simpson." Nathan heard the whine of a siren in the background.

"We didn't know her identity. She's unconscious. We're en route to Sutter's emergency room."

"What's her condition?"

"Critical. She's got multiple fractures to her legs, one compound. She's got second- and third-degree burns. Probably bleeding internally. Both her shoulders are separated. We've got her stabilized, but her head trauma is our biggest concern. Who is this again?"

Nathan ended the call. He turned toward Harv. "She's being taken to Sutter's emergency room in critical condition."

"I'm sorry, Nathan."

"Can you handle our guys when they arrive from San Diego? Get them set up?"

"Yeah, no problem."

"Will you call the bell desk and make sure there's a cab ready at the curb?"

"No problem."

"I'm sorry to dump this on you, Harv."

"I got you covered. Go."

* * *

Special Agent Bruce Henning's expression turned dark as Nathan strode into Sutter's emergency room. The man was no longer immaculate, far from it. He looked like he'd been dragged by rope down a dirt road.

"What the hell are you doing here, McBride? All of this is your fault!"

"Where's Holly?"

Henning didn't answer.

Nathan took a step toward him. "Where is she?"

"Upstairs in ICU. Hey, where're you going?"

"I don't have time for you, Henning."

"You can't go up there."

"Watch me." He approached a nurse who was running toward the ER doors.

"Where's ICU?" Nathan asked.

"Third floor." The nurse pushed through the dual swinging doors. Nathan had a brief look inside. Doctors. Nurses. Blood.

"Damn it, McBride. Wait."

"You coming, Special Agent Henning?"

The fed stepped into the elevator. "You've got a lot of nerve barging in here like this."

"Save your resentment for someone who gives a shit."

"I should arrest your sorry ass."

Nathan squared with him. "You're welcome to try."

At the third floor, the elevator chimed and the doors opened to a horrific scene. Directly ahead the nurse's station was abandoned. Several dozen gurneys containing the wounded lined the perimeter of the room. The floor was tracked and smudged with blood. What was normally a quiet place had been transformed into a battlefield triage unit. It was plainly evident there weren't enough doctors and nurses to deal with the situation. The moans of pain sounded forlorn and eerie. A uniformed officer stationed just inside the room looked ashen, his expression grim. He stepped toward Nathan and Henning, but when the FBI man flashed his badge, the officer turned away.

On the far side of the room, a doctor leaning over a wounded woman looked over his shoulder and yelled, "I need help over here."

No one came. Clearly, no one was free.

Nathan sprinted over. "What do you need?" He looked at the woman's arm where a twelve-inch gash had laid it open, exposing muscle and tendons. The skin surrounding the wound was charred and blistered. Blood was pooling on the sheets of the gurney.

"Who are you?" In his midfifties and balding, the doctor wore protective goggles over rimless eyeglasses. Nathan towered over him by a good twelve inches.

"I've got field-medic training—tell me what you need."

"Throw on some gloves. Behind you on the counter. Nurse's station."

Nathan ran over and grabbed a pair of light-green latex gloves from the box and pulled them on.

"When I pull the bicep aside, I need you to clamp the brachial artery as close to the tear as you can. The tear's just above the radial and ulnar branch. I'm pinching it closed right now with my fingers." The doctor looked at the mobile table containing instruments. "Shit, use the hemostats, they're all I got. You'll need to sponge the blood first. Ready?"

"Yes," Nathan said.

With his free hand, the doctor reached into the woman's arm just above the elbow, grabbed a handful of muscle, and pulled it aside. "Sponge," he said.

Aware of Henning's presence behind him, Nathan pressed the sponges into the opening, and watched the blood soak into them. He knew he had mere seconds to get the artery clamped before more blood would overflow the sponges and fill the cavity. "I see it," he said, opening the hemostats. He inserted the tool into the wound and applied the needlelike pliers just above the tear in the artery.

"Not too tight," the doctor said. "One click."

"One click," Nathan repeated. He pinched the hemostats to its first locking setting.

The doctor released the artery from his thumb-and-forefinger grip. "Good job."

Nathan removed the sponges without being told and set them on the table.

The doctor let the muscle slide back into place, overlaying the pinching end of the hemostats. He removed the tourniquet. "That artery will have to be repaired where it's clamped. Crushing it with hemostats makes it susceptible to clotting at the crush point, but it's the lesser of two evils. It's better to damage the artery and repair it later than to lose the arm."

"How long can you leave it that way?" Nathan asked.

"Not very long. Ischemic time for muscle is two hours max. We have to add the tourniquet time to the clamp time, so she'll need a vascular surgeon within ninety minutes at the outset. Problem is, she's tied up downstairs in the ER. We need to repeat this procedure for the other end of the tear to prevent back bleeding from collateral artery pressure. You ready?"

"Yes."

"Okay, I'm going to pull the bicep aside again. Use another pair of hemostats on the other side of the tear. Clamp it as close to the tear as you can. Get ready with a sponge again. Here we go."

Nathan had no trouble clamping the lower end of the tear. The bleeding was much less severe, but as the doctor had known, the lower end of the tear had been oozing blood from back pressure.

"I need you to wrap up this wound with gauze fairly tight, but not too tight. Don't worry about the hemostats. Just leave them where they are and work around them. Shave the area around her head wound, clean it up, and lay gauze over it, not taped. Try to keep her hair out of the cut. Keep an eye on her IV. She'll need another bag of saline in a few minutes. Can you stick around until more of our people arrive?"

"You got it. No problem."

involved considerable risk of exposing that scandal. Besides, no one knew where Nathan was being held. Containment could've been lost. So why hadn't it become a scandal? They had Nathan. Surely they must have known he was CIA. They'd had three weeks to wring it out of him. And they had tortured him to the brink of death. He didn't like thinking about it.

Stone shook his head, trying to clear his mind. Now wasn't the time to rattle this cage. If his son wanted to blame him for what happened, so be it, there was nothing he could do about it, but for now, he had more important things to worry about. If Nathan pursued this reckless manhunt of the Bridgestones and broke laws in the process, he was on his own. Impatient, he hit the intercom button again. Heidi informed him she was still waiting for return calls from Lansing and Ramsland.

"I also need you to call Commissioner Robert Price. I want the security patrolling all the Senate and House buildings tripled. If he gives you a hard time about it, put him through to me. And needless to say, no one talks to the media. I'll personally skin anyone who even looks at a reporter."

"Yes, Senator. I'll see to everything right away."

On impulse, Stone picked up the phone and called Frank Ortega.

"Hello."

"Frank, it's Stone."

No answer.

"You okay?"

"No, I'm not okay. Why would I be okay?"

Stone didn't respond. All he heard was the chime of Frank's regulator clock in the background.

Finally Frank spoke. "Why didn't your people know about the tunnel?"

The question caught Stone by surprise and he was shocked at the accusatory tone. They weren't his people, the FBI had conducted all aspects of the operation. Maybe it was better if he ended this call as soon as possible. "Look, I just wanted see how you were doing. We'll talk later."

The line went dead. Frank Ortega had hung up without saying good-bye. Stone felt sucker punched. Frank Ortega, a man he'd known for forty years, had just sounded like a complete stranger. For the first time in his life, he felt like an intruder, not a close friend. Maybe he just needed time, Stone reasoned. This was the second tragedy in his family. First his daughter, now his grandson. It had to be tearing him up.

Stone pivoted back to the muted television and shook his head at the endless parade of talking heads analyzing the bombing from every conceivable angle. The nation's first big terrorist attack since 9/11 wasn't from al-Qaeda. Domestic terrorism now occupied center stage, and the negative political fallout was going to land on his shoulders, especially after his press conference trumpeting the seizure of a huge stockpile of illegal Semtex. To make matters worse, his Committee on Domestic Terrorism had been created to prevent this very thing. Why hadn't he seen this coming? In his defense, everything he'd read in the file about the Bridgestones hadn't led him to believe they were capable of such a cold-blooded act. So why had they done it?

Deep down, part of him hoped his son would find them before the FBI did. They had it coming.

* * *

Nathan had been on a Lear before, and he felt a little underdressed in his blue jeans and white Polo shirt. The sixty-foot Learjet 60 XR was spacious, offering stand-up head room. Two rows of single tan leather seats lined both sides of the fuselage, half of them opposing one another. The rear third of the jet was set up like a small office with a table and two opposing seats facing it. Near the back, a small door opened into the head, a little cramped for a man his size, but manageable. The pilot and copilot introduced themselves as Special Agents Jenkins and Williamson respectively. Jenkins wore captain's shoulder boards with four chevrons while Williamson, the first officer, wore three. Nathan guessed they were both trained military, Navy or Air Force. As they studied their new VIP's face, they both betrayed surprise at what they saw.

"I lost an argument with a chain saw," Nathan said, easing the tension.

"That was some argument," Jenkins said. "Where are we going?"

"The airfield at Fort Leavenworth, Kansas."

The two pilots exchanged a quick glance.

"I'll check it out," Williamson said. He disappeared into the cockpit and returned twenty seconds later with a black binder. He started thumbing through the pages. "Here we are...Sherman Army Airfield. Looks like...it's a joint-use military and civilian airfield. Runway's fifty-nine hundred feet. We're good to go, gives us five hundred feet to spare for our takeoff roll." He smiled. "Shouldn't be a problem."

"Make yourselves comfortable." Jenkins waved a hand around the interior. "As you can see, there's no flight attendant so you're on your own for beverage service. I trust you'll be able to find what you need?"

"We'll manage," Nathan said. "What's our flight time?"

"Around three hours, depending on the winds aloft."

"Hell of a job you've got here," Henning added.

"We like it. To be honest, it's nice to ferry someone other than the director for a change." He lowered his voice and looked around in fake secrecy. "He's not real personable."

"So I've heard," Nathan said.

"We aren't strict enforcers of seat-belt rules, but it's best if you're strapped in for takeoffs and landings."

"Shouldn't you at least brief us on emergency procedures?" Nathan asked. "You know, emergency exits, that kind of stuff?"

"Naw," Jenkins said. "If we crash, there will be lots of exits."

Nathan smiled. He liked these guys.

"Nathan's a helicopter pilot," Henning added. "He owns a Bell Jet Ranger."

"No kidding?"

Nathan shrugged.

"I've always wanted to learn helicopters."

"Is your father really Stone McBride?" Williamson asked.

Jenkins bumped him. "We aren't supposed to know that."

"Oh yeah, that's right. Can you…uh…forget I just asked that?"

These two were real characters. Nathan hoped they took their flying more seriously. "To answer the question, Yes, he's my father."

The first officer nudged his captain. "Shouldn't we salute him or something?"

Shaking his head, Nathan took a seat facing forward and fastened his belt.

Jenkins mouthed the word *sorry* to Nathan and pivoted toward the cockpit, but before disappearing behind the cockpit door, he turned back, his expression serious. "Listen, it might seem like we're indifferent about what happened today. We aren't. We use humor to relieve stress. We're as angry as the next man, but that anger doesn't belong in here."

"Understood," Nathan said.

"We've got to file our flight plan into Fort Leavenworth, it'll take a few minutes." Jenkins studied him for a few seconds. "Did Lansing bring you in to find whoever bombed us?"

Nathan wasn't sure how to respond, wasn't sure how much he could share without violating Lansing's or Holly's trust. He hadn't been introduced as Special Agent Nathan McBride, so they knew he wasn't with the bureau. They probably figured him as some kind of VIP bounty hunter. He sensed Henning tense behind him. Walking a tightrope, he used only his eyes, moving them up and down in a nod.

Jenkins got the message. Definitely trained military.

Twenty minutes later, during the takeoff roll, Nathan let his head press against the seat as the Lear's wings bit into the midnight air. Behind him, Henning was silent. He'd been rather subdued on the short drive to the airport. Perhaps the horror of today's events had finally soaked in. Whatever the reason, Nathan welcomed the silence. Despite the catnaps he'd been taking over the last four days, a few hours here, a few hours there, a deep fatigue had crippled him. He was sluggish, both physically and mentally, and gauged his operational readiness at 50 percent. Not good. Unacceptable in military terms. Sooner or later, preferably sooner, he'd need an uninterrupted slumber of at least eight hours. But for now, another catnap would have to do. *Sleep when you can.* He reclined his seat, extended the leg rest, and closed his eyes. He hoped his personal demons would take the night off, especially in front of Henning.

* * *

The jet's PA system woke him just after 0530 Central time. "Good morning, campers," Jenkins's voice announced. "We hope you enjoyed the ride. We'll be on the ground in twenty minutes. We called ahead for a taxi, should be there by the time we touch down."

Nathan looked out the window and saw the faint glow from Kansas City to the east. Directly below, a few scattered lights here and there were the only indicators that something other than an empty black void was down there. Kansas. The heartland of America. Somewhere, amid the endless wheat fields and buffalo ranches, was a giant ball of twine. He'd seen a picture of it, but couldn't remember where, perhaps a travel magazine in his dentist's office.

Jenkins greased the landing, making the smoothest touchdown Nathan had ever felt. The thrust reversers deployed and Jenkins gunned the engine, gently applying the brakes at the same time. At the end of the runway, the jet turned onto the taxiway and rolled back toward the hangars. After the engines had spooled down, First Officer Williamson appeared and opened the fuselage door. He lowered the steps into place. Cool, damp air carrying burned jet fuel greeted them. Nathan liked the smell.

"There's our ride," Williamson offered.

Nathan looked in the direction of the hangars and saw a taxi approaching. It stopped about a hundred feet away. Its Middle Eastern driver got out, but out of respect or apprehension, didn't approach the jet.

Williamson continued. "We need a few minutes to shut down and secure the aircraft."

Nathan complimented the first officer on the landing before grabbing his overnight bag from the rear luggage compartment. Henning also retrieved his two carry-ons, an overnight bag and, from the look of the other, a laptop. Nathan let Henning take the lead exiting the aircraft. They walked over to the cab, and as usual, the driver took a little too long looking at Nathan's face.

"We need a motel," Henning said. He hadn't said hello, or how are you, or thank you for coming, or offered any other pleasantry. Nathan didn't think Henning's abruptness was intentional or purposefully rude, the man just had a lot on his mind. If the cabbie felt slighted, he hid it well.

"The Days Inn is only a few minutes from here."

"That's fine," Henning said.

The driver popped the trunk and Henning placed his two carry-ons inside. Nathan dropped his bag next to Henning's and stepped to the front passenger's seat. He wanted the front, which offered considerably more legroom. He looked at the Lear, admiring its sleek form. It had no markings identifying it as an FBI bird, which for some reason surprised him. On the way back to Sacramento, he planned to peek over the crew's shoulders and ask a few pilot-to-pilot questions. What little he'd seen of the avionics package had impressed him. He wouldn't mind switching seats with the copilot for a spell if they'd let him.

At the motel, Nathan gave the cabbie a fifty and told him to keep the change. Everyone retrieved their bags and briefcases from the trunk. Hoping to make up for Henning's lack of social skills at the airport, Nathan addressed the cabbie in Arabic.

"Thank you for the ride, my friend."

Henning's head turned quickly at hearing Nathan speak. Williamson, the copilot, didn't react at all, which in itself was a reaction.

The driver's eyes grew a little. *"You speak Arabic."*

"I do. Please excuse my friend's abruptness at the airport. We are all very tired."

"It is okay. I understand."

"Stay safe and go with God."

The driver pumped his hand and smiled. *"You too, my friend."*

After the cab pulled away, Henning stepped forward. "What did you just say to him?"

Nathan shrugged. "I thanked him for the ride and told him we're all tired."

"Well, aren't you just full of surprises. What's next, you going to pilot that Lear back to Sacramento?"

"As a matter of fact…" He looked at Jenkins.

"Sure, why not? It practically flies itself."

"No way," Henning protested. "That's not happening, not on my watch. You may be able to shoot a tennis ball at a thousand yards, land a helicopter in a palm tree, perform emergency surgery, find buried treasure, and speak Arabic, but you are *not* flying that jet back to Sacramento. Not while I'm aboard."

Jenkins cleared his throat. "Maybe we should get checked in."

* * *

Ten minutes later they were settled into their respective rooms. The first thing Jenkins did was dial his first officer's room. "Is that really what McBride said to the cabdriver?"

"Yeah, but he left something out," Williamson said.

"What?"

"He apologized for Henning's behavior. Apparently Henning hadn't been real courteous with the driver."

"Who is this guy?"

"Haven't the slightest."

"Think he's one of us?"

"I'm betting he's a spook. CIA or NSA."

"How many languages do you speak?"

"Including English, five."

"Think I should I let him into the cockpit?" Jenkins asked.

"If you asking me if he's dangerous, I'd have to say no."

"Think he bought our act?"

"Not for a second."

"Well, until Lansing changes his mind, we stick to the plan and fly him wherever he wants to go."

* * *

Nathan considered calling Harv but decided against it. It was almost three in the morning in Sacramento. He set his overnight bag on the small table next to the bed. In the bathroom, he washed his face, brushed his teeth, and plugged in his phone. He stripped down to his underwear, pulled the sheets off the bed, and made a makeshift bunk on the floor. He set the alarm clock for 0700, an hour away. Staring at the ceiling, he rehearsed the questions he planned for the Castle's shrink, hoping this little jaunt would be worthwhile. His mind moved to the pilots. When he'd spoken Arabic to the cabbie, Nathan had been certain First Officer Williamson understood every word. He'd seen it in his eyes, an unmistakable twinkle of recognition. What were the odds that one of the pilots assigned to ferry him around spoke Arabic? It seemed Lansing's trust had limitations.

Too tired to worry about it, Nathan rolled onto his side and closed his eyes. Another long tomorrow loomed. Actually, he realized, tomorrow's already here.

* * *

Despite his exhaustion, Nathan awoke before the alarm sounded. He cracked the curtains and scanned the parking lot, where a smattering of pickups, sedans, and SUVs waited beneath a red Kansas sky. At the opposite end of the room, he made a miniature pot of coffee.

After a quick shower and shave, Nathan called Henning's room. "How'd you sleep?"

"Not too well, you?"

"About the same. Hungry?"

"I called the front desk. There are several coffee shops within walking distance."

"What about our pilots?" Nathan asked.

"I didn't want to wake them."

"Five minutes," Nathan said and hung up.

Over breakfast, Henning asked about Nathan's background. Although Henning seemed to understand Nathan's need for discretion, there was a touch of resentment. The stuff in Nathan's head was doled out on a need-to-know basis, and Henning didn't need to know. Simple as that.

On the walk back to the motel, Nathan's cell rang. He looked at the screen. Harv.

"How was your flight?"

"First-class. It's a nice ride."

"No doubt. I took the liberty of arranging your meeting with the Castle's shrink. I've been on the phone all morning trying to reach him, finally did. It took a bit of coaxing, but I think I convinced him of the urgency of the situation. He's seen the television coverage of the bombing, and knows his former patient is responsible. His name is Dr. Harold Fitzgerald, and yes, that's really his name. He's agreed to meet with you at the officer's mess at ten hundred."

"Great work, Harv. What's your take on him? Will he talk to us?"

"I honestly don't know, my gut says yes, but I could've read him wrong. Our call was pretty brief. I'm sure he'll want your conversation off the record."

"I'm really hoping to learn something, anything, that might give us a starting point for tracking Ernie Bridgestone. I still need to run his girlfriend in the NCIC database. Did our guys find anything from the visitation-log info?"

"Maybe. The address she used on the log sheet was a dead end. We called the phone number and got a changed-number recording, so it's a fairly recent change. The new number is a five-five-nine area code in Fresno. When I had Mason pretend to be a telemarketer and call the number, he thought the woman who answered hadn't been honest. Mason said she hesitated for a instant before saying he had a wrong number. It might have been a girlfriend or sister, or it might have been our mark herself."

"It's possible Bridgestone has already warned her she might get a call like that," Nathan said.

"If he still has any contact with her all, he probably *has* warned her, or more accurately, threatened her. She might go underground. Maybe we should've waited on the call."

"I wouldn't worry about it too much. Telemarketers call all the time. Listen, we just finished breakfast, we're walking back to the motel. I'll call you after we've met with Fitzgerald."

Nathan tucked his phone away and filled Henning in on what he'd learned about Ernie's old girlfriend and the fake telemarketer call.

"That might have been her," Henning said.

"It's possible. We won't know until we talk to her."

"And if she won't talk to us?"

"She'll talk."

* * *

The entrance to Fort Leavenworth looked like a hundred other military-base entries. A small guard shack divided the road. MPs with sidearms approached the taxi and asked for everyone's identification. Their taxi had been expected, so the security procedure went smoothly. As instructed, the driver placed the bright-yellow temporary-vehicle pass on the dashboard. He was given a small map of the base showing the location of the dining facility.

Nathan thought the fort had a college campus feel to it, lots of green open spaces, mature trees, and historic buildings. At the dining facility's curb, Henning asked—told, really—the driver to wait for them. Army service members filtered in and out of the DFAC. Most of them wore army combat uniforms. A man in civilian clothes stepped out and approached them, Fitzgerald, no doubt. The man looked nothing like the stereotype of a shrink. No Freudian glasses, bald pate, or goatee. No white coat. He looked more like an aging California surfer than a prison psychiatrist. Dressed in tan slacks and an aloha shirt, he was in his midfifties, with sandy-colored hair, broad shoulders, and a pleasant smile.

Nathan offered his hand. "Dr. Fitzgerald, I presume?"

"The one and only."

"Nathan McBride. Thank you for meeting with us. This is Special Agent Bruce Henning from the Sacramento field office."

"I'm very sorry for the loss of your colleagues."

"Thank you, Doctor," Henning said. "I appreciate it."

"I'd prefer if we talk out here," Fitzgerald said. "The less we're seen together, the better. I know a nice spot under some trees. I eat lunch there all the time."

The cabdriver looked over with a questioning expression. Nathan asked him to keep the meter running and wait. The three men began walking down the sidewalk. After several hundred yards, they veered over to a group of oaks. There wasn't any place to sit except on the grass, so that's what they did. The meeting instantly became cordial, as though they were there for a picnic, not a discussion of national security.

"This okay?" Fitzgerald asked.

"Perfect," Nathan said. "You know why we're here."

"I do."

"I appreciate you meeting with us on such short notice."

"You realize I'm hanging my tail out on a limb, talking to you."

"You have my word as a Marine Corps officer, it doesn't go any further than us. We need to find Ernie Bridgestone and his brother. Find them fast."

"I'm not sure what I can do to help."

"There are a couple of things. First, I'm looking for any insight into his head, how he thinks."

"I've counseled hundreds of troubled souls, but he possesses a pathology we don't see very often."

Nathan waited while the doctor gathered his thoughts.

"He's what I'd consider a borderline devoid."

"Devoid?" Henning asked.

"I'll try to explain by using an example. A mother has a child, a little boy for our purposes. As the child matures, his mother starts to notice he isn't like other boys. He doesn't smile or laugh or cry or show any type of emotion at all. He's picked on by other children. They think he's stupid because he doesn't laugh when they do, and it's made worse when he doesn't react to their ridicule. So imagine the mother sitting the little boy down and explaining that when he sees other children laugh, he should do the same thing. She teaches him to curve his lips up in a smile, show his teeth, and make a heh-heh-heh sound like the other children do."

"That is seriously messed up," Henning said.

"That's right, Special Agent Henning. Just as some children are born with a childhood disease that cripples parts of their bodies, others are either born or molded into masking emotions. That's why I consider him a borderline case. I believe his emotional responses are suppressed, not missing altogether, although I can't be certain of that diagnosis."

"I'm assuming guilt would be missing as well?" Nathan asked.

"Definitely. As a child, he would've had a hard time distinguishing between right and wrong. What all of us instinctively know as being wrong, say like mistreating an animal, is missing, or more accurately, short-circuited. The safety mechanism is bypassed, or it's missing altogether. He doesn't feel any regret for the Sacramento bombing. None."

Henning visibly stiffened a little.

"What about his brother, Leonard?" Nathan asked. "What would Ernie feel toward him?"

"Loyalty isn't clearly defined as an emotion. In fact, I don't think it's an emotional state of mind per se. I mention it because Ernie Bridgestone is extremely loyal to his older brother. He talked about Leonard often."

"In what way?" Nathan asked.

"Mostly about their childhood. Their father was abusive. Brutally so, I'm afraid, and their mother didn't intervene. A common belief among psychologists is that the first year of a baby's life is perhaps the most important. I wouldn't be surprised if Ernie had also been neglected for long periods of time. Try to imagine it: An infant cries because it's hungry or lonely, but there's no one there to feed or comfort it, to give it the tactile feedback it needs to feel secure and loved. Think of it, an infant screaming into the dark, isolated and alone, for hours, maybe even days." Fitzgerald shook his head. "It's cruel beyond comprehension. I truly believe Ernie is the product of such an environment. Leonard is a few years older, so he might have filled in where his mother didn't. It would explain the strong family bond Ernie feels toward Leonard."

"Isn't it reasonable to assume Leonard was subjected to the same neglect?" Henning asked. "And wouldn't he then have the same condition?"

"Yes and no. I believe he was, but some people can overcome such trauma through intellect. My own father, for example. He was from a broken and abusive home, but he became a valuable member of society, putting himself through medical school and becoming a naval flight surgeon. He was also a loving father to me and my sisters. He broke the cycle. Some can, some can't, or more accurately, some won't. They justify their negative behavior by blaming someone else. This act of blaming, of being a victim, if you will, becomes part of their pathology."

Nathan nodded his understanding. "Would Ernie have been able to form a meaningful relationship with anyone other than his brother? We know he was married."

"The answer is yes, but it depends on what you mean by meaningful."

"Love, would he be capable of love?"

"I'd have to say no. At least not in the way we think of it. His love would be based on actions, not emotion. I'll give you an example. Let's say Ernie comes home from work and his wife hasn't cleaned up the kitchen from breakfast. She's tired or having a bad day, or whatever. Ernie would interpret the dirty dishes in the sink as a sign she didn't love him. Follow?"

Nathan nodded. "Tough situation. She'd never be able to do enough to prove her love."

"That's exactly right. A relationship like that is doomed from the start. No matter what she did, it would never be good enough because the emotional bond is missing. When people are truly in love with each other, small things are forgiven and forgotten. Not so with a devoid. Seeing those dirty dishes is like a slap in the face. He doesn't look at the dishes with compassion and ask her if anything's wrong, he just sees them as indication she doesn't love him. Living with a devoid would be the ultimate walk on eggshells."

"Why would someone stay with a person like that?" Henning asked.

"The simplest answer is love. She loved him and was willing to put up with his shortcomings. There are other reasons. She might've had nowhere else to go, or she was convinced she could change him if she only did this. None of it would make a difference. The tragic reality is, unless Ernie gets comprehensive psychiatric help, he'll never change. He'll never come to terms with who and what he is. I was beginning to make some real progress with him just before he was released. You have to remember, on some level these people instinctively know there's something's wrong with them, they just don't know what it is or how it happened. To use a simplistic example, take cats. If kittens are exposed to human love and affection within the first few weeks of their lives, they become pets. If not, they're feral. Of course, it's not that simple with humans, but the principle's basically the same. Unless an infant receives the stimuli needed to feel safe and secure, it's guaranteed to grow up with emotional problems to one degree or another."

"What's his prognosis?"

"Unless he receives comprehensive therapy, hopeless. He won't change. He can't. To use a metaphor, he'll spend the rest of his life barking at the moon."

"What did you talk about?" Nathan asked. "I mean generally. You know. What did Ernie think his problems were?"

"That's easy," said Fitzgerald. "It was the drunk-driving incident that landed him here. He claimed he was railroaded."

"Was he?"

"I reviewed the police reports and eyewitness accounts. There's no question Ernie was legally drunk, but not overly so. From everything I remember reading, it wasn't truly his fault. The woman walked out from between two parked cars. Even if he hadn't been drinking, she still would've died. She was quite drunk herself."

"But railroaded?" Nathan asked. "It sounds like you actually give that some credence."

"I do give it some credence. Some, mind you." Fitzgerald paused, trying to remember. "I don't recall her name, but I think she was from a family of some influence. Justice acted swiftly in the case, that's for sure. I kept copies of the newspaper articles in Ernie's file. He griped about it a lot, to the point of being obsessive, swore to get revenge someday. He also never believed he got a fair court-martial."

"They're all innocent," Henning said.

"Point taken," Fitzgerald said. "But if the circumstances had been slightly different, there may not have been any charges leveled at all."

"We'll check it out," Nathan said. "Please send us everything you have on Ernie's DUI conviction."

"Will do."

Nathan stood, shook hands, and gave Dr. Fitzgerald a business card with his cell and fax numbers handwritten on the back. Henning did the same. "I really appreciate you talking to us."

"To be honest, it wasn't my decision. I got a call from the USDB's commanding officer, who got a call from the fort's commanding officer, who had received a call from the chief of staff of the army."

Good old Thorny, Nathan thought. "Well, I still appreciate it."

"One last thing," Fitzgerald said. "Watch yourselves. They don't come more vicious than Ernie Bridgestone."

CHAPTER 15

On the drive out of the fort, Nathan and Henning rode in silence. They didn't want to discuss anything in front of the cabbie. Back at the motel, Nathan paid the fare and offered a generous tip.

Walking through the lobby, Nathan asked, "So, what do you think?"

Henning shook his head. "That stuff about teaching a kid to smile was creepy."

"Yeah, it's weird, all right."

"What do you think?"

"What I think," Nathan said, "is that wherever we go next, we should rent a car. It'd be better than taking taxis all over creation."

"So where do we go next?"

"Fresno, to pay Amber Sheldon a visit." Nathan looked at his watch. "I want to keep moving. When we find her, we won't have time to conduct a prolonged surveillance. We'll take the direct approach and knock on her door."

"Just like that?"

"You have a better idea?"

"Not really."

"We need to run her through the NCIC. Can you access the database from the motel?"

"Yes."

"Maybe we'll catch a break. If she's in the system we'll have a current address, even better if she's on parole or probation. If she's not at home when we show up, her PO will have her employment info."

"What do you hope to learn from her?" asked Henning. "I mean, besides the obvious, Ernie's whereabouts."

"I'm not sure yet. I won't know until I talk to her. We might be able to use her."

"Use her? Like bait?"

Nathan needed to change the subject. He didn't want to discuss this train of thought aloud. "We should call and check on your SAC, see how she's doing and give her an update."

"I was thinking the same thing."

"I'll swing by your room in ten minutes."

Back in his room, Nathan thought about Amber Mills Sheldon. Interrogating a woman involved different techniques and psychology. In truth, he hoped it wouldn't be necessary. He'd interrogated women before and in some regards found them to be more resilient than men. Despite common belief, interrogation was a mind game more than anything else. To be effective, the victim's spirit must be broken. Physical discomfort, while effective, wasn't the best method unless the information was time-sensitive.

He wished he had a female interrogator available. The psychology of having a woman present, looking on with emotional detachment and a complete lack of sympathy, worked well toward breaking a female's spirit. Having a woman present was especially effective against men. Nathan figured it was the macho syndrome. Men didn't like to appear weak and vulnerable, especially in front of women. Once again, it was all about mind games. Unless the victim had counter-interrogation training, it usually didn't take long to wring information out of them. If that held true, Amber Sheldon wouldn't be much of a challenge.

He gave Henning a few extra minutes before knocking on his door.

"It's not locked," Henning said.

Nathan stepped in and left the door partly open. Sitting at a small desk, Henning was typing on his laptop's keyboard.

"What've we got?" Nathan asked.

"Amber Sheldon is currently on probation for drunk and disorderly contact, disturbing the peace, and driving while intoxicated. Here, take a look. I didn't bring a printer."

Nathan looked over Henning's shoulder while he scrolled down to Amber Sheldon's color mug shot. As usual, she didn't look real happy. She had stringy blonde hair, blue eyes, and a hollow, sullen-looking face, probably from using. She looked hard, a summa cum laude graduate of the school of hard knocks. When the picture was taken, she definitely fit the description of *rode hard and put away wet*. The photo was a year old.

"She's got a fairly long sheet," Henning continued. "Nothing too serious. We have a current address, phone number, and place of employment. She lives in Fresno. Works at an establishment called Pete's Truck Palace. Let's see…After her arrest in 2006, her driver's license was revoked for six months. Based on her background and the trouble she's had with the law over the years, I'm not expecting her to be real friendly. Let's make that call to SAC Simpson. I think she'll want you present for the call."

Henning pulled his cell and scrolled down the numbers stored in memory. When he found the number he wanted, he hit send. He didn't put it on speaker yet. Nathan waited.

"Hi SAC, how are you feeling? Yes, he's here." Henning pressed the speaker button. "You're on speaker."

"Hi, Nathan."

Nathan sat on the bed. "Hey there." He didn't ask how she was feeling, he already knew.

"How are things going out there?" she asked.

"Good. The meeting with the Castle's shrink was helpful."

"What did you find out?"

Nathan went over the salient points of their discussion. He finished with what they found on Amber Sheldon in the NCIC.

"That's good," Holly said. "You heading to Fresno?"

Nathan nodded for Henning to take over.

"Yes," Henning said. "We're planning to rent a car, rather than call the Fresno resident agency for transportation. I'm trying to minimize Nathan's exposure."

"Hold off on that," Holly said. "Fresno's ASAC, John Pallamary, is good friend of mine. We went through the academy together. I'll give him a call."

"We're hoping to be in the air within the next half hour," Henning said.

"What's your plan once you get there?"

"We have Sheldon's current address, so we'll head over there and see if she'll talk to us."

"If she isn't forthcoming, let Nathan take over. Understood?"

"Yes," he said tightly.

"Nathan, use your best judgment when questioning her."

Translation: Don't get rough unless you absolutely have to. "No problem," he said.

Holly continued. "We've copied all the video from the bombing and sent it back east to your father's committee. They're trying to glean as much as they can. We've implemented the largest manhunt in the history of the bureau. Hundreds of agents are on the case. Three more of our people died last night, the rest are probably going to make it. Six of them will never walk again."

"I'm sorry, Holly."

"This isn't your fault. I've had a lot of to think about it."

"Maybe I didn't have to kill their little brother. Maybe I should've wounded him. I could've—"

"Nathan, listen to me, I've read all the reports. Don't do this. Sammy Bridgestone was aiming a sniper rifle at our SWAT teams. You took the proper action for the situation as it existed at the time. If our sniper team had seen him before you, they would've done exactly the same thing. Any law-enforcement officer in America would shoot to kill in that situation. Don't second-guess yourself. None of this is your fault. Clear?"

"Clear," he said.

"We've set up a hotline. Tips are coming in by the hundreds with possible sightings. We're checking them out. ASAC Perry Breckensen is in temporary command. Nathan?"

"I'm here."

"Despite all the manpower we've got, I think you're our best chance at finding them."

Nathan said nothing.

"I've got to go, my nurse just came in. Will you ask Harvey to share anything he finds with ASAC Breckensen?"

"Sure, Holly. No problem."

"Bruce, remember, you're a sworn law-enforcement officer. Where Nathan is concerned, it's don't ask, don't tell."

"Understood," he said quietly.

"If you haven't heard back from me before you leave Fresno, call me from the air."

"I will," Henning said.

"I've got to go." The cell went dead.

"She's an amazing woman," Nathan said.

Henning reached for his laptop. "Let's pack up and get going."

From his room, Nathan called Harv and filled him in. Harv said he'd follow up and make sure he received the DUI news clippings and any other documents Fitzgerald had promised to send. Harv also told him Thorny had come through with Leonard's contacts from his deployment in Iraq.

"We just talked to Holly."

"How's she doing?" Harv asked.

"She sounded tired, but otherwise not too bad."

"Listen, I got that tape of the Bridgestones torturing the two FBI surveillance techs. It's pretty ugly stuff, but I didn't hear anything we didn't already know. All the techs could tell them was your name and that your father was Stone McBride. Incidentally, our personal info isn't available. I had Mason try to dig it out. You know DMV, Social Security, IRS. He couldn't come up with anything. I think we're okay. They'd need someone on the inside of the DOD with high-level passwords to access anything on us, and I don't see that happening. Your father's a different matter. I don't know how protected his personal information is."

"Me either," Nathan said.

"If they're heading back east, it's possible they could tail him from one of his public appearances. We should warn him to stay under the radar for the time being and hire some personal security guards."

"I told him the score. Keep checking Leonard's contacts. I have a feeling one of them is our financial insider. We're looking for someone within a day's drive, two max."

"The list is pretty long, several hundred. And that's a lot of territory to cover, basically the western third of the country."

"You might need to call ASAC Breckensen and ask for some help."

"I definitely will."

"Does the FBI have a temporary field office up and running yet?"

"I don't know. I'll find out. Their building isn't a total loss, but there's no way they can operate out of there in its present condition. What about you? What's next?"

"Fresno. We'll be airborne in half an hour. I'll call once we know something."

* * *

Fifteen minutes later, everyone was boarding the Lear. As Nathan climbed the stairs, he looked at First Officer Williamson and decided to play his hand. Time for this covert bullshit to end. Nathan spoke in Arabic. *"We are on the same side. I have no agenda other than finding the Bridgestones."*

Williamson narrowed his eyes, but the spark of recognition in his expression couldn't be hidden. Nathan knew he was considering his options. There were two. Continue playing the game or come clean. Henning turned at hearing Bridgestone's name in a sentence spoken in Arabic.

Williamson came clean. *"Understood,"* he answered in Arabic. *"I am just doing my job. For what is it worth, I am not real happy about it."*

Williamson headed for the cockpit.

"What did you say to him?" Henning asked.

"I told him the same thing I told you the first time we met, that we're on the same side and my only goal is to find the Bridgestones."

Henning's expression was genuinely puzzled, and Nathan now believed he didn't know Williamson had been assigned as a watchdog. He wasn't sure before.

"How did you know he spoke Arabic?"

"When I spoke to the cabdriver early this morning, I didn't see any reaction from him at all. None. Most people show some degree of surprise."

Henning lowered his voice. "You think Lansing brought him on board to keep an eye on things? To spy on you?"

"Yeah, I do."

"Why bring in someone who speaks Arabic? Al-Qaeda isn't involved with the Sacramento bombing. It doesn't make sense."

"It does if you consider Harv also speaks Arabic."

"Good grief," Henning said. "Sometimes I think there's no limit to the cloak-and-dagger bullshit in this business."

"Don't worry about it, it's a safe play on Lansing's part. There's a lot at stake. He was concerned I might speak in a foreign language with Harv to hide things we discover about the Bridgestones. I'd be willing to bet Williamson also speaks Russian. Probably Spanish too. We aren't going to conceal anything from you guys. If your people find the Bridgestones before we do, that's fine with me. Don't get me wrong, we'd love some quality time with them, but finding them is the primary goal."

* * *

In the cockpit, Williamson lowered his voice. "He knows."

"Is it going to be a problem?" Jenkins asked.

"He seemed okay about it."

Jenkins was flipping avionic switches from a checklist as he spoke. "As far as I'm concerned, nothing's changed. We keep reporting to Lansing as ordered."

"Do we tell Lansing he knows?"

"Not unless we want egg on our faces," Jenkins said. "He'd view McBride's discovery as a blunder on our part."

"Yeah, you're right about that. McBride seems like a decent guy. It's not hard to guess how he got those scars on his face. They aren't random and he sure didn't get them from any chain-saw accident."

Jenkins started the engines, keeping his eyes on the gauges. "I think you're right, he's a spook. Someone carved him during an interrogation. Had to be hell."

"Yeah, no kidding."

* * *

Twenty minutes into the flight, Henning used the air phone to call Holly again. Nathan looked over, but there was no way to put the call on speaker. After a brief conversation, he hung up.

"She made contact with ASAC Pallamary from the Fresno resident agency. An agent's going to meet us at the airport."

"You okay with that?" Nathan asked.

"I just follow orders."

Nathan heard the frustration in Henning's voice. "Don't read anything into it. Like I said, there's a lot at stake."

Henning didn't respond, he just leaned back and stared straight ahead. Nathan felt for the guy, but knew the extra measures being taken by Lansing and Holly weren't a reflection on Henning's competence or loyalty. Although Nathan wasn't familiar with FBI methods of operation, he figured it was probably standard procedure to double up on field assets whenever possible to ensure the best chance of success. Even though he preferred working alone, he'd play along for now. The FBI Lear was too big an asset to turn down. He figured having a federal ball and chain in the form of Bruce Henning was the price of admission, but he couldn't in all honesty discount the help he'd received from Henning so far. If the time came to cut ties with his FBI friends, so be it, but for now, he was comfortable with the status quo.

The Lear touched down in Fresno a little after noon, local time. As it taxied to the general aviation transient parking area, Nathan admired the F-16C Falcons parked next to the Air National Guard hangar. They were beautiful machines, pure in form and function. Although he couldn't imagine it, he wondered if flying them ever got old.

After Jenkins parked the Lear, Nathan spotted a man standing next to a plain sedan in front of a long hangar building. Their FBI contact. He was reasonably sure the agent assigned to them would've been briefed on their objective and the rules of engagement. He had no expectations about the agent's attitude, but hoped it wouldn't be a repeat of a few nights ago when he'd first met Bruce Henning. Because the director of the FBI had given him the use of a Lear, he hoped this new agent would show some discretion. Nathan had to admit there was a definite feeling of importance associated with traveling by Lear. He could get used to this.

As the Lear's engines wound down to idle, First Officer Williamson appeared and opened the fuselage door and they said their good-byes. Unlike at Fort Leavenworth, the air was dry. A bright afternoon greeted Nathan as he followed Henning onto the tarmac. Several dozen private planes were parked to their right.

Dressed in tan slacks and a dark-blue Windbreaker to conceal his sidearm, their FBI contact began walking toward them. In his midforties, he had cropped, thinning hair with a touch of gray at the temples. Former cop or military, Nathan thought. This guy would never make it as an undercover. Their new arrival identified himself as Special Agent Paul Andrews. He looked Nathan over from head to toe before smiling and offering his hand.

Located in the northeast area of Fresno in a mixed neighborhood of residential and commercial properties, Amber Sheldon's apartment was part of a larger complex of identical structures laid out in pairs, back-to-back, with parking on both sides. Second-story walkways ran their entire lengths, accessed by concrete prefab stairs on each end. Several hundred yards to the north, the metal river of Highway 41 could be heard, but not seen. Andrews parked the sedan at the west end of the buildings, where it wouldn't be noticed from the target's apartment. According to the NCIC file, Sheldon lived in apartment number forty-six.

"If she's not here and has a roommate, we're blown," Henning said. "It's fair to assume the roommate will call her and tell her the FBI came knocking on her door."

"We don't have much choice," Nathan said. "We don't have time for a prolonged stakeout. If she's not here, we'll ask where she works—that way the roommate will think we don't know." Nathan turned toward Andrews. "Do you know where Pete's Truck Palace is?"

"It's off Highway Ninety-Nine, about twenty miles south of the city."

"Okay," Henning said. "It's probably better if only two of us knock on her door. Andrews, you cover the stairwells and watch our backs in case the Bridgestones are around. Shoot first and ask questions later."

"You got it."

They followed a concrete sidewalk paralleling the building, then cut across the grass over to the west stairs. Apartment forty-six was on the second floor. This had to be a nicer neighborhood because a Big Wheel tricycle, along with several children's bikes, was leaning against the building, unlocked. A smattering of litter was present, nothing serious enough to suggest it was a lowlife establishment. Licking its paws, a calico cat sat on the bottom step of the stairwell. She squinted in friendship as they moved past her. The windows on either side of Sheldon's door were screened by closed curtains. Nathan and Henning paused and listened to the buzz of a muffled television set.

Nathan kept his voice just above a whisper. "Bridgestone could be in there. I'll go left, you go right."

Henning nodded and grabbed the butt of his gun. Keeping to the side of the door, he knocked twice. The sound of the television went silent, followed by a forceful, "Who is it?"

"FBI, ma'am. We're just here to ask you a few questions. No one's in any trouble."

The curtains parted, revealing a slightly overweight dark-haired woman in her late teens or early twenties. Her yellow tank top revealed more than necessary.

"My mom's got nothin' to do with that man no more." From what Nathan could hear through the window, Amber Sheldon's daughter had retained most of her southern drawl.

"May we come in, please?" Henning asked.

"Y'all got some ID?"

"Yes, ma'am." Henning held up his FBI badge.

"Lemme see your gun too. All you FBI guys carry guns, right?"

"That's affirmative, ma'am." Henning pulled his Windbreaker open.

They listened to the deadbolt click back and the slide chain being removed from its slot. The door opened and the smell of cinnamon greeted them.

Gun drawn, Henning rushed into the room and pivoted to the right.

"Hey," the girl protested. "What the hell y'all doing?"

Nathan dashed into the kitchen and checked behind the counter. "Clear."

Henning checked the bathroom, a hall closet, and both bedrooms. "Clear," he called and returned to the living room. "I'm sorry for doing that, ma'am, but we had to be sure you weren't being held against your will. We're looking for a very dangerous man."

"You could've just asked me."

Both thinking the same thing, Nathan and Henning exchanged a glance.

"I apologize again, ma'am," offered Henning.

Nathan surveyed his surroundings. Although the living room wasn't a complete mess, it could've been neater. Some clothes were strewn on the furniture here and there, and a few dishes were out of place, but overall, it looked reasonably presentable. Nathan watched her freeze when she took in his face.

"What the hell happened to you?" she asked.

Nothing like a little tact, he thought. "Industrial accident."

She whipped her waist-length hair to the side. Along with the tank top, she wore blue jeans—tight in all the wrong places—and fuzzy pink slippers. Her ankles were swollen. She introduced herself as Janey "not Jane" Sheldon.

Henning asked if her mother was expected anytime soon.

"No, and I don't know where she is."

He didn't ask you that, Nathan thought.

"Does she have a cell phone?"

"Hardly, we can barely pay the rent around here. They just raised it on us by fifty bucks."

"We really need to talk with her."

Janey's face clouded. "She's a good mom and all, but she's got a problem, you know…With drinking."

"I'm sorry to hear that. Is there some place she goes regularly?"

She cocked her head, "Probably, but it isn't around here. I've already looked in all the close places."

Nathan watched her body language closely as Henning continued. "Has anyone called her lately?"

"You mean that dangerous man you mentioned?"

"Yes, ma'am."

"I can't say it was him for sure, but she did get a call the other night. She was upset afterward, got really drunk, and passed out on the floor right about where you're standing."

"Did you hear any of the call?"

"Not really, I was watchin' *American Idol.*"

Nathan took a closer look at Janey's eyes. Piercing pale blue. He ran the calculation of her age through his head.

"What time does she go to work?"

"Eight at night. She works the graveyard shift."

"Does she usually come back here before going to work?"

"Sometimes. Not always, though."

Henning turned to Nathan. "Anything more?"

"That dangerous man is your father."

Henning outwardly flinched at Nathan's comment.

Janey narrowed her eyes, disgust stealing over her face. "I think you should get out."

"You're a lousy liar, Janey."

"I said get out."

Nathan took a step forward. "And if we don't?"

"I'll call the police."

"We are the police."

"I'll still call."

Nathan took another step toward her. "That's going to be rather difficult after I've broken your jaw in three places." He quickly scanned the room for a phone, which was in the kitchen.

"Listen, asshole. You can't come in here and threaten me like this."

Nathan spoke over his shoulder to Henning. "Why don't you wait outside?"

Henning opened his mouth to respond, but hesitated, not sure what to do. "Yeah, I guess maybe I better," he said. The FBI agent stepped through the door and closed it behind him.

When they were alone, Janey glanced at the phone behind Nathan. Her lower lip trembled when she spoke. "What do you want from me?" She was close to tears.

"The truth," Nathan said. He moved between Janey and kitchen, trapping her in the living room. She crossed her arms over her chest as a tear rolled, but said nothing.

"It's like this, Janey. I believe you about your mother having a drinking problem, and I believe your life has been difficult because of it. I also believe that when you went looking for her, you found her at a local bar. And I also believe that's where she is right now."

"You don't understand, she hates cops. If you go in there, she'll freak out."

"Listen to me very carefully, Janey. I don't blame you for what your father did. You didn't ask for any of this, it just landed in your lap. It's a raw deal, but that's the hand life has dealt you." Nathan pointed to his face. "I've had a raw deal too. Life goes on. The bomb in Sacramento was made of forty pounds of Czech-made plastic explosive. We think Ernie still has three hundred pounds of it. He murdered twenty-four people and wounded fifty-five others. Six of them will never walk again. They'll spend the rest of their lives in wheelchairs. The blast wave blew people's arms and legs clean off, and the heat from the explosion was so intense, it peeled the skin from their bodies like barbecued chicken. Have you ever seen a third-degree burn victim, Janey?"

She was openly crying now. "Why are you telling.me this?"

"You know why."

"She'll kill me."

"Maybe it's time you were on your own. Don't you want to get out of this place?"

She nodded.

"Do the right thing, Janey. Break the cycle. Make something of your life."

"The Parrot's Nest. She hangs out there before going to work."

"Will you show us where it is?"

"What, right now?"

"Yes. Right now."

Henning was visibly surprised at seeing Nathan emerge from the apartment with Janey in tow. She had changed into more respectable attire, wearing a formal white-buttoned shirt with pressed jeans. Her fuzzy pink slippers had been replaced with tan walking shoes.

"Janey's had a change of heart," Nathan said. "She's going to show us where her mother is."

* * *

From the look of things, the Parrot's Nest wasn't in the best part of town. Most cities the size of Fresno and bigger had a skid row district, and this area of downtown definitely qualified. Part of an abandoned five-story building made of brick, the Parrot's Nest should've been called the Rat's Nest. The small parking lot was lousy with trash, broken glass, dented pickups, run-down hogs, and various other beaters that looked like they might or might not start when their owners finally staggered out to them, assuming they could even find their keys.

"Is that your mother's car?" Nathan asked. "The red Sentra?"

"Yes."

Henning frowned.

Reading his mind, Nathan said, "It was in her NCIC file."

Andrews parked on the curb in a red zone.

"Maybe I should go in with you," Henning offered. "It looks like a rough joint."

"They'll make you right away. Just cover the rear door. Andrews, you stay with Janey."

Andrews looked at Henning, then back to Nathan. His expression neutral, he nodded.

Nathan climbed out and walked toward the main entrance while Henning traversed the parking lot, heading for the rear of the building. The cracked sidewalk was peppered with hundreds of flattened, black gum wads. A staccato thump of bass emanated from within. Although it was the middle of the afternoon, the street was devoid of traffic. Most of the coin-hungry parking meters had been vandalized, their half-moon windows broken.

At the door, Nathan took a deep breath and stepped inside.

CHAPTER 16

Nathan's entrance ended up as clichéd as any cheesy B movie. Every head turned and the pool game stopped. He strolled over to bar and avoided touching the grimy brass rails.

The bartender scowled and pointedly ignored him. *Looks like we'll do it the hard way.* Nathan used the time to study the place in the mirror behind the bar and spotted his mark right away, a tall, stringy blonde sitting at a table with three guys in sweatshirts, jeans, and stained ball caps. Scattered around the room, twenty or so other patrons stared in ape-faced silence. Aside from the bartender, who looked formidable, Nathan didn't see any threats. Half a minute later, the bartender had made it plainly obvious he had no intention of serving someone who'd come in to case the joint.

Without looking at the bartender, Nathan walked over to the jukebox, grabbed its power cord, and yanked it free.

The machine went dark. Charlie Daniels went silent. All heads turned.

A few obscene grumbles spewed from dark corners.

"I'd like a Shirley Temple, if it isn't too much trouble."

The bartender shot Nathan a dirty look, came out from behind the bar, and plugged the jukebox back in. With his right hand, he pumped a quarter, and punched up another shit-kicker song. The music boomed again. Nathan waited for him to return to his hole, made eye contact, and pulled the plug again. The tension in the room instantly doubled, with all eyes now focused on the battle of wills unfolding. With an irritated expression, the bartender started back over.

A smile formed. Nathan McBride, in his environment.

He observed the bartender closely. Right-handed. Six-three or -four. Two hundred seventy-five plus. Weak left eye. Something was strapped to his ankle under his left pant leg, a knife or small gun. This gorilla probably runs the dive with an iron fist. As the bartender approached, Nathan saw a black nylon cord encircling his right wrist and his hand seemed to be half-closed around something, like a magician concealing a playing card. Using his left hand this time, the bartender reached down to plug the machine back in.

"Don't do it," Nathan warned.

The meaty hand froze before being retracted. The bartender straightened up, issued a give-me-a-break smirk, and swung for Nathan's jaw with an open right hand.

Nathan saw it a split second before ducking. A palm sap.

If that blow had made contact, he'd be unconscious or maybe even dead.

It happened so fast no one in the room actually saw it, although half the room heard it. In less than a second, Nathan stomped down on the man's right leg just above the ankle. The crunch of ligaments sounded like uncooked spaghetti breaking.

Howling, the bartender went down.

Nathan pounced on the downed man and rendered him inert with a right knee to the jaw. Several teeth flew. Nathan removed the man's small semiautomatic handgun from its ankle holster and jammed it into his front pocket. Half the occupants scattered for the exits, gone in seconds—bar tabs unpaid. No doubt parolees who didn't want to be caught in each other's company when the cops arrived. Two men at a corner table caught Nathan's attention. A little too clean-cut for this shabby crowd, they looked out of place. He ignored them. For now.

Amber Sheldon hadn't moved. In fact, she appeared to be enjoying the show, not unlike a kid with a magnifying glass poised over an anthill.

Nathan addressed the silent room. "Anyone else?" When no one made a move, he approached the table where Amber Sheldon was seated. Although her smile had somewhat faded at his arrival, it wasn't completely gone. He addressed the three men seated with her. "Would you gentlemen please excuse yourselves from the table?"

The politeness in Nathan's voice took them by surprise, but all three left. One of them bent over the bartender, the other two grabbed stools at the bar.

Amber Sheldon removed a cigarette from the pack sitting on the table and fired it up with a wooden match. Through a slit in her lips, she blew the smoke up and away, and nodded to a vacant chair. "Have a seat, cowboy."

Nathan sat down facing the center of the room. He caught the two men he'd noticed earlier watching him. He winked and they looked away.

She studied his damaged face for several seconds. "Been in a few fights?"

"A few."

"What do you want?"

"My own private jet."

"Cute. What do you want with me?"

"That's much more specific, but you already know why I'm here, don't you."

"I gotta pretty good idea. You a cop?"

"No."

She took another deep drag and blew it out slowly.

Nathan leaned forward slightly. "What did he say to you on the phone the other night?"

Her face showed instant understanding. "That little slut, what did she tell you?"

"I'm asking the questions from now on."

"The fuck you are. I don't have to tell you jack." She blew smoke in his face and smiled.

In a lightning-fast move, Nathan snatched the cigarette from her fingers and flicked it at her. In a shower of red sparks, it bounced off her forehead.

"Hey, asshole. Who the fuck do you think you are?"

He engaged Amber's stare. "I'm the one who's asking the questions. You're the one who's going to answer them." Nathan softened his tone. "It doesn't have to get rough. We can talk like mature adults right here and now, or you can be tortured in a soundproof room, screaming in agony. I'm good either way."

"Some cop you are."

"I'm not a cop."

"Who are you?"

"A vested third party."

"A bounty hunter? Ernie told me someone like you might come around."

"And."

"He said if I talked, he'd kill me and Janey."

"Does he know she's his daughter?"

"Hell no."

"Do you know where he is?"

"No."

Nathan watched her reaction closely.

"I don't," she said. "I'd give his ass up if I did. He's a piece a shit."

She wasn't lying. "Tell me about his old hangouts, places he liked to go, people he knew. Anything that might help me find him."

Sheldon half laughed. "Places? He liked to play pool for money, but he wouldn't be doing that now, would he? The only people he knew besides me were his brothers."

"Why'd you visit him when he was locked up?"

She considered the question for a moment before answering. "Don't get me wrong, Ernie's a first-class jackass, but he still got a raw deal. The DUI thing? His court-martial?"

"What about it?"

"That dumb broad walked right in front of his car. I know, 'cause I was there, sitting next to him, when it happened. It wasn't his fault. We weren't even speeding, and he wasn't really drunk. He got railroaded 'cause she was some sort of big-shot lawyer from a rich beaner family."

Nathan leaned forward. "I find the word *beaner* offensive. Don't use it with me again."

"Whatever. No need to get pissed off. Anyway, her dad was some kind of government fat cat. She was the one hammered that night, not Ernie."

"That may be true, but the law recognizes only the legal limit and Ernie was beyond it. He had a long history of insubordination and alcoholism."

"He still got screwed. He was real bitter about the whole thing. It's all he ever talked about. He swore to get revenge someday. I told him he should just forget about it and move on. After he hooked up with his older brother, I never heard from him again until his call the other night."

"Did you believe him, about getting revenge?"

"Yeah, I did. Still do. One thing about Ernie, he don't forget about shit like that. At the time, I felt sorry for him. I don't now, but I did back then."

"So what changed?"

"I did. I decided I wasn't going to put up with his shit any-more. After he got out, he was worse than ever. He was always yelling and screaming. I could never do anything right. Nothing was ever good enough for that man."

Nathan didn't want to pursue this line, he already knew about Ernie Bridgestone's pathology. "Is there anything else you can think of that might help us find him?"

"Not really."

"Do you mind if we put a trace on your phone, in case he calls again?"

"Knock yourself out."

Nathan grabbed a pen from his shirt pocket and wrote his name and cell number on a napkin. "If Ernie calls you again for any reason, tell him Nathan McBride is looking for him. Remember it. Nathan McBride."

"I'll remember, but I pray I never hear from that piece of shit again."

"I need your help."

"Forget about it, I'm not doing nothing to put me or Janey in danger."

"There's a million-dollar reward." That got her attention. Then he took a few minutes to lay out his plan and her part in it.

"I don't like it," she said, "even with the money you're offering me over and above the reward, which I might or might not get."

"If it doesn't work, you still keep my fifty grand, if it works, you're a million dollars richer."

"I'll think about it."

Nathan stood. "He murdered twenty-four people."

She lit another cigarette. "I said I'll think about it."

"Remember, if he calls, don't talk to him on your work or home number. Drive a few miles down the road and find a pay phone. Make sure you're not followed. Write the number down and arrange a time for him to call you back. After he calls, wait a few minutes before calling me. And be sure you mention my name, Nathan McBride."

"What so damned important about that?"

"He'll know."

She squinted her eyes and took another hit on the cigarette.

"Also, if he calls, verify that Janey's his daughter."

"I don't like that either."

"Think about it, Amber. Put the pieces together."

She was quiet for a few seconds. "You're thinking he'll want to see her."

"That's right."

"What makes you think he gives a damn? He never has before."

"That's true, but he didn't know about Janey."

She didn't respond.

"Janey's outside. Don't give her a hard time for talking to me. I didn't give her a choice. She's just trying to do the right thing. I hope you will too. Let her drive you home. If you get behind the wheel, those two over my left shoulder will probably arrest you."

She looked in that direction. "Thanks for the heads-up."

Nathan left her sitting there and walked over to the clean-cut guys. "It's a little warm in here for Windbreakers."

They didn't reply.

"She doesn't know where he is."

Keeping his eyes squarely on Nathan, the man sitting on the left slid his right hand into his waist pack. "We don't want any trouble."

"You're dressed right, but your hair and clothes are too clean. It makes you stand out in a place like this."

They glanced at each other, their expressions neutral.

Nathan continued through the bar, waved to the toothless bartender, and received a middle-finger salute.

Outside, he found Henning with his Glock drawn. All six patrons who'd bolted out the rear door were neatly lying face-down in the alley, arms out their sides. "Looks like an undersized catch," Nathan said. "I'd throw them all back."

"How'd it go in there?"

"About like I expected. Sheldon doesn't know where he is. She confirmed he called, though. Gave us permission to tap her phone in case he calls back."

"Well, that's something."

They started across the parking lot.

"What about us?" one of the barflies asked from the concrete.

Henning turned back. "Take off."

Watching them scramble in every direction, Nathan was reminded for the second time in as many days of a real-life *Cops* episode. Back at the sedan, Nathan opened the door and let Janey Sheldon out. "Your mother needs a ride home. Don't let her drive."

"What happened in there?"

He lowered his voice to a whisper. "Watch what you say in your apartment. Big Brother's listening."

"What?"

"Just don't let your mom get behind the wheel."

"That's it? You're just gonna leave me here?"

Nathan slid into the backseat of the FBI sedan and looked at Janey. "Drive your mom home."

Something occurred to him as Special Agent Andrews pulled away from the curb. Amber Sheldon hadn't asked for any sort of protection against Ernie.

* * *

The drive back to Fresno's airport was somewhat subdued. Nathan answered a few questions from Henning, but he couldn't stop thinking about the presence of the two undercover agents in the bar. It didn't pass the smell test. In fact, it stunk to high heaven. He didn't want to think about the implications, didn't want to believe what he suspected was true, that Holly Simpson had told Director Lansing of his plans.

The odds of any other explanation were astronomical. That left Nathan with a decision to make. Should he continue to share information with Holly? He found it difficult to believe Holly would knowingly betray him and act behind his back. It was more likely she had simply reported his plans to Lansing and Lansing had acted independently. Even if Holly had reported his activities to Lansing, she hadn't done anything wrong. It was her job, and indeed her obligation, to report her activities to her boss.

One thing was certain, he wanted to talk to her alone, wanted the truth.

Starting with Lansing, he began to analyze and question everything. Lansing had placed a multilingual agent on the Lear to keep an eye on his activities. Given the stakes, it was a reasonable precaution, but it felt like overkill. If Lansing wanted a watchdog, he already had one in the form of Bruce Henning. So why the doubled asset? An asset that not only spoke Arabic, but probably Russian as well. Did Lansing possess that level of mistrust? Did Lansing really think he'd speak to Harv in a foreign language to hide information? It didn't make sense. There had to be something else going on, something deeper. What was Lansing hiding?

The more Nathan thought about it, the more uneasy he became. Had Lansing given him the use of the Lear strictly as a way to monitor and control his activities? He thought back to Holly's comment in the piano bar. She'd said Lansing didn't need him. Why would he? The director of the FBI had thirty-one thousand employees under his command. She'd also said Lansing would want containment at this point, and his continued involvement would have serious consequences if it ever leaked. So why had Lansing brought Nathan in? Granted, the bombing in Sacramento had changed the equation, but did Lansing truly believe Nathan was the FBI's best bet of capturing the Bridgestone brothers? An adage flashed through his head: Keep your friends close and your enemies even closer. Was Nathan the enemy? If so, why? In the piano bar with Holly, he'd made it quite clear he and Harv were going to pursue the Bridgestones with or without the FBI's blessing. Had Lansing allowed him into the investigation only to monitor his every move?

Nathan rewound to the beginning of his involvement in the operation. Freedom's Echo and Semtex. James Ortega was discovered while undercover. The raid at the compound. The FBI's field office being bombed. Semtex being used. Semtex still missing. Semtex. Semtex. He closed his eyes and let his head rest against the seat back. Aside from the dead FBI agents, the stakes of this case revolved around Semtex. How easy would it be to get the stuff? Even if Leonard Bridgestone had made contact with a Syrian official in northern Iraq, there was still a language barrier. Unless Bridgestone spoke Arabic, which he doubted, someone would've been needed to translate conversations. He made a mental note to check if Leonard spoke Arabic. Then, if a deal was struck, the Semtex would have to be smuggled out of Syria, but not without at least a partial payment, more likely the entire payment. Did Leonard have that kind of money back then? Nathan doubted it. So how had the deal gone down? Assuming Leonard had managed to find a translator and assuming he'd made a deal with a foreign national, probably a complete stranger, and assuming he had the financial wherewithal to purchase the Semtex in advance, why wouldn't the Syrian official just keep his money and never deliver the explosives?

And how was the stuff smuggled out of there? Syria was high on the NSA's watch list of terrorist-supporting states. Smuggling Semtex to a neighboring country like Lebanon was probably difficult enough, but smuggling it into the United States had to be a million times harder. It would involve lots of people. People to create fake documents and falsify cargo manifests. People to remove the Semtex from its stockpiled location. People to pack the Semtex into disguised crates. People to transport the disguised crates down to the shipping terminal. People to load the crates into a cargo container.

Nathan couldn't remember ever seeing any type of product with a label stating *Made in Syria*. He knew Syria exported textiles and clothing, olive oil, and of course, crude oil. But anything leaving Syria on a direct path to the United States would be under much closer scrutiny than exports from other countries. It was unlikely the Semtex could be sent directly by container ship, so that meant the disguised crates would probably be sent to another country first, then transferred to another cargo container before being loaded onto a ship bound for the United States. Virtually all cargo containers were monitored and controlled by computerized inventory programs that both identified and tracked them as they were loaded and unloaded from ships. He supposed the Semtex could've been transported by a smaller private ship that met yet another ship out at sea, but how likely was that? And, again, how many people would be involved? Dozens? It simply couldn't be done by two or three people. And it would be expensive. Nathan had no idea what a ton of Semtex sold for on the black market, but whatever the number was, he doubted it would be economical based on the scenario he'd just worked out.

The Syrian connection, now that he'd had time to think it through, was looking more and more unlikely. So if the Bridgestones hadn't gotten it from Syria, where did they get it? Did someone within Freedom's Echo have a connection to international arms smugglers? If so, who? Was the FBI looking at other members besides Leonard and Ernie? Surely they had to be. The bureau would be asking the same questions as Nathan: Where did the Bridgestones get the Semtex?

CHAPTER 17

With the smell of Italian food still lingering in the air, Frank Ortega sat at his desk waiting for his phone to ring. When the damned thing finally bleeped to life, he looked at his Chelsea ship's bell clock. Four minutes late. He pivoted his wheelchair and stabbed the speaker button.

"What the hell is going on out there?" he asked. Not *hello*, or *good afternoon*, or *how are things in DC?*

"We're trying to sort it out."

"Trying to sort it out? What kind of answer is that? They burned my grandson alive."

"Frank, I'm as angry as you are. He was your grandson, but he was also my employee."

"There's a big difference."

"Damn it, Frank. I know that. Your grandson isn't the only casualty. I've got twenty-four additional unhappy letters to sign."

"Look, I'm sorry. I haven't been sleeping well. I'm…I'm so damned angry, I just want to kill someone."

"I wish I could bring him back, unwind the clock, and start over. I'd do a lot of things differently."

"Let me be clear, Ethan, I don't blame you for any of this."

"Maybe bringing McBride aboard wasn't such a good idea. He complicates things."

"Why? He's under your control, isn't he? He found my grandson."

"Yes, but he also killed the Bridgestones' kid brother. That was an unexpected twist with unexpected consequences."

Frank tried to keep his voice calm. "He did exactly what I asked of him. You'd have a dozen dead SWAT agents if he hadn't been there. I asked him to back you guys up and that's what he did, to the letter."

"You know I'm grateful for that. But the problem's different now. It's bigger, more public. What am I saying? Public? It's world-wide news. And there's over three hundred pounds of Semtex still missing."

Ortega pinched the bridge of his nose, trying to keep the conversation on track. "All the more reason to have McBride on their trail, then."

"It was that damned tunnel. If they'd shown it to James, he would've told us. As far as we knew, the Bridgestones had no way to get the Semtex out of there. Or themselves, for that matter. We had that compound under constant surveillance. This whole thing would be over if it wasn't for that damned tunnel. Hell, I don't know. Maybe I should've anticipated something like this. Maybe I should've had choppers orbiting just over the ridgeline. I could've—"

"It's not your fault, Ethan. I don't mean to interrupt, but let's stay on track. Do we keep McBride aboard?"

"At this point, I suppose we don't have much choice. It's all I can do to contain him. If he finds the brothers before we do, that's great. But I don't see that happening."

"What's he doing now?" Frank asked.

"He checked Ernie Bridgestone's visitation logs from Fort Leavenworth before going out there. He spoke to Ernie's former shrink, then came back and made contact with Amber Sheldon in Fresno, but she doesn't know where Bridgestone is."

Frank paused. When he spoke, there was a hard edge to his voice. "What did Sheldon tell him? Did she—"

"Frank, I don't know. McBride's been tight-lipped. He spotted a couple of my agents watching her, but he doesn't know for sure they're mine."

"Don't kid yourself, he knows." Frank wheeled around and looked at the photographs on his wall. "Maybe we should cut ties with McBride."

"No. I hate to admit it, but you're right. McBride's probably our best shot. Despite what we think of his methods, he gets the job done. He thinks the Bridgestones might go after his father next. He told my SAC in Sacramento he thinks the bombing is probably a diversion."

"Some diversion."

"And on our consciences."

"The hell it is," said Frank. "We didn't make those bastards do anything."

"You know what I mean. Look, if McBride's as good as I think he is, he'll eliminate the problem and we'll close the book on this."

"Let's hope so."

Three thousand miles away, Director Lansing hung up and leaned back in his chair. He needed to go home to his wife and kids. If containment weren't forthcoming, he'd be spending a lot more time there, which, when he thought about it, wasn't an altogether bad idea.

* * *

Leaving Fresno behind, the FBI Lear climbed into the clear afternoon air. Nathan pulled his cell and called Harv.

"You on your way?" Harv asked.

"Yes, we're just leaving Fresno."

"We've come up with squat on the financial insider."

"There may not be one. I'm beginning to think they've been stockpiling cash. They probably have a huge stash buried somewhere."

"That's beginning to make the most sense, but it's also going to make it a lot harder to find them."

"I know." Nathan lowered his voice. "Bear with me, Harv. I'm playing a hunch. I left my name and number with Amber Sheldon. I told her if Ernie calls back, she's to tell Ernie I came looking for him. I asked her to specifically mention me by name."

Silence from Harv.

"There's more. Amber's got a nineteen-year-old daughter. Guess who the father is?"

"No way."

"Amber never told him."

Harv paused, thinking about this new twist. "You're thinking if he discovers he's got a long-lost daughter, he'll want to see her before bugging out."

"Yep."

"Then everything depends on Ernie calling her again. What if he doesn't call?"

"I've got that covered."

"What's your plan?"

"Five-by-one," Nathan said.

"Understood. Want me to pick you up at Sac International?"

"No, Henning's got a vehicle there. I'll see you at the hotel in about an hour."

"Stay safe, partner."

Nathan settled in for the short flight back to Sacramento. He needed to talk with Holly Simpson, just the two of them. Everything hinged on her being honest. At a minimum, he was going to need the full media power of the FBI to implement his plan for trapping Ernie. He'd just have to wait and see how his conversation with Holly went. Despite everything he suspected about Director Lansing, he still felt Holly could be trusted. They'd connected on an emotional level, and he didn't think she would willingly betray him. *Willingly* being the operative word.

He turned toward Henning, who was looking at him. "I'd like to visit with SAC Simpson tonight. Alone, if you're okay with that."

"It's up to her." Henning pulled his phone and dialed the hospital. He asked to be connected to Simpson's room. "Hi, SAC," he said. "How are you feeling? Yes, we're on our way, should be landing in about twenty minutes. Nathan McBride wants to stop by... Yes, tonight...Okay. We should be there in about an hour plus or minus. Okay...See you then."

"Thanks," Nathan said.

"No problem. May I ask what it's about?"

Nathan hesitated.

"Look," Henning said. "I don't blame you for being suspicious. There hasn't been a lot of trust around here."

"I'm an unproven asset. It's a safe call on Director Lansing's part."

"If Lansing had seen you in action at Sutter Hospital, he'd feel differently."

"For what it's worth, I've got no problem with you."

"Well, at least that's something. What does five-by-one mean?"

"It means I'm uneasy with the current situation and don't want to discuss the subject aloud. I have a plan, but I want to run it by SAC Simpson first."

"Why not run it by me too?"

"I will when I'm able. I can tell you this much. My plan's risky and I'm going to need some luck to pull it off, but it's all I've got."

"I want to help."

"It'll be Simpson's call. You and I have worked well together."

* * *

The first thing Nathan noticed when he entered Holly's hospital room was the cheerful atmosphere. Flowers and heart-shaped helium balloons were everywhere. Despite the monitoring machines and intravenous stands, the room looked colorful and bright. Holly was sitting up in bed with an FBI file in her lap. She set the file down.

"Thank you for the flowers and balloons," she said.

He paused, but recovered quickly. *Harv.* "You're welcome. Feeling better?"

"Tons."

The top of her head hosted a new bandage wrapped in gauze. The external supports on her legs were still there, suspended by a cable system of stainless-steel supports that looked like jungle-gym bars. Some of the balloons were attached to them, swaying gently in the processed air. The room had a conflicting odor, antiseptic versus floral. Nathan thought she looked better. Her eyes were brighter and more alert. When he first visited, she'd looked like death warmed over.

He grabbed a chair and sat facing her. "Director Lansing beat me to finding Amber Sheldon. When I arrived at the bar, two special agents were already inside watching her."

Holly stared, her mind working. "Are you sure they were ours?"

"Am I one hundred percent sure? No."

"Then why do you think they were ours?"

"Lansing put an agent on the Lear with me, the copilot. He came clean and told me he was reporting directly to Lansing on my activities. Look, I'm not trying to be confrontational. I think it's a safe play on his part, but before I go any further, I need to know who I can trust and who I can't. And right now, Lansing's in the negative column."

"Of course I told Director Lansing where you were going and what you planned to do, but I didn't know he'd take that kind of action."

"He's in the hot seat for any political fallout. He has to be cautious."

"Overly, it seems."

"I have a decision to make and I wanted to talk with you first. If we're going to catch these guys, we can't be working against each other. If Amber had spotted those undercover agents in the bar, the entire dynamic would've been different, she might not have talked to me. You understand where I'm going with this."

"Yes."

"Because I don't want you to compromise your position with Lansing, I'm reluctant to continue with the status quo, especially if you feel you have to report everything I'm doing."

"I don't have to report everything."

"Good, because I need your resources for the next phase of my plan."

"If I'd known what Director Lansing was planning, I would've told you."

"Like I said, I'm not pointing fingers at anyone, especially you, but the surveillance needs to stop."

She reached out and grasped his hand. "I'll find out what's going on. That's a promise."

"Don't compromise your relationship with him over this. You and me? We're still good."

"I'm glad to hear that." She released his hand. "You mentioned the next phase?"

"I'll be honest. It's a long shot, but it's all I've got. I need Ernie Bridgestone to call Amber again."

"She already called?"

Nathan had told her about Amber's first call. He credited her memory lapse to the heavy drugs in her system. Surgical anesthetics had a certain amount of amnesia associated with their use. "Ernie called and told her not to talk to the authorities or he'd kill her. I'm going to tap into that."

Holly listened while Nathan laid it out. It took several minutes.

"It's a good plan," Holly said, "but you're making a huge assumption about Ernie's character."

"It's all I've got. And aside from Leonard, Janey's all Ernie's got, in terms of family. If we set this up right, I think there's a good chance Ernie will feel compelled to call. I told Amber not to talk with him on her home or work number. I told her to have Ernie call back on a pay phone. She's also being shadowed. Let's hope Lansing's people aren't using rifle mikes on her every move."

"It's a little cruel, what you're planning."

"To pull this off, it has to be spontaneous. She can't know it's coming. I can't worry about hurting her feelings. In fact, I'm counting on it. I'm hoping she *will* be angry about it."

"Why?"

"Because I broke my promise."

"What promise, what are you talking about?"

"Remember our conversation in the piano bar? The part about me not making myself a target?"

"Nathan, what did you do?"

"I added an insurance policy. During my interview with Dr. Fitzgerald at the Castle, he said Ernie was obsessed with revenge for being railroaded. I'm hoping to tap into his tendency toward revenge, this time for his little brother, Sammy. If Ernie calls Amber, I told her to specifically mention my name, that a guy named Nathan McBride came around looking for him."

"I really wish you hadn't done that."

"I'm sorry, Holly, but I made that promise before they bombed your field office. This isn't a simple manhunt anymore. It's a fight to the death. The FBI is now the hunted, not the hunter. If the family loyalty angle doesn't work, I'm hoping Ernie's desire for revenge will. Think about it, they could've taken their cash and bugged out, but they chose to stay and avenge their kid brother. Although they don't know it yet, they didn't kill the person directly responsible. After Ernie finds out I'm still alive, it probably won't sit well with him. If I can just get Ernie to call Amber again, things will fall into place."

"In any case, we need to protect you. You know what they're capable of."

"I can take care of myself. Hey, I've got to run."

"Nathan?"

He waited.

She smiled and waved at the decor. "Thank Harvey for me."

Nathan smiled. "You don't miss much."

CHAPTER 18

Nathan entered his hotel room and collapsed on the bed. He knew Harv would hear him.

"That you, Nate?"

"Yep."

"How's Holly doing?"

"Better. And thanks for sending the balloons and flowers. Her room looked nice."

"I figured it might brighten things up a little."

"I need a shower and some chow. Have you eaten?"

"Not yet. Let's grab a bite down in the restaurant. Dr. Fitzgerald promised to fax everything he has on Ernie Bridgestone's drunk-driving accident. We don't have it yet, but it might be here by the time we finish dinner."

Nathan rubbed his face. "I keep having this feeling...Doesn't it seem like there's something's missing? Something we're not seeing? I mean, think about it. Lansing's gone to a lot of trouble to monitor my every move. The use of his Lear. The agent on the Lear, the two agents in the bar. I wouldn't be surprised if he's tapped our phones. They're probably listening to us right now."

Harv nodded. "Whatever the case, we should probably go stealth from now on."

"Agreed. Also, I was thinking about Frank Ortega. When was the last time you talked with him?"

"I called him early this afternoon."

"How's he doing?"

"Hard to say. He seemed calm. He was very curious about your trip out to the Castle and your chat with Fitzgerald. He was especially interested in your meeting with Amber Sheldon. He really grilled me over it."

"Grilled you? What about?"

Harv pointed at the ceiling. "I'll tell you on the way to dinner."

In the elevator, Nathan resumed their conversation. "What did Ortega want to know about Amber Sheldon?"

"Everything. He wanted to know what you two talked about. Word for word."

"What did you tell him?"

"I thought it best not to get too specific. I basically told him you asked Amber about Ernie's background, anything she could share that might help us find him. I said she didn't have much to offer. I didn't say a word about Janey being his daughter."

"Good thinking. We need to keep that under wraps."

"I'm uncomfortable withholding information from him."

"I'm not. Something tells me Lansing and Ortega are closer pals than we realize. I've been thinking about that too. How much clout would you need to involve a couple of outsiders like us in top-secret bureau business?"

"A lot."

"Exactly. Ortega's been cashing in a big debt Lansing owes him. I wish we could find out what it is."

"With all due respect, Nate, why would we care? We don't need to know."

Nathan sighed. "I suppose you're right. I guess all this cloak-and-dagger crap is getting to me."

Neither of the Hyatt's restaurants were open yet, so they walked a few blocks to the Hard Rock Cafe. It was still a bit early for dinner, so the place wasn't crowded, which suited them just fine. They were escorted to a corner table by a hostess who looked sixteen years old. In reality, she was probably in her late twenties. *I must be getting old*, Nathan thought as he watched her walk back to her station. When the server came, he ordered a Caesar salad with the dressing on the side. Harv ordered a teriyaki-sticks platter, pot stickers, a shrimp cocktail, a bowl of New England clam chowder, a calamari steak sandwich with fries, and a chocolate shake.

Nathan just stared.

"What," Harv said.

"You got a hollow leg or something?"

"I'm hungry. What about it?"

"I'll bet you fifty bucks you can't eat all that."

"You're on."

Forty minutes later, Nathan fished out his wallet.

On the walk back to the Hyatt, Nathan shook his head. "You amaze me."

"I know."

Nathan switched to Russian. *"You spot the two agents watching us in there?"*

"Yes," Harvey answered. *"Opposite side of the room. Male-female combo sitting at the bar. They were good. I thought maybe you had missed them."*

"What are we going to do about them?" Nathan asked.

"You want to mess with them?"

"It is tempting, is it not? Did you see them while I was out of town with Henning?"

"No."

"Means they are watching me, not you."

"Probably, but I could've missed them."

"You are better at this than me."

As they chatted, they passed a homeless man sitting against the brick wall of a liquor store. "Gol-darned for-ners," he muttered.

Nathan smiled at the comment, removed his wallet, and took out a twenty. "Don't spend it all in the same place," Nathan said in English. He used the opportunity to glance back at the Hard Rock's entrance. Their tails were just walking out the door. They turned and started down the sidewalk, holding hands. Yeah, right.

Harvey kept walking without turning. *"They coming?"* he asked in Russian.

"Yes. I will divert over to the registration desk and let them catch up. You head into the bar and order a glass of wine. I will head up to the room. Give me three minutes, then come up."

"What are you going to do?"

"Waste some taxpayer money."

At the registration desk, Nathan spoke softly to the woman behind the counter. She was in her midthirties and slightly over-weight. Her dark hair was in a bun. As usual, she did a double take at Nathan's face, but recovered quickly and forced a smile.

Nathan leaned forward and spoke quietly. "There's a man and a woman following me. When they come through the doors, give me a nod."

"You want me to call the police?"

"No, just nod when they come in. They work for an insurance company, they're harmless, but don't make it obvious you're notic-ing them."

Ten seconds later she gave Nathan a nod.

"Thanks," he said.

Nathan walked over to the bank of elevators and pressed the button. At the sixth floor, he hurried to his room and let himself in with the electronic card key. He grabbed his 9-millimeter from the duffel bag and unloaded it. After opening the door on his side of the adjoining room doorway, he placed an ear against the sec-ond door. Sure enough, he heard the room's door open and close.

With a smile, he stepped back, raised his foot, and kicked the door with all his strength.

The door splintered away from its jamb, flew open, and smacked the dresser hard.

Nathan burst through. The woman he'd seen in the Hard Rock was just setting her purse and sidearm down on the bed.

She made a move for her gun, but Nathan pointed his Sig at her chest.

She held her hands up. "FBI special agent."

"I know that. Where's your partner?"

She hesitated. "In the lobby, watching Mr. Fontana."

Nathan held his gun up. "Do I need this?"

"No."

"I've got your word on that?"

"Yes."

"Good, 'cause it's not loaded."

"When did you spot us?"

He tucked the gun behind his back. "In the Hard Rock. Your partner kept using the mirror behind the bar to watch us." He smiled, but it wasn't returned. He gave her a closer look. She was actually quite attractive. Around the same age as Nathan, she wore jeans and a white silk shirt under a black leather jacket. Her blonde hair was cut shoulder-length and she had piercing blue eyes behind a Slavic face.

Nathan looked around the room at all the surveillance equipment. Half a dozen black boxes were stacked on the dresser next to the door, all of them connected to a digital recorder.

"Okay, Special Agent…"

"Grangeland."

"How do you want to play this out? We have a couple of options. The first, I smash every piece of equipment in this room and you'll have to explain its destruction to whoever you're reporting to, presumably Lansing. The second, we maintain the status quo. Harvey and I will be careful what we say and no one needs to be the wiser. I'll tell the hotel staff I lost my footing and fell against the door."

She crossed her arms. "What makes you think I'd allow you to break all this equipment?"

"Because I outweigh you by a hundred pounds."

A smile touched her lips. "I have a counterproposal. You and me. Right here. Right now. The winner decides the outcome." She slipped out of her coat and tossed it on the bed.

Nathan stared, not sure he'd heard it right. Was she challenging him to a physical contest? He'd make mincemeat of her. He narrowed his eyes. "May I assume there will be no closed fists and no groin or head blows?"

"Sure, why not."

Nathan tossed his gun on the bed next to hers.

It happened fast.

One second she was six feet away, the next she was on him. He parried her palm punch aimed at his solar plexus and realized his mistake too late. Before he could react, she had dropped down and swept his legs out from under him. He went down hard, landing on his butt with a grunt. Two seconds later, he found it difficult to breathe. Pinned against the base of the bed, his mind tried to register what had happened, but his vision was already graying. He was pretty sure he felt her left forearm across the back of his neck and her right hand squeezing his throat, but he couldn't be sure. Somewhere in the growing black tunnel he heard her whisper in his ear, "You can cry uncle anytime."

Nathan would've laughed and responded with a witty retort, but he was immobilized in a half nelson executed by an opponent half his weight. He braced his legs against the base of the bed and thrust out, flipping them both onto their backs. Grangeland was now underneath him, her grip on his throat unrelenting. His mind was fading fast. He figured he had ten to fifteen seconds to break the hold or be rendered unconscious. If they hadn't agreed to no head blows, he could have easily driven the back of his head into her face and smashed her nose, but he wouldn't do that to her, even it meant losing this struggle.

He sucked in what air he could and saw an opportunity to break her hold. Yeah, it could work. Using the space between the bed and the dresser, Nathan rolled to his side and braced his feet against the bed. With his free right hand, he reached behind her back and grabbed the belt above her butt. With Grangeland still clinging to his back, he began simultaneously pulling her jeans up while starting a crushing leg press. All 130 pounds of Special Agent Grangeland ended up pinned between him and the dresser. He was hoping the intrusive distraction of her jeans, coupled with the pressure on her torso, would drive the air from her lungs. Feeling his mind begin to plummet into the void, he pushed his legs harder and yanked her jeans higher. In a desperate, last-ditch effort, he doubled his energy, giving it all he had.

It worked.

He felt a hiss of air escape her lungs on the back of his neck. Her arms loosened, giving him just enough room to wrench his head sideways. When her grip on his windpipe failed, he jerked his head free, and sucked in a precious lungful of air.

Red-faced and panting like a dog, he gasped, "Let's call it a draw." He managed to gain his hands and knees just before his Caesar salad came up in projectile fashion. When he finished vomiting his dinner, he wiped his mouth and half laughed. "Damn it, woman, that was some trick."

She rolled onto her back, her legs bent at the knees. "You cheated, giving me that wedgie. I had you."

"The hell you did."

"No doubt you enjoyed that little stunt."

"You'll never know." They both looked up at the same instant. Harvey was pointing his Sig at a man who was pointing his Glock at Nathan's head, the four of them frozen in time like waxwork figures.

"It's a good thing you showed up when you did," Nathan said. "I might have killed her."

Grangeland held up a hand. "Stand down, Agent Ferris. This isn't what it looks like."

Somewhat reluctantly, Ferris holstered his gun and looked at Harvey.

Harvey tucked his gun into the small of his back and looked at Nathan, then to the woman, then to the pool of vomit. "I see you two have been properly introduced."

Still breathing heavily, Nathan said, "Special Agent Grangeland, meet Harvey Fontana."

Harvey shook his head. "What is it with you, Nathan? Didn't your mother hold you enough as a baby?"

"Hey, it was her idea."

"Uh-huh."

"Well?" Nathan asked her.

With a grimace, Grangeland sat up. "I guess we'll keep the status quo."

"Good choice," Nathan said.

"Would someone please tell me what the hell is going on?" Ferris asked. He looked at the splintered door jamb, then back to Nathan. "Looks like a clear case of breaking and entering to me."

"Tell me about it," Grangeland said. She staggered to her feet and limped into the bathroom.

Nathan rubbed his throat. "She'll be okay." Even though Ferris was formidable looking, Nathan towered over him. In his midthirties, Ferris had the same intensity in his eyes that Henning had shown several nights ago. He was clean-cut, dressed in tan Docker-type slacks with a long-sleeved buttoned shirt. Nathan knew Ferris didn't like the idea of his partner rolling around on the floor with a complete stranger.

"Sorry about the mess," Nathan said. "Tell me something. Where'd she learn to wrestle like that?"

"Alternate for the 2000 Olympic team."

"No kidding," Nathan said. "You ever go a round with her?"

"Once."

"And?" Nathan prompted.

"Got my ass kicked in ten seconds. She's also holds black belts in three different forms of martial arts."

"I'm in love," Nathan said. He looked at the processed romaine lettuce on the carpet. "Want me to call housekeeping?"

Ferris just stared.

Harvey grabbed Nathan's handgun from the bed. "Come on, Nathan, let's get the hell out of here." Harvey turned toward Ferris, then pointed at the electronic surveillance equipment. "This is *bullshit*."

"Easy partner, don't shoot the messenger."

"Why not?" Harvey said. "We've been open and honest." He waved a hand at the black boxes. "And this is the thanks we get?"

"It's just business," Nathan said.

Harvey grunted and walked out of the room.

Nathan addressed Ferris. "This doesn't have to go any further than the four of us. We'll let you save face with Lansing, but we're onto you now. If you want to know what we're up to, just ask." Nathan joined Harv and closed the door behind him. Still rubbing his throat, he sat on the edge of the bed.

Harv was standing at the window, staring at the state capitol. "I'm sorry I snapped at you." He turned and smiled. "Your mother held you a lot, you were an only child."

"No, you're right, I acted childish in there. I didn't have to spar with her. I could've said no."

"Why didn't you?"

"Not sure. I'll tell you what, she's tough as nails."

There was a soft knock at the door. They both turned at the same time. Half-expecting to see the hotel manager standing in the hall, Nathan went to the door and peered through the peephole. It was one of their own security guards. Nathan opened the door and the tech handed him a fax. It was from Dr. Fitzgerald at Fort Leavenworth.

"Let's see what we've got." Nathan sat down at the desk while Harv looked over his shoulder. The first piece of paper was a copy of the Pensacola police department's incident report. Ernie Bridgestone had been going the speed limit, the skid marks on the road verified it. From what they could glean from the report, a woman had entered the street from between two parked cars. The right bumper of Ernie's Camaro had clipped her, sending her head over heels. She died instantly from a broken neck. Her BAC, or blood-alcohol concentration, had been .35, over four times the legal limit of .08. Ernie's BAC had been .10. Just as Amber Sheldon had said, he hadn't been truly drunk, but he'd been over the legal limit and that's all that mattered. The responding officer had written in his notes that Ernie had been extremely indignant, stating over and over that he wasn't drunk and that it wasn't his fault. He'd used profane and derogatory language about the dead victim's ethnicity, which was Hispanic. Things quickly turned ugly. After resisting arrest, he'd been Tasered by a backup officer. Booked for felony drunk driving, his bail was set at ten thousand dollars.

The next documents in the file concerned Ernie's civil-court matters. His driver's license had been revoked for eighteen months and he'd been fined two thousand dollars, the maximum allowed by law. Because Ernie had been in the military, Nathan knew his troubles were only beginning. As an active member of the US armed forces, Ernie had been subject to the Uniform Code of Military Justice, no matter where the accident had happened. On or off base, it didn't matter. He'd been surrendered to the military police of Pensacola Naval Air Station and placed in the brig. Notes from the transporting MPs also indicated Ernie had been belligerent, profane, and generally uncooperative. In the court-martial that followed, the presiding military judge showed no leniency. Had Ernie possessed an outstanding military record with no prior offenses, things might have been different. But Ernie had a long history of insubordination. The bottom line: the Marine Corps made an example out of him, sentencing him to five years in the USDB at Fort Leavenworth, Kansas. Basically, the Marine Corps version of good riddance, dirtbag. The final sheet of paper was a copy of a newspaper clipping, complete with a photograph of the victim. Nathan's eyes grew as he stared at the low-resolution photocopy.

"I've seen this face," he said.

Behind him, Harv whispered, "No, it can't be."

Nathan rewound his mind, trying to place it. Then he had it. Staring up at him from the lifeless sheet of paper was an image he'd seen for the first time only days ago.

The face of Frank Ortega's daughter.

CHAPTER 19

Harv barely managed a whisper. "Do you know who that is?"

Nathan nodded.

"Do you know what this means?"

"Yes."

"I've never felt so...betrayed. This whole thing, it's, it's—"

"Dirty."

Neither of them spoke for several seconds, each running the events of the past week through their minds.

"We risked our lives for Frank Ortega at the Freedom's Echo compound. We could've been killed, almost were killed. Nathan, I'm sorry."

"Harv, this isn't your fault."

"How could—" Harv cut himself off and pointed to the door interconnecting the rooms.

Nathan nodded.

Without saying another word, they both left the room. In the elevator, Harv said, "How could the Ortegas have done this to me, to us?"

"Blood is thicker than water," Nathan said quietly. "A lot thicker, it would seem."

"Greg and I go back fifteen years. *Fifteen years*. We spent night after night together looking at satellite imagery when you were missing. I knew Frank's daughter had been killed, but Greg never talked about it. I never knew the circumstances."

"How deep does this go, Harv?"

"You mean Lansing? Ortega must have cashed in that IOU earlier than we imagined. Getting his grandson assigned to the Bridgestone operation…" Harv gave Nathan a double take. "You mean your dad? I can't fathom him betraying you like this."

"I can," Nathan said. The elevator dumped them into the lobby. Nathan kept his voice low. "We'll take a cab over to Sutter Hospital. Holly needs to know about this right away."

"Nate, she could be involved."

He shook his head. "She's not. I can't explain it, but I'm sure she's not."

After the bellman called the cab, it took several minutes for it to arrive. Their moods identical, neither of them spoke during the late-afternoon ride through rush-hour traffic.

Nathan sensed Harv's anger mounting. Anger and pain at being used like a pawn and betrayed by a trusted friend.

Nathan grasped Harv's arm. "We'll get through this."

Harv shook his head and closed his eyes. "I'm so damned angry, Nate. I can't…"

Nathan squeezed his arm. "We're going to turn this around on them, Harv. You hear me? We own their asses now."

* * *

Nathan knocked on Holly's door.

"Come in." Her cheery tone ended the moment she saw the expressions on their faces.

"What happened? Did they hit us again?"

"No," Nathan said. He pulled a chair over from the corner. Harv did the same.

"You two look like you've seen a ghost."

"We have."

"What's happened?"

"Ernie Bridgestone killed Frank Ortega's daughter."

"Oh, no. When?"

"Eighteen years ago."

"Eighteen years ago?"

"Drunk-driving accident. It's why he went to prison. This whole thing's about revenge. Frank Ortega set Ernie Bridgestone up for a fall."

"No, I don't believe that, I won't believe that."

"It's true, Holly. Everything makes sense now."

"Director Lansing?" she asked.

"Right in the middle of it."

"Are you absolutely sure about this. Is there any possibility you could be wrong?"

"None."

"Do you know what this means? What it means for the FBI? For my field office, for my agents?"

"Holly, listen to me. Harv and I aren't going to do anything that would compromise or embarrass the FBI. We aren't whistle-blowers. You have our word."

"Nathan, I—"

"Just listen for a sec. We've been thinking about this, working it out. Strictly speaking, what Lansing and Ortega did wasn't illegal. It may be a terrible lapse in good judgment, but it wasn't illegal, we all need to understand that. But it raises some other questions. What exactly were the Bridgestones doing prior to dealing in Semtex?"

She sat up a little. "Where are you going with this?"

"Stay with me here. Think back. What did the Bridgestones initially do to get the attention of the FBI?"

"I can't remember exactly, but I'm sure I got a call from Director Lansing to begin surveillance up there."

"Is that normally how things work? A call from Lansing?"

"No. My boss is in the Los Angeles field office, he's an assistant director. The call should've come from him."

"Right, but it didn't, it came from Lansing himself. It would be like a brigadier general giving an order to a battalion commander, bypassing the regiment commander. He bypassed the chain of command, left your assistant director out of the loop. Do you remember what he said?"

"Vaguely. Something about a new militia-type group he wanted to watch."

"Do you see where I'm going with this?"

"No, I honestly don't."

Nathan looked at Harv, then back to Holly. "We read the file on the Bridgestones' operation. Frank Ortega gave it to us prior to the raid. Freedom's Echo was tiny, way under the radar compared to other militia groups in Montana, Idaho, Ohio, you name it. Those big groups have hundreds, sometimes thousands, of members. The Bridgestones were small potatoes. They dealt mostly in small-arms conversions, semiautomatic to full auto, that kind of thing. It wasn't until the last few months that they started dealing in bigger things." Nathan watched understanding take Holly's face.

"You're saying James Ortega wasn't just undercover, he was their contact for the Semtex."

Nathan nodded. "Yes. It was more than a deep-cover operation. It was a sting. The FBI was both the seller and the buyer of the Semtex." He paused to make sure she was absorbing it all. "Ortega and Lansing set the Bridgestones up for a fall, for a very personal reason. They thought they had it all under control until two things went wrong. First, the Bridgestones discovered James Ortega was undercover. Second, when the raid came, the FBI had no idea about the tunnel. No matter what happened to James Ortega, the Bridgestones should've been cooked. But with the tunnel, the targets escaped with a bunch of the Semtex, leaving Lansing and Frank Ortega with a nightmare scenario, their personal little war gone amok. There's more. We have to assume James Ortega cracked under the torture and spilled his guts. I don't fault him for it." He looked down at the floor. "In Nicaragua, I told my interrogator more than I should've. I'm not proud of it, but I'm only human. After a certain point, you just can't take it anymore."

"So he told them everything."

"That's right. The brothers found out about Frank Ortega's plan to bring them down. James caved under the torture and told them who he was and who his grandfather was. Think about it, Holly. How angry would Ernie Bridgestone be at finding out who the FBI had sent to bring him down? The grandson of the man who railroaded him eighteen years ago. How angry would he be? Would he be angry enough to bomb your field office? Suppose it hadn't been James Ortega? What if it had been any other agent? Would the Bridgestones have let it go? Would they have just taken their money and run?"

"It's more complicated than that," Harv said. "We also killed their little brother, which may have been the last straw. Could've been the deciding factor."

"That's absolutely possible," Nathan agreed. "We may never know the truth. But here's what we do know. After he got out of prison, Ernie Bridgestone had thirteen years to avenge what he claims was an unfair imprisonment for killing Frank Ortega's daughter. But he didn't. I think it's fair to assume he'd let it go, put it behind him. My point is this: it was very bad judgment to use James Ortega at Freedom's Echo against the Bridgestones. Undercover agents are always facing the threat of discovery and interrogation. Frank Ortega should've known that if his grandson were ever captured, he'd reveal his identity under duress. He had to know that would trigger Ernie Bridgestone's old vendetta."

"You'd think so," Holly said. "He just never thought they'd fail, that the brothers might get away. This whole thing..." She paused, shaking her head. "Selling those people Semtex? You may be right, Nathan. From a legal perspective, Director Lansing's clean. Ethically, it's a different matter. It was a severe conflict of interest to involve James Ortega. It may not be illegal, but it's a career-ender. The real question, I guess, is what are we going to do about it."

"Nothing," Nathan said.

"Nothing?"

"I don't see anything constructive in blowing this wide open right now, or ever. As much as Harv and I resent being used as pawns, it doesn't compare to the pain Frank Ortega has endured. He's lost both a daughter and a grandson to the Bridgestones."

"You amaze me, Nathan. I would be far less forgiving in your shoes."

"This isn't about me or Harv. It's about justice. Justice for the dead SWAT agent, for James Ortega, your two techs from the van, and twenty-four other slain FBI employees. I'm not above using the information to keep Lansing off my back, though."

"Then we stick to the plan," she said.

"We stick to the plan," Nathan said. "We've got a big day tomorrow."

"Nathan, I'm sorry about Director Lansing and Ortega."

"It's not a reflection on you. You and me, we're still good."

"I appreciate your trust, especially after all the BS you've been through."

"I don't need to tell you this, but I will anyway. Be careful, Holly. Watch what you say." He squeezed her hand and got up. "The walls have ears."

* * *

Under a flawless afternoon sky, the press conference was staged on the steps of Sacramento's capitol. The podium held over two dozen microphones, six of them from foreign countries. The bombing of the Sacramento field office had made international news. The reporters and cameramen were set up in ten semicircular rows of seating fifteen feet away from the podium. Assistant Special Agent in Charge Breckensen was being introduced by Governor Schwarzenegger. The ASAC looked sharp and focused, his tailored suit gleaming in the afternoon sun. He shook hands with the governor and took the podium.

* * *

Leonard and Ernie Bridgestone were still holed up in the same cabin they'd broken into after the raid on their compound. While charting their next moves, they'd been watching the near-constant news coverage of their handiwork, compliments of the cabin owner's satellite dish. They agreed their best course of action was no action. They needed to let things cool down before heading up north to Canada, but when they did leave the United States, it would be for good. Getting to the location of their hidden money cache in northern Montana had been the topic of many conversations. The longer they stayed put, the better chance they'd have of quietly slipping through the net. Leonard found it ironic he was the antsy one, while Ernie seemed quite content watching the television coverage.

Ernie sat forward in his chair. "This oughtta be good."

"We aren't out of the woods yet, Ern."

"Shit, these feebs couldn't find their own ass with a mirror on a stick." Ernie cranked the volume and sat back.

ASAC Breckensen's face filled the screen. "Thank you, Governor Schwarzenegger. I'd also like to thank the press for attending on such short notice. As you know, on October seventeenth, our Sacramento field office was bombed with catastrophic results. The blast killed twenty-four people and wounded fifty-five others, many with career-ending injuries. Our thoughts and prayers go out to all of our employees and their families."

"Breaks my fuckin' heart," Ernie said.

Leonard increased the volume.

Breckensen continued, outlining the chain of events leading up to the bombing. "One of the reasons we called this conference was to make a plea to the general public to come forward with any information, no matter how insignificant it may seem. As an example, I'd like to introduce Ms. Amber Mills Sheldon." He gestured off-camera to his right.

Ernie jumped up from the sofa. "What the fuck?" Then he yelled at Leonard. "What the fuck is this?"

His mind already working, Leonard squinted and said nothing.

The camera followed Amber Sheldon as she stepped up to the podium. The makeup artists had earned their pay, Leonard thought. She actually looked good. She placed a piece of paper on the podium and thanked Governor Schwarzenegger and ASAC Breckensen. She looked visibly nervous. Reading from a prepared statement, she began.

"My name is Amber Sheldon. I was married to Ernie Bridgestone in Pensacola, Florida, where he worked as a drill instructor training naval-aviator candidates at the NAS. I am both shocked and horrified at the bombing of the FBI's field office. I would not have thought him capable of such an act."

Sheldon looked up and stared into the camera for several seconds with the haunted look of a woman in emotional pain. "I wish to express my deepest sorrow and condolences to the colleagues, friends, and families of the slain FBI employees. I have fully cooperated with the FBI." Her lip quivered and a tear rolled down her cheek. She wiped it away and looked off-camera. Breckensen stepped up to the podium and put his arm around her.

"Look at that son of a bitch," Ernie hissed. "He wants a piece of that. I can't believe this shit."

"Shut up, Ernie," Leonard said. "He's just comforting her."

"Yeah, right."

Breckensen leaned in toward the microphones. "Ms. Sheldon has agreed to take a few questions." He pointed to a reporter seated in the middle of the first row.

"Ms. Sheldon, have you had any contact with Ernie since the bombing?"

"No," she said.

The same reporter fired a second question. "When was the last time you spoke with him?"

She looked at Breckensen, silently asking if it was okay to answer. He nodded. "Years ago. After he was released from the Disciplinary Barracks at Fort Leavenworth. I haven't heard from him since."

Breckensen pointed to another reporter.

"Ms. Sheldon, is there anything from Ernie's past that might've led up to this?"

"Not really. He was very angry about his court-martial, but that happened a long time ago. I don't think this is about that."

Just as Breckensen was about to point to a third reporter, a question boomed out from one of the back rows. "Have you told Ernie Bridgestone that he's the father of your daughter, Janey Sheldon?"

The sudden anger in Amber's face couldn't be hidden. "That's none of your damned business." She twisted away from Breckensen and stormed from the podium. The camera showed Governor Schwarzenegger running to catch her.

Leonard looked at his brother, who was staring at the television with his mouth hanging open. "Ernie? You okay, man?"

"She never told me. How could she never fucking tell me?" He hurled the TV remote across the room.

Leonard didn't know what to say, didn't want to provoke Ernie, who seemed dangerously poised at the moment.

"She never told me. I knew she had a daughter, but I didn't know she was mine. She said she got knocked up by accident in my first year in the Castle."

"Hey, man, it doesn't matter."

"It doesn't matter? Doesn't matter? What do you mean, it doesn't matter?"

"Take it easy, Ern."

"I had a right to know."

"I'm not disagreeing with you, but we can't let this change anything. We've got too much to lose."

"I can't fucking believe this shit."

"This isn't a coincidence, Ern. Can't you see this whole thing is staged? They're trying to bait us, to flush us out. It could be bullshit."

"I can't believe this."

"It's a trap, they're baiting us. You know that."

"Yeah, I know. Shit. This really sucks."

"What can you do about it? Do you honestly think Janey's going to welcome you into her life with open arms? She doesn't even know you other than what she's seen on TV, and that hasn't exactly been favorable lately. Think about it, Ern. You were out of Amber's life. She wanted a divorce, and you agreed. You must know Janey can never be a part of your life. Let's not blow everything we've worked for over this."

Ernie nodded, but didn't respond.

Leonard walked into the kitchen and poured himself a glass of water. On the television, Breckensen was wrapping up the press conference. He watched his brother closely. What a disaster. He had to admit it, though. It was a brilliant move on the FBI's part. But it only worked if Ernie took the bait.

Leonard thought through his own options. It might be wise to put some distance between himself and Ernie, but he'd need to do it carefully, so it didn't look obvious. He wasn't willing to lose everything they'd earned over this. He didn't plan on rotting on death row over a long-lost niece that he neither knew nor cared about. If Ernie became a liability over this, he'd be on his own.

He went back to the TV room. "We might want to accelerate our plans. Are you okay for a few hours? I'm gonna get our cash near Quincy. We're gonna need it. We'll pick up the big stash on our trip up north."

"Want me to go with you?"

"Safer if you don't. We shouldn't be seen together, even in disguise." He came over and patted Ernie on the shoulder. "I know you got a lot to think about. I'll be back by sundown. If you haven't heard from me, don't assume the worst, just head up north to the rendezvous point. We'll meet there. How much time do you have left on your cell?"

"I don't know, a few hours."

"Me too. I may not call, depending on the situation. Keep your cool."

"I will."

He looked Ernie in the eyes. "I know you want to call Amber. I'm not even gonna tell you not to. But be careful when you do it. Make sure she calls you back from a pay phone to your cell. Don't use the phone in here. Keep your conversation under thirty seconds. Don't do anything until we've had a chance to work out a plan. I'm serious, Ernie, stay put. Everything's going to be fine if you keep your cool. I'll see you in a few hours."

Ernie nodded.

"One more thing."

"What."

"If the owners of this place show up, don't kill them."

"Yeah, yeah. I won't."

As Leonard drove away from the cabin, he looked in the rearview mirror and wondered if he'd ever see his brother again.

CHAPTER 20

Rather than order room service, Nathan and Harv decided to head downstairs to Dawson's American Bistro, a nice place with a classy atmosphere. The hostess seated them in a corner table. A few couples, engaged in quiet conversation, were present.

They hadn't been real talkative with each other, and for good reason. They both felt deeply. Nathan took a swig of iced tea and again wondered why Frank Ortega hadn't told them the truth. Ortega must've thought they wouldn't take the assignment. The truth was that they would have helped him find his grandson, no matter what his motivation had been. None of this deception had been necessary. He really felt bad for Harv.

Nathan set his glass down. "You okay, partner?"

"Yeah, I'm just embarrassed I got us into this mess."

"Harv, forget about it."

"I can't. I've known the Ortegas for over twenty years. Maybe I should've seen this coming."

"Be careful, you're starting to sound like me."

Harv raised his glass in a toast. "I consider that a compliment."

Nathan smiled and clinked his glass. "Everything's in place, we've done what we can. Let's hope Ernie takes the bait."

"He probably knows it's a trap."

"No doubt he does."

They both turned at the same time and saw their two FBI friends enter the restaurant. When Grangeland noticed them sitting across the room, she seemed to hesitate. Nathan was sure they weren't here to keep an eye on them: that game had ended in a wrestling match. He motioned them over with a nod. Harv switched sides and sat next to him.

"Will you join us?" Nathan asked.

Grangeland managed a smile. "Are you sure? We don't want to impose."

"Not at all." Both he and Harv stood as Grangeland slipped into her chair.

"Such gentlemen," she said.

Ferris seemed all business. To each his own. Nathan addressed Grangeland. "Are you okay? No broken ribs, or…other damage?"

"I'm not a china vase. But to answer your question, yes, I'm fine. I was raised with three older brothers who sometimes fought dirty. I'll live."

Nathan thought Grangeland looked stunning. Her red cocktail dress was cut low and tight. Below her blonde hair, half-karat diamond studs adorned her ears. Nathan grinned. "I was…just wondering where your piece is concealed."

She leaned forward and whispered, "It's a secret."

"I'll bet it is."

"Do you want Ferris and me to leave?" Harvey asked.

"No," Nathan said quickly. "That would be dangerous."

"Agreed," Grangeland added.

Harvey looked at Ferris. "I apologize for snapping at you up there."

"Already forgotten."

"So," Nathan continued. "Ferris here said you were an alternate for the 2000 Olympic team. I'm assuming it wasn't for synchronized swimming?"

"Yes, that's a fair assumption."

"Look, I know we didn't get off to a good start. I'm sorry for busting in on you like that. I was frustrated with the surveillance. Not a very good excuse, I know."

Grangeland placed her napkin in her lap. "Understandable, given the circumstances."

"Were you guys in the building when it blew?" Harvey asked.

Ferris shook his head. "No, we're from the Fresno resident agency."

"We've been under a lot of stress too," said Grangeland. "I feel like I wake up every morning with a gun in my face. I guess that's why I challenged you. I shouldn't have done that. At least there's one saving grace to all this," she said, looking around. "This hotel's first-class. We've stayed in some real fleabags before."

"I can imagine," Nathan said.

Their server arrived and took their orders for dinner. Grangeland and Ferris ordered iced tea. Officially, they were on duty.

"Harv and I discussed it, and although we don't think very highly of Director Lansing's tactics, we don't extend that resentment to you. We'd like to work with you, if you're willing."

"What do you have in mind?" Grangeland asked.

"We've set a trap for Ernie Bridgestone. If he calls Amber Sheldon again, I specifically told her to mention my name. She didn't know why that was so important. Do you?"

Grangeland looked at Ferris, then back to Nathan. "No, should we?"

"During the Freedom's Echo SWAT raid, we killed their little brother."

"You were there at the compound when the claymores went off?"

"Yes," Harvey said. "Sammy Bridgestone was seconds away from shooting the SWAT team when we nailed him."

"I see."

Nathan leaned forward slightly. "We can't tell you everything that's happened, but we can tell you this. We're going to need your help if my plan is going to work."

"To avenge his little brother, you're thinking Ernie Bridgestone will use Amber to set you guys up."

"That's right."

"It sounds like another SWAT job. Why use us?" Ferris asked.

"Because we don't know who we can trust."

"But you can trust us?" Grangeland asked.

"I don't know, can we?"

An awkward silence settled around the table. No one spoke for several seconds.

Grangeland broke the silence. "You're already working with one of our agents, Bruce Henning. Why involve us?"

"Because five is better than three. Simple as that."

"I'm not sure we can do this without clearance. I'm assuming you don't want Director Lansing to know."

"You assume correctly."

She shook her head.

"Would it help if SAC Simpson gave you a green light? You're technically under her command, aren't you?"

"Technically, yes."

Nathan waited.

"I suppose that would give us some protection," she said, "but we have orders from Director Lansing to report only to him."

"Doesn't that strike you as odd?" Harvey asked

"It's not protocol, but when the big man gives you an assignment, you do it without question."

"So you should," Nathan said. "Let me ask you something. What's the ultimate goal here? To capture the Bridgestone brothers and recover the missing Semtex, right? What if you were in on it? It wouldn't look too bad on your résumés if you helped collar both men at the top of the FBI's most-wanted list."

"No argument there," she said.

"Needless to say, it's going to be dangerous. Vest work for sure. Shots will probably be fired."

"When do you think it's going down?"

"I'm hoping tonight," Nathan said.

She and Ferris exchanged glances. "We're in," she said, "but we're not doing anything without SAC Simpson's orders."

Nathan made the call.

* * *

As much as she'd mentally prepared herself for it, Amber Sheldon wasn't ready for Ernie's call when it came. She must have gone over what'd she'd say dozens of times and yet she found herself totally unprepared. When Ernie called her at work a little after 8:30 PM, she told him to call her back in ten minutes with the number she gave him. With irritation in his voice, Ernie had agreed and seemed to understand the need for it.

Amber was many things, but stupid wasn't one of them. She'd seen the sedan following her and assumed it was the FBI. Who else could it be? Both she and Janey had driven to Pete's Truck Palace together, parked in a dark area of the parking lot, and walked into the restaurant. Janey had a large purse slung over her shoulder. She scanned the area, not sure what she was looking for. Over fifty trucks were parked in the transient lot. Several dozen had their motors idling to keep their compressors supplying refrigerant to their cargo boxes. Diesel fumes hung in the air like fog. To her left, the diesel-fueling area was brightly lit by mercury vapor lights suspended under a flat metal canopy.

It was time to call Ernie.

* * *

A plain four-door sedan lurked in the northwest corner of the complex facing the restaurant. The two FBI agents inside the sedan watched Amber park her car and walk into the restaurant.

"Looks like her daughter's with her."

"Yep."

"Now we wait."

"Yep."

Their wait wasn't long. Five minutes later, Amber Sheldon marched across the parking lot and slid into her car.

"Here we go, she's on the move." At a safe distance, they followed her onto Highway 99 heading south. After three miles or so, she used her turn signal and exited the highway at a convenience-store gas station. Screened by mature eucalyptus trees, they stopped on the exit ramp. The driver watched through field glasses as Amber pulled into the gas station's parking lot and climbed out. She walked over to a pay phone on the side of the building and stood there, as if waiting for a call. Like a bad actress trying to look impatient, she kept glancing at her watch every few seconds. The agent on the passenger side pointed a clear, sixteen-inch parabolic mike at Sheldon's location and donned a headset.

"She's waiting for a call," the driver said.

"Yep."

Somewhat irritated, the driver asked, "You ever say anything other than *yep*?"

"Nope."

"Funny. Real funny."

"What the hell?" the driver said. He watched Amber Sheldon reach up to her head and pull off a blonde wig, exposing dark-brown hair. She held it high in the air and waved it like a flag. "Shit. We've been had. That's not Amber Sheldon, it's her daughter."

* * *

Would the real Amber Sheldon please stand up? Driving her supervisor's car, she grinned as she pulled into the McDonald's driveway seven miles north of Pete's Truck Palace. Her smile faded as she realized this trick worked only once. She kept telling herself she was doing it for Janey, but she had plans for McBride's fifty grand. Even if she never got the million-dollar reward for Leonard and Ernie, McBride's money wasn't peanuts. Had it not been for Janey, she would've told Nathan McBride and his FBI pals to stuff it. With a little luck, this would all be over tonight, and she believed in her heart she was doing the right thing. When the pay phone rang, she quickly picked up the receiver.

"Ernie?"

"Yeah, it's me."

"Thanks a lot for everything. My life's turned to shit."

"Why didn't you tell me about Janey?"

"I can't believe you're asking me that! Were you a part of my life? Were you ever going to be? You never gave a shit about me, it was always about *you*, what *you* wanted."

"I had a right to know."

"You disappeared after you got out of prison. I can count on one hand the number of times you called to ask how I was."

"You're the one who called it off."

"Can you blame me? Yeah, I guess you can. Nothing is ever your fault, right? It's always my fault. I made you get behind the wheel that night. I made you resist arrest. Pull your head outta your ass and take a look in the mirror."

"You gotta lot of nerve talking to me like that. You think I can't get to you?"

"I'm not afraid of you anymore. It's you who should be afraid."

He laughed. "Afraid of what? The FBI? You?"

"Of Nathan McBride."

There was silence on the other end for several seconds. "How do you know that name?"

"He stopped by and we had a little chat about you."

There was venom in his voice. "What did you tell him?"

"What do you think? I told him you're a piece of shit."

"That cocksucker killed Sammy."

"What're you talking about?"

"Sammy!" Ernie screamed. "You know, my little brother?"

Amber froze, suddenly understanding why Nathan McBride had insisted she use his name. She'd been used again. Anger flared. "Well, he didn't tell me that. Must have slipped his mind."

"He's a dead man."

"Yeah." She laughed bitterly as she put it together. "He set me up. They set me up. That whole press-conference thing, the question about Janey. It was all staged. Total bullshit."

"And you were dumb enough to buy it?"

"I needed the money."

"What money?"

"McBride offered me money to do the press conference."

"How much?"

"Ten thousand," she lied.

On the other end, Ernie chuckled. "Ten thousand."

"It's a lot of money. I'm not exactly swimming in greenbacks, Ern."

"It's peanuts."

"Peanuts? Who do you think you are, Donald Trump?"

"Shit, I could give you ten times that much. In cash."

"There's no such thing as a free lunch. What do you want?"

"I want to torture Nathan McBride to death."

"Well, good luck with that. I wouldn't mess with him. That's what he wants. In fact, I'm supposed to call him after I talk with you. He gave me his cell number."

"Give it to me."

"It's your funeral." She pulled the cocktail napkin from her jeans and read the number.

"I'm sure he'd love to hear from you. Now, good-bye."

"Wait, here's what you're going to do."

"Screw that. I ain't doing shit for you anymore."

Ernie was silent for a moment. Amber knew she should hang up, but didn't.

"I'm serious about the money," Ernie said. "Leonard and me are buggin' out. We don't have much time. If you want the dough, here's what you're gonna do."

"I don't want your money. It's dirty."

"It's not for you, it's for Janey."

"Yeah, right, like you care."

"This can go one of two ways. The first, you and Janey can live happily ever after. The second, you don't."

"Don't threaten me."

"Oh, it's not a threat, sweet Amber, it's a promise and you know I'll make good on it. What does this asshole look like?"

Amber gave him Nathan's description. "I wouldn't mess with him if I were you."

"Yeah, right. Now shut up and listen. Here's what you're going say to McBride."

* * *

Nathan couldn't formulate a plan to collar Ernie until after Amber called, if she called at all. Until he knew Ernie had taken the bait, all he could do was wait. Nathan hated waiting. It grated on his nerves like a headache. As a sniper team, he and Harv had been masters at waiting, often for days at a time until their mark materialized, but this felt different.

He knew Harv preferred to stay busy during downtime. Currently, Harv had all their equipment laid out on the hotel room's bed, checking and double-checking everything. He'd broken down their Sig Sauers and thoroughly cleaned and oiled their actions. He'd replaced the batteries in their night-vision scopes, RF detector, handheld thermal imagers, and radios. He then used a lens cloth to clean their field glasses. Although it wasn't necessary, Harv pulled their Predator knives and checked sharpness. He applied a fine coat of gun oil on their menacing surfaces and sheathed them with more force than needed.

Nathan just stared.

"What?" Harv asked.

"I didn't say anything."

"I'm just making sure they're ready."

Nathan's cell rang. He didn't recognize the number and held it out for Harv to see.

Harv shook his head. Nathan answered it. "Hello?"

"Well, well, well, if it isn't old scarface himself."

"Am I speaking with the loosest ass from cell block D?"

"Fuck you, McBride."

"Come on, Ernie, can't you think of anything more original than that? Do me a favor and put Leonard on the phone. I'd rather talk to him. He's the brains of your operation. You're just an errand boy."

"Oh yeah? Well, here's a message for you. I'm going to kill you real slow with a dull knife."

"That's going to be rather difficult after I've severed all your fingers."

No response.

"Tell me something. Did your baby brother die right off, or did he squeal on the ground like a little girl?"

"We'll see who does the squealing."

The line went dead.

The coldness and lack of emotion sent a shiver through Nathan. "Well, at least this confirms he called Amber. She gave him my cell number. I love it when a plan comes together."

Two minutes later, his phone rang again. It was a 559 area code, probably Amber Sheldon calling. He took the call. "Don't say anything. Give me the number you're calling from."

She rattled off the number.

"Sit tight. I'll call you back in five minutes." He ended the call. "Let's go find a pay phone a few blocks away, I don't trust the ones in the lobby."

Nathan rapped on the door adjoining his room with the two FBI agents and opened it. Grangeland and Ferris were waiting for him. They'd obviously heard everything he'd said. "We're going out to call Amber Sheldon from a pay phone. We'll be back in a few minutes. Cross your fingers, with a little luck we'll be able to formulate a plan."

They took the elevator down to the lobby and diverted over to the registration desk to get some quarters. They found a pay phone outside a liquor store. Ignoring the green wad of gum jammed into the receiver, Nathan dialed the number.

"It's me again," he said. "How did it go?"

"About like I expected." There was sarcasm in her voice. "He wants to give me and Janey some money. He said it's his way of making up for all the shit he's put us through over the years."

"Do you believe him?"

"Ernie's done plenty of bad things, but yeah, I believe him."

"How much money?"

"Twenty thousand," she lied.

"How're you supposed to get it?"

"He said he'd leave it in a paper bag in a trash can at the gas-pump island at Pete's."

"Which one?"

"He didn't say. We have eight islands if you include the commercial diesel pumps. I guess I'll have to rummage through all of them."

"When?"

"He said sometime after midnight."

"Listen to me very carefully, Amber. Don't do anything. Do not approach the trash cans. Understood? I mean it, stay away from them."

"I will."

"What else did he say?"

"He said he's bugging out with Leonard and that I'd never hear from him again."

"Good job. Sit tight. You won't see us, but we'll be there. Don't do anything."

"I won't."

Nathan replaced the cradle and turned to Harv. "He took the bait, we're on."

"It's a trap. He told her what to say. You know that, right?"

"Yep."

"And now you're taking the bait."

He smiled. "Wrong. *We're* taking his bait."

Harv stopped cleaning their field glasses and shook his head. "Why do I get the feeling I'm going to regret this?"

"Relax, Harv, I've got everything under control."

"I was afraid you'd say that."

* * *

It would be a two-and-a-half-hour drive down to Fresno. For tonight's action, both Nathan and Harv were dressed in their woodland pants, black T-shirts, and combat boots. Nathan considered using his helicopter but there was no way to land anywhere near Pete's Truck Palace without alerting the entire area. Besides, fog was in the forecast for the early morning hours. Nathan and Harv were in the lead, driving a rented Ford Expedition. Henning, Grangeland, and Ferris followed in a Crown Victoria. As usual, Harv drove. Until they surveyed Pete's Truck Palace, they couldn't plan anything in detail.

Nathan felt Harv was right. Amber Sheldon hadn't been completely honest. When he'd asked how much Ernie had offered, a slight change in her tone gave it away. Twenty thousand dollars wasn't chump change, but he was certain Ernie had offered more than that. How much, he didn't know or care. All that mattered was her dishonesty. And if she were lying about the money, what else was she lying about? For all Nathan knew, Amber had made the call under duress, with Ernie's knife at her throat.

Prior to beginning the drive to Fresno, Nathan had given Henning one of his radios in case they needed to stop for any reason. As they descended the on-ramp onto Highway 99 south from Highway 50, Nathan keyed the radio. "Radio check."

"*Copy,*" came Henning's response.

"We're going to exceed the speed limit. I trust you'll use your FBI credentials if we're stopped by the CHP?"

"*No problem.*"

Nathan set the radio on the seat and settled in for the drive. "I miss my dogs," he said. "When this is over I'm going to spend some quality time with them."

"Yeah," said Harv. "I know what you mean. I miss my family too." Harv moved into the fast lane and accelerated up to ninety miles an hour.

CHAPTER 21

On the drive south, they'd been forced to slow down through patches of fog, some of them several miles long. At the exit for Pete's, Harv coasted down the off-ramp and turned right, away from their target. Anyone coming down the off-ramp at this hour would probably turn left, heading to Pete's. Harv drove another hundred yards and killed the headlights. Nathan craned his neck and saw they were obscured from Pete's by the Highway 99 overpass berm. Harv pulled the Expedition onto the shoulder and slowed to a stop. The Crown Vic pulled in behind them.

Nathan keyed the radio. "It's fair to assume Amber gave a description of me to Ernie, so Harv will conduct a reconnaissance report back to us. I'll wait in your vehicle until he returns."

"*Copy*," Henning said.

"Harv, you're on. Locate all the trash cans at the islands. Fill the gas tank and check out the restaurant and convenience store. You know the drill, make a mental picture of everything."

Nathan opened the door and stepped out.

"Ten minutes," Harvey said.

Nathan watched his partner execute a U-turn and head east under the freeway overpass. He climbed into the backseat with

Henning and looked at his watch. As he'd predicted, the dome light in the Crown Vic was disabled.

Harv was back in just over eight minutes and pulled in behind the Crown Vic. Making room for Harv, Nathan slid into the middle of the backseat. Harv climbed in and asked for a notepad and pen. Grangeland passed a legal pad from her briefcase. Ferris held a small penlight to illuminate the pad as Harv drew a quick sketch of the site, circling areas of potential threats. There were five: The transient truck parking area. The roof of the main building. The customer parking area. The truck-washing bays. And a warehouse building across the street to the north. Harv told them he believed the greatest threat came from the truck parking area because it was dimly lit and noisy. It would be easy to hide between the rigs, especially if their occupants were sleeping.

"We have a difficult assignment," Nathan said. "We have to cover each other without looking like it. If Ernie's already here, he's looking for plainclothes undercover agents. Grangeland and Ferris will act like a couple and take up a position inside the restaurant. You guys will watch Amber's every move and report anything she does except her normal restaurant duties. Henning will drive the SUV in case Ernie's already seen Harv come and go. Harv will be in the front seat, I'll be ducked down in the back. Henning will pull up to a fuel island, pretend to fill the tank, and then park in the customer parking area and go in for a cup of coffee and return a few minutes later. We'll disable the dome light in the SUV to keep the interior dark when the doors open. We're at a distinct disadvantage here—we don't know when or where Ernie will show, if he shows at all. If nothing's happened by zero thirty hours, I'll make an appearance to draw him out."

"He might have an NV weapon scope," Harvey said.

"It's a chance I'll have to take. I'll be relying on you guys to cover my back."

"Nathan, we can't watch every square foot of this place. It's spread out over ten acres. It's impossible."

"I hope it doesn't come to it, but we may have to force his hand. Amber told me he's bugging out tonight. That's the one thing I did believe. If we don't get him, we may never get another chance. Grangeland and Ferris, you go in first, we'll follow in few minutes. Use the radio if Amber makes a move. One last thing. Lansing had a couple of agents watching Amber. They're probably still around. Let's try not to get killed by friendly fire. Good luck, everyone."

"You too," she said.

Henning, Harvey, and Nathan got out of the Crown Vic and piled into the SUV. Grangeland made a U-turn and drove under the overpass. In the backseat, Nathan used his knife to remove the plastic cover of the dome light and disconnect the bulb. Henning disabled the driver's-side dome while Harvey got the passenger side.

* * *

Two minutes later, Harv made a U-turn, crossed under the freeway, and parked the SUV in the northeast corner of the property, fifty yards from Grangeland's Crown Vic. Even though he couldn't see much from his hidden position in the SUV, Nathan sensed this place encompassed a huge area. From the map Harv had drawn, he knew that the restaurant where Amber worked was in the same building as the convenience store. There were three gas-pump islands for noncommercial traffic and five diesel islands designed to handle large commercial trucks. The truck-washing bays occupied the southeastern corner of the property. Just north of the washing bays was the transient truck parking area. Harv also said there were dozens of trucks lined up in rows, many of them with their engines idling. Nathan heard the collective drone of their motors rumbling across the asphalt.

Per the plan, Henning stepped out and walked into the convenience store and served himself a cup of coffee. He returned two minutes later. "It's all quiet in there, I was the only customer. We might have a problem. Amber's daughter's in the restaurant. I saw her when I walked past the connecting doors."

"Did she see you?" Nathan asked.

"No, she was looking in the other direction, toward the gas pumps."

"This complicates things," Nathan said.

* * *

Amber Sheldon grew more and more annoyed by the minute because she couldn't keep a constant eye on the gas pumps. Janey was watching them, but she might not recognize Ernie. Between seating new customers, waiting and bussing tables, and acting as the cashier, she was earning her pay tonight. When a lull in her duties came, she asked her supervisor if she could take a smoke break. He reluctantly agreed, giving her five minutes. She walked over to Janey's table, informed her she was going out for a cigarette, and told her to stay put.

* * *

Nathan's radio earpiece crackled to life. It was Grangeland. "*Sheldon's on the move, she's walking out the front door.*"

"Copy," Nathan said.

"*You see her?*"

"She's lighting a cigarette and walking toward the rear of the building," Nathan said. "I've lost sight of her. Can you pick her up?"

"*No, she might make us.*"

"Can you make it look like you're using the bathroom?"

"*No,*" Grangeland replied, "*it's the wrong direction.*"

"Go through the convenience store in case Janey's watching. Go the opposite way around the building. Watch yourself, Ernie might be back there."

"*Copy.*"

Nathan watched Grangeland exit the convenience store and turn right. She disappeared from his line of sight. "Grangeland, report."

Five seconds went by. Silence.

"Grangeland, do you copy?"

A few seconds later, her whispered voice came through the radio. "*She's leaning against the rear wall, smoking. She's alone.*"

"Hang back and stay in the shadow of the building."

"*If anyone pulls in the main driveway, their headlights will light me up.*"

"Get out of there then. Harv will take over from this side. He can use the landscaping and block wall for cover. Wait thirty seconds, then head back into the restaurant."

"*Copy,*" she said.

Nathan estimated the light fog had reduced visibility to just under two hundred yards. It was thinner in some areas and thicker in others. He knew as the dew point and temperature closed in on each other, it would only get worse.

Harv slid out of the passenger seat and stayed low amid the parked cars. Nathan peered out just above the passenger window-sill and watched his friend work his way to the north edge of the property and dash across the driveway, where he vanished in the shadows of a head-high concrete block wall screened by mature oleander bushes.

"Harv, report," Nathan said.

"*I can smell her cigarette, wait one.*"

Nathan waited through a long fifteen seconds of silence.

"*She's leaning against the rear wall of the restaurant with her arms crossed, smoking. She keeps looking left and right.*"

"Harv, stay with her. Grangeland?"

"*I'm back inside with Ferris. Her daughter hasn't moved.*"

"Copy," Nathan said.

"She's on her way back," Harvey reported. *"Grangeland, I'll lose sight of her as she rounds the corner. Let me know if you don't see her within the next five seconds."*

"Copy," Grangeland confirmed. *"I've got her. She's reentering the restaurant through the convenience store."*

Using field glasses, Nathan watched Grangeland approach the convenience-store checkout counter. She was purchasing something to cover her absence from the table, a DVD or paperback book, he couldn't tell which.

Nathan conducted a 360-degree sweep of his surroundings with the handheld thermal imager. The HHTI could pick up the heat signature from a vehicle at over twenty-two hundred yards or a man-sized target at eight hundred yards. The HHTI used in tandem with night vision became an extremely effective combination. Although a person could hide from the night-vision scope, they couldn't hide their thermal signature. The HHTI nailed them every time. Sure enough, it had no problem seeing through the light fog obscuring the area. The truck parking area shone extremely bright from all the heat signatures of the engines. In the open field behind Nathan, it picked up eight to ten cattle lying several hundred yards distant. As he turned the device off, he keyed the radio.

"Harv, you on your way back?"

"Affirm."

"Grangeland, what's Sheldon doing? It looks like she's just standing at the door."

"She keeps looking at her watch, she seems irritated. Wait. She's going back outside. You see her?"

"Affirm. Where the hell's she going? Oh shit, she's heading for the trash can at the island. Grangeland, Ferris, stop her. Don't let her approach that island."

* * *

Amber Sheldon was thoroughly pissed off, more at herself than anyone else. She felt like an idiot. Ernie Bridgestone would never give her any cash, let alone a hundred thousand dollars, as payment for setting up Nathan McBride. She must've been out of her mind to believe anything that jackass said. The lure of money had clearly blinded her. The one thing she believed was Ernie's desire to kill Nathan McBride. He'd made that quite clear. An image of the devastation in Sacramento flashed in her mind. She shivered. Coming anywhere near this damned place tonight was stupid. Stupid and crazy.

It was time to leave.

Ignoring the trash can, she marched across the gas-pump island on the way to her car, but suddenly remembered Janey was with her. She started back toward the restaurant, back across the island.

* * *

Grangeland stepped through the restaurant's door at the same time Amber reached the island.

Nathan's voice buzzed from her radio. "Grangeland. Get down! *Now!*"

She dropped to the concrete.

Amber Mills Sheldon disappeared in a bright flash.

For an instant, the air shimmered. Grangeland's mind registered the explosion and something else. Something hideous. Charred and smoking, Sheldon's upper torso smashed into the brick wall right next to her.

* * *

Every window along the storefront shattered inward, showering the occupants in a horizontal hail of glass. Car alarms sounded from every corner of the property. The SUV fueling at the northern part of the island was lifted into the air and flipped onto its roof. Its gas tank exploded two seconds later. A huge mushroom of burning gasoline roiled into the air.

* * *

"Son of a bitch," Henning hissed as the Expedition's windows shattered inward.

Then Nathan heard something chilling.

Children screaming.

The burning SUV had children in it.

Nathan dashed across the pavement, tearing off his shirt as he ran. He wrapped it around his hand and used it on the door handle of the overturned SUV. After two hard yanks, the passenger door opened. Hanging upside down, two small girls were strapped into car seats, screaming bloody murder as flames licked at their skin. Nathan reached into the SUV and singed his arms unclipping the seat belt holding the first girl's car seat. It fell into his grasp and he yanked it out of the flames.

Harvey and Henning sprinted over.

"Get the other side," Nathan yelled, and hauled the car seat away from the burning wreck. He set the child down and rushed back to the SUV. Ferris was running from the convenience store with a fire extinguisher. He pulled its pin and flooded the interior of the SUV with carbon dioxide gas. Harvey reached into the cloudy discharge and freed the second car seat. When Harvey pulled back from the interior of the SUV, his shirt was smoldering. Ferris nailed him with a discharge of CO_2. Grangeland ran around the island and grabbed the first car seat. She sprinted for the restaurant and disappeared inside. A few seconds later, she returned for the second little girl and ran her into the restaurant. Nathan looked for the SUV's owners but didn't see them. He suddenly realized he hadn't checked the front seats.

Nathan yelled over the crackling of flames, "Ferris, nail the front seats."

Ferris stepped forward, stuck the nozzle through the broken driver's-side window, and pulled the trigger. White cloudy gas filled the cab, starving the flames of oxygen. The reddish-orange glow from the interior winked out. Nathan grabbed his shirt and used it on the door handle. It wouldn't move. With a roar of anger, he pulled with all his strength and the door screeched open. A woman was crumpled into a ball on the SUV's ceiling, which was now the floor. Her clothes and hair were burned and smoking. Fortunately, her skin wasn't too bad. As Nathan and Harvey dragged her away from the SUV, she cried out for her daughters.

"We got them out," Nathan said. "They're okay."

Running from window to window, Ferris continued to spray the SUV's interior.

"Get the tires."

Ferris aimed high and doused the flaming wheels. He hurried to the opposite side and sprayed those tires as well.

Nathan looked up and saw the blacktop moving all around him. No, not the blacktop. SWAT teams. What the hell were they doing here? Lansing…

MP5s at their hips, at least ten SWAT agents were advancing toward their position, some of them fanning out to cover the property's exterior boundaries.

At the exact moment Nathan turned back toward the SUV, he heard the supersonic arrival of a bullet combined with the boom of the discharge.

His right arm jerked. Shit! "Sniper!" he yelled.

Harvey scooped the woman up from the pavement and dashed for the restaurant.

Grangeland, Ferris, and Henning crouched down, but they were out in the open.

Nathan dived for the cover behind the smoldering SUV as another shot cracked through the air. The bullet missed. It careened off the asphalt three inches from his head. Just above his elbow, warm liquid ran down the bare skin of his arm.

The entire SWAT team had hit the deck. "Dowdy, Collins," he yelled, "did you see a muzzle flash?"

"Behind you, five o'clock, plus thirty."

"Give me some cover fire."

Bursts of MP5 fire hammered the air as Nathan scrambled up and dashed for the safety of the restaurant. A giant bullwhip cracked again as the third bullet whizzed by him. He sensed it miss his torso by less than an inch as he entered the building. The floor was littered with broken glass. Janey was screaming. The other server cringed behind the counter, shaking glass out of her hair. Harvey knelt near the rear wall, tending to the injured mother and her little girls. Nathan looked back and saw Henning, Grangeland, and Ferris running in a full sprint for the door.

A fourth rifle report echoed across the pavement.

Twenty feet from safety, Henning tumbled.

Nathan ran back toward the door. "Henning's down." He slipped past Grangeland and Ferris as they rushed inside.

"Nathan, wait!" Harvey yelled. "I'll get him."

"No time." Steeling himself for the bullet that would end his life, he raced across the asphalt, bent down, and hoisted Henning's two-hundred-pound body over his shoulder.

More bursts of MP5 fire echoed off the surrounding trucks and buildings.

A fifth shot tore the air.

This one found its mark. Shit! Nathan's right calf jerked with the impact, but he kept his balance and made it back inside. Harv took Henning from Nathan's shoulder and laid him against the rear wall with the other wounded. Grangeland had grabbed a first-aid kit from the convenience store and was about to apply a large bandage to the flesh wound on Nathan's arm.

"Later," he said.

"You're bleeding bad."

"There's no time, we have to get Bridgestone."

"You've got two gunshot wounds, you may not have time."

"Ferris, can you handle Henning?"

"The bullet went through his vest, but it missed his lungs. He's still in a bad way."

The convenience store's supervisor said, "I called nine-one-one. An ambulance is on the way."

"Harv, Grangeland," Nathan said. "Bridgestone's on the roof of the building north of the property. We'll use the rear exit and stay against the perimeter wall for cover. When we get to the driveway, Harv will retrieve the SUV. Ferris, let your SWAT teams know what we're doing. Tell them to hold their fire until we're in the SUV. We've got to hurry, let's move."

The three of them passed through a stockroom and burst through the rear door facing the freeway. They hugged the wall as they traversed to the northwest corner of the property. All of them heard it. An engine started, followed by the squeal of tires as a vehicle accelerated toward the east. Nathan was limping but kept up with Harv and Grangeland as they ran toward the SUV. Blood had already soaked his sock and shoe.

"Harv, you drive. Grangeland, follow us in the Crown Vic. Let's move."

Just as Nathan closed the passenger door, another deafening explosion rocked the night.

The island at the diesel pumps vanished in a white flash. The freight truck parked at the island was blown ten feet sideways and knocked onto it side. Its fuel tanks exploded, sending a fiery mushroom up to the bottom of the metal canopy covering the islands. Eerie flame spread along the underside of its surface and shot skyward at the edges. Some of the truckers parked in the transient area began driving their rigs out of the danger zone. Men and machines were going every direction. People were screaming and running for cover. Like black ants against a red background, the SWAT team sprinted for the protection of the convenience store, two of them dragging a wounded comrade.

Harv turned right out of the parking lot. With the windows of the SUV gone, they could hear the roaring headers of Ernie's retreating vehicle. It was running east with its lights out.

"That's him. Punch it, Harv." He flipped on the thermal imager and immediately saw the heat signature of the fleeing vehicle's exhaust. "Straight ahead, four or five hundred yards."

The Expedition's engine answered the call. Within ten seconds, they were doing eighty miles an hour. Harv stomped the accelerator and brought their speed up to a hundred and ten. "Stay with him, Harv. Wait one. He's slowing, turning south. I've still got him. We're coming up on the turn in five hundred yards."

"Nate, put the NV visor on my head, we should go dark."

Nathan reached into the duffel bag on the seat between them, grabbed the night-vision visor, and saw blood covering the lower half of his arm. He turned the device on, removed the lens cap, and placed it on Harv's head before pivoting the scope down to his partner's eye.

Harvey made a slight adjustment and said, "Good to go."

Nathan keyed the radio. "Grangeland, we're switching to night vision. Hang back a little. We're going dark."

"*Copy.*"

Harv killed the headlights and the road disappeared into blackness. Behind them, Grangeland also went dark.

"Turn here, to the right," Nathan said. Confirming what he already knew, fresh skid marks marred the pavement where Bridgestone had made a four-wheel slide around the corner. They were now paralleling a sandy dry wash on the eastern side of the road, thick with oak trees and underbrush.

"How you doing, Nate?"

"I'm okay. Stay with him."

Nathan glanced over his shoulder and saw Grangeland make the turn. Through the thin fog, he saw several other vehicles leaving the driveway from Pete's Truck Palace to join the pursuit.

Bring it on. The more the merrier. The cold wind rushing in the windows against his bare skin became an issue. Compounded by the blood acting like water, Nathan was losing body heat quickly. He fought back a shiver and leaned forward as much as he could to avoid the worst of the wind.

"You okay?" Harvey asked.

"Never better. Keep closing, Harv. We'll intercept him in thirty seconds."

"I'm on it."

CHAPTER 22

Ernie Bridgestone whooped in triumph when he lost sight of the headlights pursuing him. He'd lost them.

"Fuckin' pussies," he said aloud. "Now who's doing the squealing?"

He was sure he'd scored at least one hit, maybe two, on McBride, the big man with scars on his face. With a little luck they'd be fatal shots. *Bleed out slowly, you piece of shit.*

Leonard had been wrong about him getting caught after all. Sometimes he wondered if his older brother truly had the balls for this type of thing, trained Ranger or not. He'd been conveniently missing when the time came to head down here and take care of business. Ernie shook his head. He'd actually enjoyed blowing Amber to smithereens. The lousy bitch. She'd betrayed him for the last time. He'd easily spotted the two FBI agents tailing her. Besides, she had it coming for lying to him all these years. Hell, Janey was an adult, she could take of herself. He wasn't worried about her at all. In fact, she was better off without that sleazy—

He looked in the side-view mirror. "What the fu—?"

* * *

Nathan pulled his Sig and hung out the window. When Harv closed to within twenty-five yards, Nathan took aim with both hands and emptied a magazine at the fleeing pickup truck. Each shot he fired illuminated the hood of the SUV in stroboscopic flashes. He aimed low and right, hoping for a skipping shot off the asphalt into the rear tire. He didn't want to shoot the cab because they needed Ernie alive. He couldn't risk a lucky head shot. He had an appointment with Ernie's fingers—an appointment he intended to keep.

Nathan passed the empty gun to Harv and received a fully loaded weapon in return. The chill on his exposed skin felt like a million ice picks. He ignored the hideous sensation and took careful aim. Ernie had begun to swerve back and forth, which actually improved Nathan's odds of blowing out a tire. Harv kept the Expedition on the centerline of the road. Nathan let loose with another full magazine. Got it. Rubber began to peel away from the punctured tire. A baseball-sized piece whizzed past his head and he pulled himself back into the interior. Shredded chunks of rubber thumped off the Expedition's shattered windshield.

"Good shooting," Harv said.

Ernie's truck swerved right, then back to the left before he regained control. It skidded to a stop on the left shoulder. Ernie jumped out and took off into the dry wash. Harv braked hard and pulled in behind the truck.

"He's wearing a sidearm, Harv. Looked like a nineteen-eleven."

"I saw it."

Nathan was in no shape for a foot chase. Although not life-threatening, his right-calf wound was bleeding at a damned ugly clip. "Get him, Harv, we could lose him in there. Take the thermal imager. I'll be right behind you."

Harv didn't have time to strap on his holster, so he jammed four magazines into his front pockets. "His ass is mine."

Nathan watched him disappear into the blackness. *Be careful, old friend.*

Grangeland pulled in behind the SUV and killed the engine. She rushed to the passenger door and saw Nathan donning a night-vision visor.

"No way," she said. "Give that to me. You're in no shape to go out there. Your color's nearly gone and you're shaking like a leaf."

She was right. He wasn't in good shape—in fact, he was in terrible shape. The blood loss combined with the shock and adrenaline wearing off had hammered him. He handed her the visor. "Harv's got a ten-second head start. He's got a thermal imager and night vision with him. We need Bridgestone alive, understood?"

"Yes," she said. Three seconds later she vanished into the moonless void.

Nathan gathered as much strength as he could and shouted, "Grangeland's coming, Harv, not me." He didn't expect an answer and didn't get one.

He limped to the Crown Vic and found Ferris's coat in the backseat. The flesh wound on his arm just above the elbow was burning and throbbing. He was pretty sure the bullet had passed clean through without hitting any bones or major blood vessels, but he wasn't positive. His lower calf wound was a different story. He was tempted to take a look with a flashlight, but decided against it. It was better if he didn't know. He returned to the SUV and looked for something to slow the bleeding on his leg. Settling for Harv's Windbreaker on the front seat, he wound it up like a towel about to be used for a prank whipping in a locker room. He decided to leave his ankle sheath in place—it might offer some stability. He wrapped his lower leg and tied a knot. Tight. He also needed something for his arm. Nathan scanned the backseat of the SUV and saw his shirt he'd removed at the truck stop. Although he had no memory of it, Harv must've picked it up on their way back to the SUV after the explosions. Using his teeth on one end, he tied it around the wound on his arm. Next, he strapped on his gun belt and reloaded his Sig. He holstered the weapon and checked to make sure his spare magazines were secure in their slots. Finally, he turned off his cell and slipped it into his pocket.

At Ernie's truck, the dome light from the open door revealed an HK-91 assault rifle with a night-vision weapon scope. He wondered why Ernie hadn't taken it with him. *Panicked*, he thought. *He's probably regretting leaving it behind. Too bad for old Ernie.* He leaned in, grabbed the weapon, removed the magazine, and cycled the bolt. A live round flew from the breech and landed on the pavement. He picked it up, pushed it back into the magazine, and inserted the magazine into the receiver. After turning the weapon scope on, he cycled the bolt, shouldered the rifle, and looked through the scope. Beautiful, with a capital *B*. The Bridgestones were many things, but cheap with their weaponry wasn't one of them. The night-vision scope was ultramodern, third-generation. He used it to survey the wash and saw Harv picking his way through the underbrush like a wraith. Every so often, Harv would bring the thermal imager up and scan the area in front of him before moving forward. In the image of the night-vision scope, the glow from the thermal imager lit Harv's face like a spotlight. *Attaboy, Harv. Just like old times.*

Through the scope, Nathan could see the dry wash gradually turned in a westerly direction. Several hundred yards up the road, the wash went under a bridge and continued wrapping around to the north. Wide-open fields lay on both sides. If Ernie left the cover of the underbrush, he'd be in plain sight and vulnerable. Nathan pulled on Ferris's coat and started across the field, heading for a copse of mature oaks. With a little hustle, he'd get there before Ernie.

The FBI vehicles in pursuit had missed the turn where Ernie made his four-wheel slide and were heading east. He heard the distant whine of approaching sirens on Highway 99 and the telltale *blat* of a fire engine's air horn. Nearly a mile away, the orange glow from the inferno at Pete's Truck Palace backlit the oaks he was limping toward. They looked like giant mushrooms against a sunset sky. Every so often he'd bring the weapon up and sweep the wash, but he saw no movement. The pain in his calf was distracting, but when he thought about Ernie's bomb at the gas pumps and the screams of the little girls trapped in the burning SUV, he hardened his resolve and kept pushing forward.

Halfway across the open field, Nathan heard two shots off to his left. He recognized them as the distinctive reports of a large-caliber handgun. Ernie's 1911. They came in rapid succession. A few seconds later, two more shots rang out. Ernie was shooting at either Harv or Grangeland, or both. No fire was returned. Bridgestone was probably shooting blindly, gambling for a lucky shot. At least that's what Nathan hoped. He quickened his pace, doing his best not to lose his footing on the parallel mounds of plowed earth. He estimated he'd be at the copse of oaks within two minutes. Once there, he'd lay low and wait for Harv and Grangeland to drive Ernie to his position. He needed to be careful: getting nailed by friendly fire would definitely ruin his evening. The saving grace? Harv and Grangeland had night vision, Bridgestone didn't.

By the time Nathan made it to the stand of oaks, his lower calf was really throbbing. He was pretty sure the bleeding hadn't slowed because his shoe was overflowing with blood. He worked his way over a barbed-wire fence and crouched down beside the top of the wash. At this location, the wash was about fifty feet wide and five feet lower in elevation than the surrounding plowed fields. Islands of thick brush were scattered through the dry riverbed. Fallen leaves from the oaks covered the ground. He shouldered the weapon and swept the sandy expanse in the direction Ernie should be coming from. Nothing. No movement at all.

As though a camera flash had gone off, the area flared bright green in the NV scope. A second later, the thump of Ernie's handgun report reached him. Nathan knew sound traveled at close to one thousand feet per second, which meant Ernie was roughly three hundred yards away. He tried to spot Harv or Grangeland, but couldn't see them.

Directly in front of him, a long strip of brush would make a perfect ambush location. It dawned on him like a slap in the face. He hadn't removed the keys from his SUV or Grangeland's Crown Vic. If Ernie circled back...He silently cursed himself for being so careless and scanned the plowed field between his position and the parked vehicles. No sign of Ernie. If Nathan positioned himself down in the wash, he wouldn't be able to see the vehicles. He gambled that Harv had Bridgestone in sight. If Ernie made a beeline for their SUV, Harv would intercept him. He slid down the sandy bank, limped in a crouch over to the strip of brush, and shouldered Ernie's rifle.

"Got you," he whispered. Bridgestone was running along the eastern bank of the wash, ducking for cover every so often and pointing his gun back at his pursuers. Nathan spotted Harv and Grangeland about fifty yards behind, advancing in leapfrog movements. It looked like they were trying to flank him. He had to let Harv know he was here. He stepped out from the cover of the brush and waved Ernie's gun back and forth like a flag. He kept repeating the gesture for ten seconds. When he shouldered the weapon and peered through the scope, he saw Harv waving in recognition. Nathan returned the wave and pointed to the place where he planned to ambush Bridgestone. Harv gave him an "okay" hand signal. He watched Harv turn his head toward Grangeland's position and she closed the distance. They huddled in a crouch for a few seconds before Grangeland sprinted to the western side of the wash and began working her way forward through the underbrush. Two more flashes lit the landscape. Grangeland dived for cover, but Harv didn't move. *The man's got nerves of steel*, Nathan thought. Although Ernie was firing blindly, he could still score a lucky hit.

In a two-story farmhouse, five hundred yards to the west, the porch lights snapped on. The locals were responding to the gunfire. It was only a matter of time before sheriff deputies or the

FBI SWAT team from Pete's Truck Palace arrived. The situation could get sticky. Friendly fire would become a serious problem. As if sensing Nathan's thoughts, Harv let loose with three quick shots. Through the NV scope, he watched Bridgestone duck for cover, then begin a full sprint toward Nathan's position. Harv fired again.

Attaboy, Harv, drive him home.

If Ernie kept his current pace, he'd close on Nathan in about thirty seconds.

That's it. Keep coming.

Nathan squinted and steadied himself.

* * *

It wasn't cinematic. It didn't have to be.

Just as Bridgestone reached Nathan's position at the island of underbrush, he extended his good leg. Simple. Elegant. Effective.

Arms flailing, Bridgestone fell flat on his face. Nathan pounced on the man's back, grabbed his wrist, and wrenched it up all the way to his neck. The handgun fell from Ernie's grasp and thumped into the sand. Nathan both felt and heard Ernie's shoulder dislocate. Ernie cried out and tried to roll over, but Nathan kept his entire weight centered.

"Well, well, well, if it isn't the cell-block sweetie himself."

Harv and Grangeland arrived ten seconds later and joined the restraint. Harv forced Bridgestone's other wrist behind his back and Grangeland handcuffed him.

"You stupid motherfuckers," Ernie hissed. "You're dead, you're all fucking dead."

"Oh, we'll be fine," Nathan said. "But you, Ernie, old boy? You're going to wish you were dead. Trust me on that."

"Fuck you."

"Sorry, you're not my type, but I'll get Doc Fitzgerald to call up some of your old inmate buddies, if you like."

"I'm not afraid of you."

"You will be," Nathan said. "*You will be.*" He held his hand up and started counting. "I count fourteen knuckles, Harv. Sound about right?"

"Fourteen on each hand," Harv corrected.

"Brutal. Think he can take it?"

"Don't know, only one way to find out."

"What are you guys talking about?" Grangeland asked. Like Harv, she was breathing hard from the sprint up the sandy wash.

"I'm going to start cutting this jerk's fingers off. One knuckle at a time."

"The hell you are, McBride. The FBI doesn't torture its prisoners."

"We aren't FBI."

"I want my fucking phone call," Ernie said.

"That's what your cousins said before you killed them." Harv shoved Bridgestone's face into the sand.

"You are *not* torturing this man," Grangeland said.

"Special Agent Grangeland, take a walk with me. You got him, Harv?"

"Oh, I got him all right." Harv kept his knee on Bridgestone's back and leaned on the dislocated shoulder. Ernie grunted and spit sand.

Nathan led Grangeland fifty yards up the sandy wash and stopped. "I need the truth. Is my cell phone being tapped?"

"I don't know," she said.

He pulled it from his pocket, turned it on, and entered a Washington, DC, number from memory. Holly had given him Director Lansing's cell number.

It rang four times. The voice answering was sleepy and a little annoyed. "This had better be good."

"It's good," Nathan said.

"Who is this?"

"Nathan McBride."

"Do you mind telling me why you're calling at...four in the morning?"

"I've got Ernie Bridgestone in custody."

"Right now? You have him in custody right now?"

"That's right."

"Damned good news, Mr. McBride."

"I need to interrogate him."

"I see."

"I'm not sure you do. I mean *interrogate* him."

"If I understand what you're implying, we don't do things that way."

"I think you'll make an exception."

"And why would I do that?"

"Because I know about the Ortega-Bridgestone connection."

Lansing said nothing.

"And the Semtex."

More silence.

"You still there?" asked Nathan.

"Yes, I'm here."

"Are we on the same page now?"

"Yes."

Nathan kept his tone even. "May I ask why the FBI was at Pete's Truck Palace?"

"Amber Sheldon wanted the reward money. There's a million-dollar reward on the brothers. Half a million each. She called and told us about tonight's money drop."

Nathan shook his head at the two-dimensional double-cross Sheldon had pulled off. "Well, I guess that money belongs to Harv and me now."

"What about Sheldon?"

"Bridgestone turned her into red mist."

"Then yes, the money's yours. You collared him. It's yours."

"One of your field agents is with us. She needs clarification on our arrangement." Nathan handed the phone to Grangeland.

She took it, walked a few paces away, and kept her back to Nathan, but he could still hear her end of the conversation.

"This is Special Agent Grangeland from the Fresno residence office," she said. After a few seconds, Grangeland tensed as if she wanted to object, but said, "Yes, sir. Understood." She handed the phone back to him.

"You've got one hour, Mr. McBride."

"I don't need that long. One more thing, Director Lansing."

"What?"

"Keep this under wraps. Tell absolutely no one we have Ernie until we've got his brother. Leonard can't know Ernie's been apprehended. If it leaks, he'll bolt and we'll never catch him. Play along and you'll get your front-page headline and no one will be the wiser. You have my word on it."

"All right, agreed. I want you to call me back when you've got something to report."

"Will you put Special Agent Grangeland under my command for the remainder of this operation?"

"Yes."

"She'll need to hear it from you." Nathan handed her the cell again.

She listened for several seconds before saying, "Yes, sir."

Nathan took the phone back. "Thank you, Director Lansing. We'll collar Leonard if you play along."

"No mutilations, McBride."

"We'll see." Nathan ended the call. "You're welcome to stay, if you think you've got the stomach for it."

"I'll stay."

"Suit yourself, Grangeland, but don't interfere. Are we crystal clear on that? No matter what you see."

She nodded tightly.

They hustled back to Harv's position.

"Are you ready, Mr. Bridgestone?"

CHAPTER 23

There were moments in life when you found yourself totally unprepared. This was such a moment for Special Agent Grangeland. Nothing in her FBI training or competitive athletic background could've prepared her for the horror unfolding before her. She found it difficult to watch, but more difficult *not* to watch. Ernie Bridgestone lay facedown in the sand. Harvey had dragged a large piece of wood over from the dry riverbank and placed it beneath the man's cuffed hands. He then dragged a second piece over and placed it under Bridgestone's chin so he wouldn't inhale sand and choke. She watched in horror as Harvey removed a menacing knife from his ankle sheath and handed it to Nathan. Harvey then placed a knee on Bridgestone's upper back and applied his full weight. Facing Harvey, Nathan sat on Bridgestone's legs and grabbed one of his hands. Ernie tried to resist, thrashing about and swearing like a madman, but he was pinned and couldn't get any leverage.

She watched in abject disbelief as Nathan forced the tip of the knife into Bridgestone's ring-finger knuckle and shoved, rocking it back and forth as if cutting through a tough piece of steak. She'd never heard a grown man scream bloody murder. She clenched her jaw so tightly her head began to throb. Although Nathan wasn't actually severing Bridgestone's fingers, he was coming damned close. Bile rose in her throat as she tried to separate her mind from her body, but the two kept clashing back together. How could she allow this to continue? Surely Director Lansing hadn't approved what she was watching. What kind of men were these guys? How could they brutally torture another human being with such casual indifference? Was it worth her job, a lifetime's worth of achievement, to put a stop to this? How could she live with herself knowing she could've ended this and didn't? She looked down in shock and disgust as they started again on the next knuckle up.

* * *

"How does it feel, you piece of shit?" Nathan hissed. "Did you enjoy cutting James Ortega's fingers off as much as I'm enjoying this? Well, did you?"

In truth, he wasn't angry, and in truth, he didn't enjoy it, but he wanted Ernie to think he did. He actually found it repulsive, but he needed Ernie to believe otherwise. He hadn't asked Ernie any questions, nor did he intend to. It was all part of the mind game he was playing.

Nathan pushed the knife.

Bridgestone shrieked in agony. Blood flew from his mouth where he'd bitten his tongue. The tortured man whipped his head back and forth, tearing his cheeks on the log.

Nathan removed the knife after going halfway through the second knuckle and started on the final knuckle. Within two minutes, Bridgestone had been reduced to a sobbing wretch. He was crying like a child and begging for Nathan to stop. He promised to tell Nathan anything he wanted if he'd stop cutting his fingers.

Nathan looked up at Harv. "What do you think?"

"I think he's full of shit. We've got twenty-five knuckles to go. Let's see how he feels in say.... twenty minutes or so."

Nathan reached down and grabbed Ernie's hand again.

"Stop!" Ernie screamed. "I'll tell you whatever you want, man."

"What makes you think we want information?" Nathan asked. "This isn't about information, it's about payback for James Ortega."

"The Ortegas fucked me in Pensacola," Bridgestone wailed. "It wasn't my fault. I did my time. I was willing to let it go but they fucked me again. Ortega set us up. His grandson sold us the Semtex."

"Is that why you burned him alive?"

"It was an accident, we didn't mean to, I swear."

"Save it for someone who gives a rat's ass."

"I'll tell you where Leonard is, just don't cut my fingers anymore. He took off for Montana around six o'clock tonight. I'm supposed to meet him up there tomorrow night."

"We already know where he is, he's being arrested right now. Do you think we're stupid?" Nathan looked up at Grangeland, "He thinks we're stupid." Nathan grabbed his hand and forced it against the driftwood.

"Wait! There's money. Over three million in cash."

"I'm worth twenty times that. I don't need your blood money."

"It's cash, man! Buried in ammo cans near the Canadian border."

Nathan looked at Harv again. "What do you think, do you believe him?"

"Hell no."

"I don't either." Nathan jammed the knife into the first knuckle of finger number two. Ernie screamed again, rawer this time. His voice was failing.

Grangeland turned away and threw up. Falling to her knees, she heaved in violent spasms.

Nathan grabbed Ernie's hair and yanked his head back. "Where's the rest of the Semtex?"

"My truck. Leonard has the rest."

"How much is *the rest*?"

"Ten bricks. That's it, man. I swear."

"Does he have blasting caps?"

"Yes."

Nathan looked up. "Grangeland, let your SWAT team know Leonard's got ten bricks of Semtex before they take him down."

She didn't respond.

"Grangeland!"

She slowly pulled her cell phone.

This is it, Nathan thought. *She's either with the program or she's going to blow it.* He couldn't risk it. "Give me the phone."

"What?"

"Give me the phone."

She wiped her mouth and stepped forward. When she was close enough to see his face clearly, he winked at her.

She nodded an understanding. "They're under my command, I'll make the call."

Nathan knew she'd make a fake call and hoped it would sound convincing.

"It's Grangeland." She paused. "Yeah, we got him and he's talking. He said Leonard's got ten bricks of Semtex and blasting caps." She paused again. "Where? Okay, don't approach him until SWAT arrives. Understood? I say again, do not approach him...All right, good work, I'll call you in ten minutes."

Perfect. Nathan couldn't have played it better himself. Ernie had soaked up every word. Now that he believed his brother was being captured, he'd have no reason to hold back.

Nathan pulled Ernie's head back again. "Where's the money?"

"It's buried near an abandoned ranch in Montana near the Canadian border."

"Montana's a big state, that doesn't tell me squat." He reached for Ernie's hand.

"Wait! I got GPS coordinates."

"Well?" Nathan asked.

Ernie rattled off the numbers. Grangeland pulled a penlight, secured it in her mouth, and wrote the coordinates down on a small pad of paper.

"If you're lying, we'll upgrade to a butter knife and use a plumber's torch to cauterize the stumps. I've got fifty-seven more minutes with you, and trust me, I'll savor every last second."

"I'm not lying, I swear."

Nathan got off of Ernie's legs and stood up. "Harv, keep him company for a minute."

"No problem."

"Grangeland, let's take another walk." He led her across the sand, working his way through the islands of underbrush. After a hundred feet he stopped and kept his voice low. "We don't have much time, we need to get going. Like I told Lansing, we have to keep Ernie's capture under wraps. It's vital it doesn't leak. If Leonard believes Ernie escaped, he'll head for the cash, I'm sure of it. Maybe even wait for him there, for a time."

She pointed to the orange glow from Pete's Truck Palace. "There's no way to keep that under wraps. It's probably on the news already."

"Here's what we'll do. We leak to the press that all we got from the scene was Ernie's cell phone and his sniper rifle, that Ernie's still at large, and that your people are analyzing the call logs."

"Leonard will think Ernie's phone has been compromised, so he'll ditch his. They'll have no way to communicate."

"That's right."

"What's next?"

"I'm going to take custody of Ernie until we have his brother."

"What? That wasn't part of the deal with Lansing. I—"

"Think about it, Grangeland. You, me, Harv, and Director Lansing are the only people on the planet who know Ernie's in custody. He's number one on your most-wanted list. How long could something like that stay under wraps? People talk, the walls have ears. We can't risk it. Don't worry, I'll make sure you get the credit for the collar."

"I'm not worried about getting credit, I'm worried about going to prison."

"Director Lansing put you under my command, so I'm giving you a direct order. Ernie stays with us until we've got Leonard."

She nodded tightly.

"We need to get up to those coordinates. Just the four of us. We'll take my helicopter."

"You own a helicopter? I guess you weren't kidding when you said you're worth twenty times that much."

"We need to bug out of here before the cavalry arrives. By the way, you did a great job with the fake call."

"How's the arm?"

"All things considered, not too bad."

They started back to Harvey's position. "Bridgestone might need a hospital. And you certainly do."

"I'll clean myself up once we've made it back to Sacramento. With a little luck, I'll only need some stitches and antibiotics."

"Stiches and antibiotics? You were shot twice."

"I appreciate your concern, but right now, we need to get moving."

They returned to their prisoner. Grangeland grabbed Ernie's 45, shook the sand out of the barrel, removed the magazine, and ejected the round. She stuffed the gun and its magazine into her front pockets. Harv took charge of Bridgestone and started marching him toward the vehicles. Five minutes later, they were back at the SUV. Just as Ernie had said, they found nearly three hundred pounds of Semtex and several dozen blasting caps. The orange-colored bricks were packed into cardboard boxes. The blasting caps were in a smaller box. Before Harv transferred the boxes of Semtex and the blasting caps into the trunk of the Crown

Vic, Grangeland grabbed the first-aid kit. Not all of the boxes fit into the trunk, so Harv stacked the remainder of them into the rear of the SUV. Nathan would have Grangeland relay the location of the boxes to her FBI counterparts once they cleared the area. He didn't like leaving the Semtex unsecured, but thought it'd be safe for the next few minutes or so. He laid Ernie's assault rifle atop the boxes in the trunk.

Grangeland pulled on a pair of latex gloves and told Ernie to hold still. The cuts on Ernie's knuckles were streaming blood and needed to be wrapped to stanch the flow. Holding the penlight in her mouth, she applied several tight layers of gauze around Ernie's two mangled fingers and secured them with white tape. Ernie grunted from the pressure.

"You'll live," she said.

Nathan kept a close eye on their captive as Grangeland tucked him into the backseat of the Crown Vic and closed the door. Ernie seemed subdued during all of this. Maybe it was shock or the false news about his brother's capture. More likely, it was the reality of his fate sinking in. He was headed back to prison, only this time to death row. Depending on how cooperative he was on their trip up north to Montana, Nathan might give him an alternative to the living hell awaiting him.

Nathan reluctantly agreed to let Grangeland look at his wounds. He shucked off Ferris's coat and held out his arm. Once again holding the penlight in her mouth, she pulled on a fresh pair of gloves. When the beam swept across his chest, she frowned at seeing the network of crisscrossing scars. She obviously hadn't noticed them earlier, when the truck stop went up in flames.

He winked at her. "I lost a bet."

"Must've been some bet."

"It was." He let her remove the blood-soaked shirt and apply a dozen wraps of gauze around the torn flesh and secure it with tape.

"Better let me see that leg."

He put his foot on the lip of the open trunk and pulled his soaked fatigue up.

"Did you have a knife like Harvey's?" she asked.

"Yeah, why?"

"Take a look." She shone the penlight on the wound.

"I'll be damned," he said. The knife was gone, but the sheath was still there. The bullet must've hit the knife and broken it free before fragmenting outward, shredding the flesh with shrapnel. All the bleeding had been from lacerated skin, not a bullet hole. "Luck favors the well-prepared," he said. After Grangeland removed the sheath and wrapped the wound, he turned toward Harv. "Let's take a quick walk. Grangeland, you've got Bridgestone. I need you to relay this position to your team at the truck stop so they can retrieve the Semtex from the back of the SUV."

"No problem," she said.

They walked a good fifty feet down the road.

"Based on what Ernie told us, I figure Leonard's got a six-hour head start on us," Nathan said. "We should assume seven. That has him arriving at the money drop in Montana by three in the afternoon tomorrow at the earliest. I can't see him driving up there any faster than that. He'll drive the speed limit to avoid being pulled over. Whatever disguise he's using, it's probably good enough to fool the average law-enforcement officer. Colored contacts, facial hair, whatever. He'll have fake IDs too. We should assume he'll make it up to the drop. I've driven through that area of I-Fifteen, it's remote. You could drive for hundreds of miles without seeing a state trooper."

"You're thinking he'll drive straight through?"

"No doubt about it. He wants to recover his money and bug out. He'll pump himself full of over-the-counter caffeine pills for the drive. We need to be one hundred percent certain we arrive there first."

"We'll also need satellite images of the area." Harv paused meaningfully.

"Damn it, Harv, he could be involved in all of this."

"Do you honestly believe that? Deep down?"

Nathan didn't answer right away. "No, I guess not." Harv was right, they did need satellite images. Without them, they'd be going in blind, without knowing the terrain. Although she could arrange it, he couldn't risk asking Holly because, quite frankly, he didn't trust the FBI. More accurately, he didn't trust Director Lansing.

"I know you don't want to ask, but we could really use his help. It could make or break this operation."

Nathan said nothing.

"You want me to make the call?"

Nathan sighed. "He's my father. I'll make the call. You realize we'll have to tell him everything."

"Nate, it's me, okay? I know you've been wanting to patch things up for a long time. Here's your opportunity. Give the man a chance."

"He's a politician."

"Has he ever lied to you?"

"No, I can honestly say he hasn't." His cell rang. Nathan unclipped it from his belt. He recognized the phone number on the LCD. It was Holly Simpson. "We have Ernie."

"Nathan, thank God. The truck stop is all over the news. Every network's covering it."

"Holly, I can't talk right now."

"Are you okay? Special Agent Ferris just told me you were shot twice."

"I'll call you back in a few minutes. Don't talk to anyone about this. No one."

"Nathan—"

"A few minutes, Holly, I promise." He ended the call and looked at Harv. "The cat's out of the bag. It's a good bet Leonard's heard about this on the radio by now."

"He'll avoid the money cache until he hears from Ernie."

"I've got that covered. We're going to leak to the press that Ernie got away and all we recovered from the scene was his sniper rifle and his cell phone. We'll also leak that we're analyzing the cell company's call logs. I'm betting that will make Leonard ditch his phone."

"They must have some contingency meeting location if they're separated for a long period of time."

"No doubt they do."

"Leonard could lie low awhile. He might wait a week or even a month before he approaches the money drop."

"That's a real possibility, but I'm betting his love of money will force his hand. For Leonard, this whole thing's about money, not revenge. As long as Leonard believes his brother's on the run, we've got a chance to nail him."

"Bringing Ernie along complicates things."

"We'll put Grangeland in charge of him."

"She'll love that. How's the arm?"

"Better than the leg. When we get back to Sacramento, can you preflight the chopper while I get our gear from the Hyatt and clean myself up a little?"

"Not a problem."

"I'll drop you guys off at Sac Exec Airport and make the call to my father on the way over to the Hyatt. I'd better call Holly back." He dialed the number from memory and quickly recapped the events at the truck stop leading up to his current situation. She kept turning the conversation to his gunshot wounds, and he kept reassuring her he was okay. He told her about his call to Lansing after collaring Ernie.

"Lansing knows I know about Ortega and the failed sting," he said. "I used it to persuade him I needed some quality time with Ernie."

"Be careful, Nathan. Lansing can be a formidable enemy."

"We made a deal. He looks the other way for a spell and I keep quiet about the Semtex business. It's a good arrangement for him.

He knows what's at stake if this ever leaks. He put Grangeland under my command."

"Nathan, I could get you SWAT backup. You don't have to do this alone."

"No. Harv and I can handle it. I don't want the situation complicated by having friendlies in the area. It's a shoot-to-kill situation now."

"I don't like the sound of that."

"Neither do I, but frankly, it's easier than trying to capture him alive."

She had no response to that.

"We tricked Ernie into believing we have Leonard in custody and that all we're doing is going up there to recover the cash."

"Smart move."

"I need your office to leak some information to the press right away. Tonight. Right now, if you can. Leonard has to believe Ernie is still on the run or he'll never show at the money drop. You need to leak that Ernie got away and all we recovered from the truck stop was his sniper rifle and his cell phone and that the bureau's analyzing the call logs from the carrier. Leonard will ditch his phone. He won't risk the FBI tracking it."

"That's a good plan. ASAC Breckensen is dating an anchor at News Ten. I'll take care of this right away."

"Needless to say, don't tell Breckensen the truth."

"He won't like it when he finds out."

"We can't worry about that right now. Leonard has to believe Ernie escaped. If it leaks he's in custody we can kiss Leonard good-bye. He'll disappear. This is our only chance to bag him. We won't get another opportunity. Ever."

"Nathan, we lost another SWAT agent at the truck stop. Three civilians too."

"I'm sorry, Holly."

"I didn't know SWAT was going to be there or I would've told you. ASAC Breckensen was under direct orders from Lansing. They left me out of the loop again."

"The beat goes on…"

"End this, Nathan, before anyone else gets killed."

"You can count on it." Nathan ended the call. "We need to get moving." He pointed to the west, where several sheriff's cruisers were racing down the road with their light bars flashing blue and red. "We've got less than a minute to clear the area. You get everything we need out of the SUV?"

"Yes."

They hurried back to the vehicles. Nathan was thankful the Crown Vic's windows had survived the blast. He was in no condition for a freezing drive back to Sacramento. Grangeland took the rear seat next to Bridgestone while Nathan slid into the front. Harv left the headlights off as he pulled onto the road. He flipped the night-vision scope down to his eye and stomped the accelerator.

"All the roads in this area are laid out at ninety degrees to one another," Grangeland said. "Take a right at the first major road we come to. That should take us back to the freeway or its frontage road."

After another mile or so, Harv turned right and said, "Shit."

The northbound lanes of the freeway were stopped dead. A string of headlights stretched to the south for at least a mile. Emergency vehicles were using the shoulder to advance. The inferno at Pete's Truck Palace must have closed down the freeway.

"Keep going under the freeway," Grangeland said. "We'll take a parallel road until we're past this."

They had to go several miles until Harv could make a right turn. Flat farmland lined both sides of the road. Harv gunned the sedan up to seventy miles an hour. Other drivers had the same idea. The once-quiet country road now looked like a prime arterial. Following the pack, Harv made a right heading north and saw the same string of bumper-to-bumper headlights in the southbound lanes of I-5. After another right turn heading east, they passed under the freeway and accelerated up the northbound on-ramp.

Ernie remained silent. Nathan knew how he felt. Hell, he'd lived it. Immediately after his capture in Nicaragua, he'd been beaten senseless and thrown into the bed of a truck under armed guard. Angry faces had sneered down at him, some spat. The drive through the jungle had seemed endless.

Nathan turned his head and addressed Ernie. "Why don't you give us the real GPS coordinates now."

"What are you talking about?" Ernie said.

"I'll be honest with you. You've got a nasty ten years ahead of you before you get the needle. And you *are* getting a needle. Think about it, death row at San Quentin with Scott Peterson, your brother, Leonard, and the rest of the tattooed mutts. Within your first week, Big Bubba will make you his wife and swap you with all of his friends for packs of cigarettes."

"Shut the fuck up, McBride."

"Give me the real GPS coordinates and I'll give you another option."

"What other option?"

"A bullet to the head."

Ernie said nothing,

"See, it's like this," Nathan continued. "I'm not turning you over to the FBI just yet. I've decided you're coming with us to the coordinates, and if you're lying about them, we'll start over. I've still got fifty-seven minutes left with you." He made eye contact with Grangeland, who looked stressed.

Harv jumped in. "It costs the state of California a million dollars to go through the death-row appeals process. Isn't that money better spent somewhere else?"

"I can't argue with that," she said, "but I need to be insulated from what you're doing here."

"Special Agent Grangeland, consider yourself insulated. I don't care how you deal with it. Plug your nose, look the other way, pretend it never happened, whatever works."

"I've got your word you won't take me in?" Ernie asked, closing the deal.

"Marine to marine. Now give me the real coordinates."

CHAPTER 24

After dropping Harv, Grangeland, and Bridgestone at Sacramento Executive Airport, Nathan pulled his cell and looked at his watch. It would be a little after 0700, Eastern time. He dialed his father's mobile number.

"Hello?"

"Hi, Dad."

"Nathan. Are you okay? The explosion and fire at the truck stop are all over the news."

"I need to talk to you."

"Okay..."

"Look, I know we haven't always seen eye to eye. For what it's worth, I feel like it's my fault. I have trouble trusting people. Trusting you."

"Nonsense. You're my son. Just because we don't always agree on things doesn't mean we can't trust each other."

"I need to trust you. Now more than ever."

"You can."

"What I'm about to tell you can't go any further. Tell no one. Absolutely no one else can know. It's life-and-death, Dad. My life, and Harv's."

"What's happened?"

"I need your word."

"You don't have to ask for that."

"Your word." He heard his dad sigh.

"I give you my word."

It took five minutes for Nathan to tell the story and describe the plan going forward. He knew with certainty the news of the Ortega conspiracy to entrap the Bridgestones by selling them Semtex both shocked and angered his father. The only thing that surprised Nathan was how good it felt to know his dad hadn't been in on it.

"Are you absolutely sure about this?" Stone asked when Nathan had finished. "I mean, absolutely sure?"

"Yes."

"You think you know someone. Frank and I were in Korea together, fought side by side. I can't believe this whole thing is about revenge against Ernie Bridgestone."

"It hurts, I know. Harv feels betrayed too. There is some good news. We recovered most of the missing Semtex. Nearly three hundred pounds."

"That's good news."

"Leonard still has ten bricks and some blasting caps."

"What can I do to help? Name it."

"We need satellite images of the location where they stashed their cash."

"I'll get to work on it right away. Do you have exact coordinates?"

Nathan rattled them off. "I need twenty-four by twenty-four-inch prints at three meters per inch, ten meters per inch, and one hundred meters per inch. Radial from point zero. Did you copy that?"

"Yes, I'm writing it down."

"Get me a fourth print at five hundred meters per inch. We'll be airborne within the hour. Communication will be critical. My cell's tied into the NavCom of my helicopter. It usually works over urban areas, but in the more remote locations, all bets are off."

"Nathan, it'll be hard to keep this under wraps once the military's involved."

Nathan didn't respond.

"Don't worry, I'll think of something."

"Do your best, Dad, that's all I can ask. I think Malmstrom Air Force Base in Montana is our best bet to download the images."

"I know Malmstrom well. We put our first Minutemen silos up there."

"Listen, I've got to go. We've got a long flight ahead of us."

"Nathan, thank you for trusting me. I'm sorry for the things I said to you the other night."

"Me too."

"I'll call you as soon as I have something to report."

"Tell Mom I love her."

"You can tell herself when this is over."

Nathan said nothing. He didn't have to.

"I'll tell her," Stone said.

* * *

After dropping off Harv, Grangeland, and Bridgestone at Sacramento Executive Airport, he returned to the Hyatt and cleaned himself up as best he could. There was nothing he could do about his head-turning trek through the lobby. He grabbed the duffels, returned to the sedan, and drove back to the airport. Grangeland looked concerned and asked about his arm. He told a white lie and handed her the medical supplies he'd stopped for on the way over.

"She ready to go?"

"Ready," Harv said.

"This is everyone's last chance for a pit stop. We'll be in the air for several hours."

Grangeland looked around in an exaggerated manner. "Hmm, no restroom."

Nathan nodded to the hangar buildings.

She jogged over to the hangars and disappeared around the corner.

Nathan turned toward Ernie. "What about you?"

He shook his head.

Harv removed their duffel bags and Nathan's aluminum rifle case from the Crown Vic's backseat and secured them in the baggage compartment.

"Listen up, Ernie," Nathan said. "I'm willing to cuff your hands in front for the flight provided you behave yourself. Do we have an understanding?"

"I ain't gonna make no trouble," he said.

Without being asked, Harv pulled his Sig and pointed it at Ernie's chest. Using the handcuff key Grangeland had given him, Nathan re-cuffed Ernie's hands in front of his stomach. Even though he had it coming, leaving the condemned man's wounded hands cuffed behind his back for the long flight seemed cruel, especially with his dislocated shoulder. Harv pushed Bridgestone into the right rear seat, behind the pilot's position. He fastened Ernie's seat belt and shoulder strap.

Once Grangeland returned from her business, Nathan pulled her aside and kept his voice low. "I cuffed Ernie's hands in front for the flight. Guard your weapon closely."

She nodded and strapped herself into the left rear seat.

"What about the Crown Vic?" Harv asked.

"Yeah," Nathan agreed. "Park it over by the hangars with the other vehicles."

"There's Semtex in the trunk," Harv said.

"Grangeland can relay its location once we've landed at our first fuel stop. We'll just have to risk that no one steals the car within the next few hours or so. As a precaution, we'll take the blasting caps with us."

"Good thought," she said.

When Harv returned from parking the sedan, he secured the blasting caps into a duffel bag and handed Grangeland a Bose headset with a boom mike. He plugged it into the console over her right shoulder. Bridgestone didn't receive a headset. Although engine and slipstream noise would be loud, it wouldn't be overly so, but more important, it allowed Grangeland, Harv, and Nathan to communicate without being overheard, which was far more important than worrying about Bridgestone's ears. Besides, he wouldn't need them much longer anyway.

While Nathan went through the start-up checklist, Harv connected Nathan's cell into the audio interface that would allow them to patch calls through their flight helmets. Harv entered the GPS coordinates Ernie had given them into the Garmin G600 NavCom. The glass avionics in Nathan's helicopter were state-of-the-art. Along with flight-control data on the left screen, the G600 employed built-in terrain and navigation databases on the right screen, providing a precise moving map of where they were at any given time and where they were going. With the GDL-A data-link receiver, they could access high-resolution weather information anywhere within the United States.

"While you were at the hotel, I did some rough flight planning," Harv said. "It's a three-leg trip. Winnemucca, Nevada; Idaho Falls, Idaho; then into Great Falls, Montana. Our destination coordinates are close to a town called Dupuyer on Highway Eighty-Nine. We'll fuel up in Great Falls. I checked the airport listing binder. At each airport, self-service pumps are available if the jet centers are closed. All of them have Jet-A available, night or day."

"Good job. We might be landing at Malmstrom Air Force Base instead of Great Falls."

Harv consulted the charts. "That's…no problem. It's only a few miles to the east."

Within two minutes of starting the engine, Nathan had the two-and-a-half-ton Bell 407 in a stable hover.

"Clear on the left?" Nathan asked.

"Clear," Harv answered.

They were on their way.

CHAPTER 25

Minutes after their stop in Winnemucca, Nathan's cell rang. It was close to 7:00 AM. Harv patched it through the NavCom.

It was Stone McBride. "I've got the satellite intel all set up for you."

"Great work, Dad. Thanks."

"I'm glad to do it. When you get within one hundred miles of Malmstrom, change to this frequency and announce your call sign as Civilian Delta." Stone rattled off the numbers and Harv programmed the frequency into the ninth preset on the NavCom unit.

"Got it," Nathan said.

"An Air Force Black Hawk will intercept you and escort you onto the base. It would be useful if I could tell them when to expect you up there."

"Wait one," Harvey said and began scrolling through menus. "We'll be crossing Interstate Ninety in approximately...four hours, assuming our fuel stop in Idaho Falls goes as expected."

"Got it," Stone said. "Once you're at Malmstrom, they'll fuel you up and give you the latest photos of the area. They'll probably be twenty to thirty minutes old by then, but that's the best they can do. Also, if anyone shows up at the location after you leave Malmstrom, they'll radio you."

"Perfect," Nathan said.

"Major General Mansfield is the base commander. I told him this is a classified operation on a need-to-know basis. The number of people involved is minimal. He assured me there will be no leaks or quote, 'heads will roll.' Don't take any unnecessary risks. Bridgestone isn't worth your life, or Harvey's."

"Thanks for your help, Dad. I'll call you later."

"Be careful, Nathan."

* * *

After a quick refuel and head call in Idaho Falls, they were on their way north again. The weather was perfect, not a cloud in the sky, and it looked good all the way to the Canadian border. Nothing was forecast for the next forty-eight hours. Nathan wondered why he hadn't flown up this way before. It was truly beautiful territory. He made a mental note to go camping up here. River-washed valleys and rocky canyons dominated the landscape. In the distance off to the west, snowcapped peaks lined the horizon.

Harv worked the NavCom. "We'll be coming up on Interstate Ninety in about twenty minutes. That's a good place to call our Air Force escort."

"Sounds good."

"How's the arm?" Harv asked.

"A little sore, but the bleeding has almost stopped. Thanks for the TLC, Grangeland." She'd insisted on changing his bandages at each fuel stop.

"You're welcome, I wish I could do more."

"How's our passenger doing?"

"About the same," she said. "He's been staring out the window the whole time."

Not surprising, considering what lay ahead for him. One way or another, this was a one-way trip for Ernie Bridgestone.

* * *

At I-90, Harv pressed the ninth preset button for the frequency Nathan's father had given them. He toggled the transmit trigger on the cyclic control. "This is Civilian Delta on heading zero-one-zero crossing Interstate Ninety at eight thousand five hundred."

The response came back immediately. *"Civilian Delta, squawk three-two-two-five and ident."*

Harv repeated the instructions, entered the numbers into their transponder, and pressed the ident button.

The metallic voice came back. *"Civilian Delta, radar contact confirmed. Maintain current heading and speed and await further instructions."*

They flew for another ten minutes before the controller came back. *"Civilian Delta, your escort is five miles at one o'clock. Maintain heading and speed. Advise upon visual contact."*

Harv repeated the instructions. "You got him yet?" he asked Nathan.

"No, but we're closing fast. We should see him in the next minute or two."

"There he is," Harv said. "One o'clock high."

Harv's eyes were better than Nathan's. It took him another ten seconds to find the tiny black spec. "Got him," Nathan said.

Harv called in the visual contact and for the third time, they were told to maintain heading and speed. The black speck grew into the recognizable shape of a gray UH-60 Black Hawk. It began a sweeping 180-degree turn, dropping altitude as it formed up off their port wing.

"Impressive sight," Harv said.

Grangeland leaned forward to look out Ernie's window. "He's awfully close to us," she said.

"He's just looking us over, making sure he likes what he sees." Their escort was about one hundred feet away, matching airspeed and altitude. Harv gave the Air Force pilot a crisp salute, which was returned.

A different voice came through their flight helmets. *"Civilian Delta, this is Air Force Escort Five. Maintain position off our starboard side."*

Harv copied the instructions.

This was the first time Nathan had ever flown in formation with another helicopter. He liked it. Forty minutes later, with Great Falls off their port side, they were approaching Malmstrom Air Force Base. Their escort handled all the radio communication with Malmstrom's tower and they were given clearance to land. The two helicopters made a straight-in approach from the south. Malmstrom's huge runway ran diagonally from the southwest to the northeast. They crossed it and settled into controlled hovers over a large expanse of concrete near some off-white hangar buildings. Once on the tarmac, Nathan went through the shutdown procedure, flipping switches and turning off avionics. After the engine had cooled, he shut it down. Harv opened Grangeland's door and she climbed out, keeping her attention sharply focused on Ernie.

An Air Force sedan parked between the two helicopters, and a major climbed out to meet them. The pilot's door of their escort Black Hawk swung open and a two-star in flight fatigues began walking toward them. Major General Mansfield, no doubt about it. Out of habit, Nathan and Harv issued salutes. Mansfield, a six-footer with cropped gray hair and pronounced crow's-feet at the edges of his hazel eyes, returned their salutes. "At ease, gentlemen. Welcome to Malmstrom." The general introduced his aide as Major Reid and handshakes were made all around.

Nathan looked at the Black Hawk and then back to Mansfield.

Mansfield smiled. "Would you like to give her a test drive?"

The Black Hawk was significantly bigger than his own ship and far more powerful. He'd love to strap her on for a spell. "We're in a time-critical situation, sir. May I have a rain check?"

"That's a promise. Your father's a good friend to the military. He fights for every red cent we get."

Nathan nodded.

Mansfield addressed his aide. "Top off Major McBride's fuel tanks."

"Thank you, sir." Nathan asked Grangeland if she'd guard their prisoner for a few minutes.

"Who's your handcuffed passenger in the backseat?" Mansfield asked. "He doesn't look real happy to be here."

"For your ears only?" Nathan asked.

"My ears only."

"Ernie Bridgestone."

"You're kidding. He's been all over the news. I heard he escaped from the Fresno truck stop. That was some show. The live news clips looked like a napalm attack." Mansfield addressed his aide. "Major Reid, you didn't hear any of this."

"Hear what, sir?"

"The FBI leaked his escape to the press," Nathan said. "We're hoping to collar his brother, Leonard. That's why we're here. Leonard needs to think Ernie got away. We think they're planning to meet at the coordinates my father gave you. We figure he'll be arriving in about two or three hours."

Mansfield noticed the blood soaking through Nathan's shirtsleeve. "What happened to your arm?"

"I took one at the truck stop."

"You were shot? You flew six hours with a bullet wound?"

"It's not bad. It went clean through."

"Major Reid, get a medic over here double-time."

"Yes, sir." The aide climbed into the driver's seat and made a radio call.

"General, I'm fine. Really."

Mansfield held up a hand. "Don't argue with me, son."

Nathan zipped it. You didn't argue with general officers. Ever.

Mansfield pulled a large envelope from the passenger seat of his gray sedan. He spread the color photos on the hood. They were oblique shots taken from the south. "These are fifteen minutes old. I had my aide look them over. As far as we can tell, there's no one in the area. We didn't spot any vehicles or any engine or human heat signatures on the infrareds. It's harder to detect them during the day, but sometimes we can. They sure chose a remote location. These coordinates are just south of the Blackfeet Indian Reservation. They were wise to stay off tribal territory. The Blackfeet are protective of their land." Mansfield pointed to a dirt road. "This is Dutch Creek Road, it connects to Highway Eighty-Nine several miles to the east. This track up here is Sweet Dam Road, it also connects to Highway Eighty-Nine. It's probably why they chose this location. They could approach the coordinates from the north or south. It also gives them two possible routes of escape."

"This is perfect, General. Just what we need."

Mansfield bent over the photos a little. "Point zero looks like some sort of spirelike rock formation on the south wall of the canyon. You can see its shadow here." He stabbed a finger on the most detailed photo, the image at ten meters per inch.

"It's easily recognized from the ground," Harvey said, studying the other photos. Nathan knew his partner was scoping potential shooting locations and looking for an LZ to set their chopper down.

"What else can I do to help?" Mansfield asked.

"Just keep us updated if anyone approaches the coordinates."

"We're on that. Right now we're checking with NORAD to see what birds we've got overhead. There might be some dark intervals. In all honesty, we won't be able to reposition any of them. They're needed over the Gulf."

"We'll make do, General."

"Ernie Bridgestone," he said slowly. "Public enemy number one. I'm glad you caught the son of a bitch. That Sacramento bombing was cold-blooded."

"Yes, sir, it was. Special Agent Grangeland probably needs a pit stop. We all do. Harvey and I also need to change into our MARPATs. Can we trouble you for some chow and coffee?"

"It's no trouble."

Mansfield told Reid to round up some sandwiches and coffee from the dining facility on the double. Reid jogged back to the sedan and sped away.

"Should be about ten minutes."

"That's fine, General, thank you."

As they walked back over to Nathan's helicopter, he was acutely aware of the passage of time. Although he didn't think Leonard could get up here in less than twenty-two hours, he wasn't 100 percent sure. A sense of urgency seized him. Did they really have time for this? If Ernie had lied about Leonard's departure time from California, it could cost them their lives. Although the satellite images were devoid of human activity, it didn't mean Leonard wasn't already there, cash in hand, planting Semtex charges and trip wires. How long would he wait? A few hours? Longer? Or would he wait at all? The Canadian border would be whispering his name.

A gray aviation fuel truck pulled up to Nathan's helicopter and the driver climbed out and attached the ground wire to a skid. Nathan made sure Jet-A was being fed to his machine.

Mansfield nodded over his shoulder. "There's a latrine and locker room in the hangar."

Harv and Nathan helped Grangeland extract Ernie out of the Bell and followed Mansfield to the hangar. General Mansfield carried Nathan's duffel.

Mansfield's medic arrived at the same time Reid returned with lunch. She sat Nathan on the lunch table, where he received eighteen stitches in his arm. Nathan refused a local anesthetic, claiming he didn't want any part of his body numb. Occasionally wincing, he endured the tightly spaced stitches while eating a turkey sandwich. The medic wrapped his lower calf wound as well. Thankfully, she didn't comment on the crisscrossing network of scars on Nathan's torso, even after doing a fairly shocked double take. When he noticed Grangeland staring, he feigned innocence and asked, "What?"

She rolled her eyes.

After he and Harv changed into their MARPATs, General Mansfield took them out to Nathan's chopper and asked, "Are you sure you don't want any backup out there?"

"Positive, General," Nathan said. "We prefer to work alone."

"Monitor the frequency we gave you. We'll keep you apprised of any activity at the coordinates. And I'll keep a squad standing by just in case you give us a nine-one-one call."

* * *

Ten miles southeast of Dupuyer, Nathan dropped the helicopter down to one hundred feet. "Watch for power lines," Nathan told Harv. "Did you find an LZ on the photos?"

"I think so, we'll have to check it out. It's about a mile and a half northwest from ground zero. It's an island of trees in our canyon and kinda horseshoe-shaped. It screens the chopper from three directions."

"I'm dropping down to fifty feet. Keep your eyes peeled." Nathan lowered the nose. Ten seconds later they were skimming the grassy landscape at nearly 140 miles an hour. The ground rush was intoxicating. As dangerous as it was, Nathan loved flying low and fast.

Harv worked the NavCom screen. "Adjust heading to three-four-five."

"Three-four-five," Nathan echoed.

"Guys?" Grangeland asked.

Harv pivoted toward the rear seats. "You okay back there?"

"I hate to be the weak link, but do we have to fly this low? I don't feel so good."

"Sorry, but yeah, we do," Harvey said. "Look straight ahead, don't look out your window."

She grunted an acknowledgment.

A small herd of elk dashed underneath them. The animals tried to stay in a group, but several peeled off in different directions.

"Keep an eye out for birds, Harv. Striking an eagle at this speed will definitely ruin our day." Nathan's brow furrowed in concentration. "Do you see any transmission or antenna towers?"

"Negative. We're good to go."

"Let's call Malmstrom and ask for an update."

General Mansfield himself answered the radio and reported all was quiet except for the thermal image of their exhaust. He informed them that in ten minutes, they'd experience a thirty-minute blackout as the current surveillance satellite dropped below the horizon.

Harv had the five-hundred-meter-per-inch photo in his lap. "I seriously doubt Leonard's arrived yet. To get here before us, he'd have to drive eighty miles an hour the entire way, straight through. There's no way he could do it and he certainly wouldn't risk getting pulled over."

"Agreed," Nathan said, though he shared Harv's apprehension. "If what Ernie said is true, then we're beating him here by at least one hour, possibly as many as three."

"What's your gut on what Ernie told us?" Harv asked.

"Obviously we can't know for sure, but I don't think he was lying about the second set of coordinates."

"We assume nothing," Harv said.

"Right."

"Think Leonard will have an RF detector?"

"Hard to say, but I doubt it. If he does, he'll pick up our handhelds for sure, but unless it's a contemporary device, he won't have signal strength or direction—he'll just know there's radio chatter in the area. There's not much we can do about it unless you want to skip the radios. Since our handhelds can't interface with the helicopter's NavCom, I'm thinking we keep Grangeland and Ernie at the chopper. We'll need her to relay anything Mansfield sees from the surveillance birds. I'd say using the radios outweighs being blind out here. Lesser of two evils."

"Booby traps?" asked Harv.

"I've thought about that too. I think it's unlikely they'd have any kind of long-term trip wires or pressure-triggered devices because of all the wildlife in the area. They wouldn't want a random accident to call attention to their cache. They might have something at the actual location of the buried money, though. If he does, it'll be a bomb-disposal job. Can your people handle it, Grangeland?" Nathan already knew the answer, he just wanted to distract her from her airsickness.

No answer.

"Grangeland?"

"Yeah, I think so," she said tightly.

"You okay back there?"

"I'm feeling really woozy."

"There're barf bags in the seat pockets. Harv, how far to Dutch Creek Road?"

"Maybe four thousand yards." He looked down at the satellite image. "Adjust heading to three-four-zero. That should take us pretty close to the LZ."

Nathan pushed the cyclic slightly to the left and watched the LCD screen's digital compass rotate. "Copy...Three-four-zero." He snuck a look out the port window. The snowcapped peaks of the Flathead Range were a damned beautiful sight. *Where the mountains meet the prairies*, he thought. Buffalo and Blackfeet Indian territory.

"Should we risk a visual pass down the canyon to the money drop and back?" Harv asked.

"It won't help us that much. For the kind of detail we'd need, we'd have to move slightly faster than a hover. Let's set her down right away."

"You'll have my undying gratitude," Grangeland said.

"Reduce speed to sixty knots," Harv said.

"Sixty knots." Nathan lowered the collective, pressed the right antitorque pedal, and pulled back on the cyclic control. Maintaining its altitude, the helicopter flared and rapidly bled off air speed.

"Oh shit," Grangeland moaned.

"Hang in there," Harvey encouraged her.

"I'm gonna be sick."

"We're ninety seconds from being on the ground."

She didn't make it.

Nathan heard violent retching sounds as Grangeland leaned forward and vomited into a barf bag. The distinctive odor filled the cabin.

"Don't worry about it," Nathan told her. "Happens to all of us. Keep track of your weapon, Ernie might try something." She didn't respond. "Harv, what's happening?"

Harv whipped around.

"She's okay," Harv said. "Crossing Dutch Creek Road. Slow to thirty knots."

A dirt track passed beneath them, no more than twenty feet below their skids. Sixty seconds later, the landscape suddenly dropped off as they cleared the canyon's southern ridgeline.

"Set her down inside that copse of trees at two o'clock," Harv said.

"Power lines?" Nathan asked.

Harv scanned the area. "Clear."

Twenty seconds later, leaves cartwheeled away from the LZ as Nathan set the chopper down. "Shutting down," he said. "Any bullet holes in us yet?"

Harv grinned. "The afternoon's still young."

* * *

Grangeland heartily agreed with being delegated to guard duty. The nausea left her weak and in no condition for physical exertion. With Harvey covering, she handcuffed Ernie to the skid support just below the rear door and sat down in the sand, facing him. The cord was stretched tight, but her headset was still plugged into the ceiling console.

Dressed exactly as they were at Freedom's Echo in their ghillie suits, they parted company with Grangeland and headed east along the northern edge of the canyon's streambed. Nathan estimated the canyon's width at three hundred yards, tighter in places, wider in others. Because the north wall of the canyon caught more sunlight, the underbrush was thicker with more trees present. In the middle of the canyon, a small stream flowed toward the east. The canyon's seventy-foot limestone walls were steep in places and shallow in others, where smaller streams fed the main creek. In hundreds of places, striated layers of rock were exposed in a series of ten- and twenty-foot ledges like giant steps. Dark recesses in the rock formations created ideal shooting positions for a potential sniper.

They moved quickly along the tree-lined bank of the sandy wash, stopping every three minutes or so to scan the area in front and behind them with their field glasses.

"Ground zero is on the south side of the wash about thirty feet above the bank," Harv said. "In the oblique shot, it looked like a giant stack of flat boulders."

"How far?"

"Another thousand yards or so. We should be able to see it once we clear the next bend in the wash. I don't like being down low like this with the sun in our faces."

"That's affirmative, neither would Leonard. But don't worry, if he's already here, he can only nail one of us at a time. Your odds are fifty-fifty."

"The hell they are," Harv said. "He'll shoot the man carrying the rifle first."

"Maybe you should carry it."

"Nice try."

Nathan toggled his transmit button on the radio. "Grangeland, radio check."

"*Copy,*" came her response. "*I gagged Ernie just in case he has the notion to sound off. He's livened up a bit. Mad as a hornet.*"

"Good thinking. Five-minute check-ins from now on. We left the helicopter's master switch on. In the event Malmstrom calls, you'll hear it through your headset. If you need to contact Malmstrom for any reason, all you have to do is pull the red trigger on the cyclic, the control stick. Copy that?"

"*Copy,*" she said. "*Good hunting.*"

"Despite her gritty personality," Harv said, "I kinda like her."

"Me too. She's a trooper. We're going stealth from here on. Ten-meter separation, I'll take the lead. You've got my six. How long before our next surveillance bird's overhead?"

Harv looked at his soap-smeared watch. "Twelve minutes."

CHAPTER 26

With her nausea gone and equilibrium back, Special Agent Grangeland felt a lot better. She surveyed her surroundings. Light-to-moderate tree cover surrounded the helicopter to the north, east, and west. From the south rim of the canyon, the helicopter was in plain sight. From the other directions, it wasn't totally screened. Unless someone was purposely looking for a parked helicopter in the middle of nowhere nestled within a canyon surrounded by trees, they'd never spot it from those directions. She supposed Leonard could be looking for just such a situation. She'd overheard Nathan and Harvey talking. This spot was nearly a mile and a half from the money stash. Would Leonard Bridgestone reconnoiter out to this range? Would he start at such an extreme distance and spiral in, checking the perimeter? No doubt, he'd be exhausted from a twenty-two-hour drive and need to get some sleep, unless he was wired on drugs.

Shit. Too many questions without answers. She felt vulnerable in her current position, exposed from the south. She had a patchy view through the trees and overhanging branches. Given all the variables, she felt the north side of the helicopter was the best place to wait. Or was it? Maybe she should be inside the trees, under deeper shadow, but then she remembered her headset. The uncoiled cord wouldn't reach more than five feet from the helicopter. She wasn't going anywhere. If Leonard Bridgestone spotted her, there was little she could do about it. Besides, the Air Force was watching the place. If anyone approached, they'd give her a heads-up.

Except during the satellite blackout.

She looked at her watch, cursing herself for not knowing the blackout period. Was the blackout just starting? Or ending? What were the odds of Leonard arriving during the blackout period? To distract herself, she tried to calculate them. Thirty minutes of three hours is the same as one-in-six odds. Would she bet her life on one-in-six odds? Hell no. She fought an overwhelming urge to look behind her. *Relax*, she told herself, *you're just being paranoid*. Besides, she had a vest under the Windbreaker. She'd be fine.

Two seconds later, an invisible brick smashed her torso at the same instant the air cracked.

She struggled with the truth.

Before blacking out, the last thing she saw was Ernie lean under the helicopter and smile behind his gag.

* * *

The high-power rifle report ripped down the canyon, echoing off thousands of exposed limestone ledges. Nathan and Harvey hit the deck simultaneously.

From the prone position, Nathan whipped around. "Harv!"

"I'm okay."

Nathan pressed the transmit button. "Grangeland, you copy?"

No response.

"Grangeland, do you copy?"

Nothing.

"Harv, form up. I think Grangeland's down."

Harv ran in a crouch over to Nathan's position and settled in.

"That was a rifle, not a handgun."

"Agreed," Harv said.

"I'm going back. Stay here and keep your head down."

"She's dead, Nate."

"I'm going back. Radio silence from now on. We have to assume Grangeland's radio's compromised." Nathan knew changing frequencies was useless: the devices had scanners and would automatically switch to any active channel.

"We should go together."

"Harv, the endgame is at that rock formation down the canyon. It all comes together there. Ernie will tell Leonard there's only two of us out here. They'll try to take us down and recover the money. Leonard knows if he doesn't get his money now, he never will. He won't leave without it."

"Shit," Harv said.

"I'll stay on the north side of the canyon and try to flush them down the south side. I doubt Leonard has a ghillie suit, but he'll be in a woodland combat uniform. Ernie will be easier to see in his civilian clothes. Stay concealed and wait for me."

"Nathan—"

"No matter what happens, I won't leave the north side of the canyon. If you get seen or pinned down, give me three quick shots with the Sig and stay put. I'll come get you."

"Nathan." Harv shook his head. "Man, we're brothers. Closer. I just want you to know…"

Nathan grasped both of Harv's shoulders. "Keep your head in the game. We're going to win." Nathan opened and closed the bolt of his rifle in two crisp movements, chambering a round. "They don't stand a chance."

* * *

He forced his mind away from Grangeland and concentrated on stealth. Moving from tree to tree, bush to bush, and boulder to boulder, Nathan worked his way back upstream to the west, always staying in deep shadow. In one sandy streambed feeding the main creek, he had to drop to his belly and crawl across the open ground. He hated being exposed, even though his ghillie suit made him all but invisible. The thirty-foot-wide area of sand offered only thinly scattered buck brush for cover. From the opposite side, he'd have a three-hundred-yard visual look at the helicopter through its eastern tree cover. If Grangeland was down, it was good bet Ernie would be long gone. It was also a good bet Ernie would tell Leonard everything he'd seen about his captors. Leonard would now know what kind of weapons they carried, what they were wearing, and the direction they'd gone. He hoped the bastards wouldn't take time to destroy his helicopter. It was more likely Leonard would make a mad dash, free his brother, and get back into cover as soon as possible.

Once out of the sandy wash, Nathan crawled the last few yards through thick underbrush and oak fallout, being careful not to bump any bushes or dead branches. He also kept an eye out for ants. Crawling through a fire ant nest was never a good idea. He felt stinging and dampness on his right arm. The stitches had torn and he was bleeding again.

Ignoring the renewed pain in his arm, he cleared his thoughts and put himself into Leonard's head. *I'll take the high ground on the opposite side of the canyon with the sun to my back. The enemy knows I'm here, he heard my shot. McBride will double back to check on the woman and Ernie. When he approaches the helicopter, I'll nail him from a bench-rested position on the southern rim of the canyon.*

Wrong, Leonard. Sorry to disappoint you.

Secured in deep shadow, Nathan slowly brought his rifle up, shouldered the weapon, and flipped the front and rear lens caps up. Three hundred yards distant, Grangeland was down. Her back was to him. He steadied his rifle and tried to determine if she was breathing. He couldn't tell. She looked like a lifeless heap. Wait...

Movement. A slight motion of her left arm. Her hand lifted above the sand for a moment before falling. Nathan kept watching until he saw her move again.

She's alive.

And of course Ernie was gone. Anger began to flare, but he forced it aside and slowly pivoted his rifle through an arc covering a one-hundred-yard radius centered on the helicopter. Nothing. No movement at all. Approaching the helicopter was suicide, an obvious trap. He couldn't make a mad dash to Grangeland and tend to her. Not against a trained shooter like Leonard.

Gritting his teeth at the fire in his arm and leg, and at Grangeland's situation, he backed away from his current position and tucked himself behind a fallen log offering solid cover from the south rim of the canyon. He couldn't leave Grangeland. Nor could he save her. He could almost feel Leonard's rifle scope sweeping back and forth past his location.

Two can play this game...

Moving with a caterpillar speed, Nathan maneuvered himself into a cross-legged position and bench-rested his cloth-wrapped weapon atop the log. He began a slow, sweeping scan of the canyon's opposite rim beyond the helicopter, zigzagging back and forth from the ridge down, concentrating on rocky spots with deep recessed shadow.

There. A flash of white.

Possibly Ernie's T-shirt. He swung his rifle back and focused on a spot where two huge slabs of fallen limestone formed a narrow triangular area of shadow.

There it was again.

"Got you," Nathan whispered.

Through his Nikon scope, Nathan watched as Ernie slowly ducked up and down with a pair of field glasses in his good hand and a handheld radio in the wounded hand. The white flash Nathan had seen was the gauze wrapping on Ernie's hand. Good ol' Ernie had wisely removed his white T-shirt, but overlooked the gauze.

He turned the elevation knob of the scope, counting ten clicks for a four-hundred-yard, slightly elevated shot. He gauged the wind as calm, maybe two to three miles an hour from the northwest. He'd be shooting into the wind, so he didn't make a correction.

"You're blowing it," he whispered to Ernie. "You're being too regular with your movements." Every fifteen seconds Ernie would come up from his hiding place, focus on the helicopter for five seconds, and then duck back down.

Nathan placed the crosshairs where Ernie's head would appear in the next ten seconds and waited.

Nothing happened.

Ernie didn't come back up.

Well after the fifteen-second interval had passed, there was still no Ernie. What the hell was he doing? He couldn't leave the crag of rock without Nathan seeing him. Thirty seconds went by. *Have I been made? Shit. No way. No way Leonard's seen me. Not in this soldier's world.*

Forty seconds.

Fifty.

A full minute.

Patience, he told himself. Breathe in deeply. Let it out slowly. In deep...Out slowly...Stay focused. Ernie's still there, he'll be back up. Patience...

After ninety seconds, Nathan had his answer. It was almost as if Ernie had sensed Nathan's presence, for when he reappeared, the bright white gauze on his hand was gone. But it was too late.

"That's a bingo," Nathan whispered.

The Remington 700 bucked against his right shoulder and sent a white-hot jolt of agony through his stitched wound. For a few seconds, his vision blurred and dimmed. When it cleared, he didn't see Ernie, but he saw what was left of him on the limestone wall behind his hiding place—the unmistakable pattern of a head shot.

"Promise kept," he whispered. "Marine to marine."

Feeling the sudden flood of moisture on his arm, he knew the wound was open. How long did he have before blood loss became a concern? He couldn't worry about that right now because the struggle had just begun. Removing Ernie was moderately helpful in the battle against Leonard Bridgestone, as much psychologically as logistically, but there was no safe transit past an entrenched sniper. Leonard was playing a waiting game, counting on Nathan's compassion for Grangeland. Leonard would know his sole means of transport and communication was the helicopter, so his opponent would also be counting on that to draw him into the kill zone. *Sorry to disappoint you, Leonard, but that's not happening.*

Nathan saw another way. To reach Grangeland, he'd need to create a diversion, and that meant getting back to Harv. Two against one, they might just pull it off.

Like oozing molasses, Nathan slid himself away from the log, hunkered down behind its cover, and slung his rifle over his shoulder for the return crawl to the east. *Hang in there, Grangeland, we aren't going to abandon you.*

How much time had passed since she'd been shot? Twenty minutes? Thirty? He wasn't sure. He thought back to the image of her prone form and didn't recall seeing any blood. She'd been wearing her dark-blue FBI Windbreaker to conceal her piece and her ballistic vest. Her vest was probably the only reason she was still alive. How long did she have?

* * *

Harvey turned his head toward the sound of the shot. "Nathan," he whispered. Had Leonard just killed Nathan, or had Nathan killed one of them? He considered moving back up the canyon toward the source of the report. Nathan could be down, wounded. Slowly bleeding out. If he stayed put, would he be condemning his lifelong friend to death? He wanted to use the radio, needed to use the radio, but Nathan had called for silence. He weighed the repercussions. Leonard had Grangeland's radio, and there's no way he couldn't use it to triangulate. The receiving transmission would be silent, coming out of Nathan's tiny ear speaker.

Decision made, he pressed the transmit button. "Five-by-five?"

A few seconds later, he heard, *"Five-by-five. Stay put. I'm coming to you."*

Relief washed over Harvey like warm wind. Although he doubted Leonard possessed Nathan's shooting skills—only a handful of people in the world did—Leonard could've seen Nathan first, and in a long-range sniper duel, the shooter who spots his opponent first, wins.

Stay put.

Nothing so simple had ever been more difficult.

* * *

Nathan didn't blame Harv for breaking radio silence. From a tactical perspective, Harv needed to know he was okay and still in the fight. Had he been killed, Harv would have an agonizing decision to make: stay and fight and possibly die, or bug out and possibly die. Nathan doubted Leonard would let either of them just fly out of here. Harv was a family man and had more to consider than his own life. But family or not, Harv would never abandon the fight if he knew his partner was still alive, Nathan was certain of that.

Nathan's plan was simple. Since Leonard couldn't be in two places at once, he and Harv would separate. He'd head toward the money cache while Harv doubled back to the helicopter. Through a series of purposeful ploys, he planned to lure Leonard to his end of the canyon, leaving Harv free to fly Grangeland to safety. He hoped Harv was ready for his first solo flight.

Setting that thought aside for now, Nathan crawled down the length of the fallen log, shouldered his rifle, and scoped the canyon's southern wall. Although he had a pair of field glasses, he always used his rifle. If he saw his mark, he was instantly ready to send a bullet. If his opponent was on the move, he didn't see any evidence of it. The few sandy areas he could see were virgin, lacking discernable footprints. He steeled himself for what lay ahead, that damned thirty-foot expanse of sand and brush. If he were going to get nailed, he knew it would happen out there. It looked as vast as the Sahara Desert, but there was no avoiding it and no way around it. He had to traverse it. Simple as that.

Here goes…

Moving no faster than a foot every five seconds, he started his crawl across the sand.

He ran the math through his head to distract himself from the pain and wet sensation in his arm. Thirty feet times five seconds per foot. One hundred and fifty seconds. Two-and-a-half minutes. That's not so long really, after all, it's—

Halfway across the sand, he froze.

Had he heard something behind him?

A crunch of leaves?

If Leonard was back there, he was a sitting duck out here in the open. He knew his ghillie suit transformed him into a shrub, but what about the tracks he left crawling out here? Moving his head slowly, he snuck a look over his right shoulder and was surprised when he didn't see any deep tracks. He hadn't remembered brushing them flat with his legs as he moved, but he must have. He'd done it on autopilot, on pure instinct from his old training. *I'll be damned*, he thought.

There it was again.

A crunch of dried leaves.

He was certain this time.

Staring through the thinly spaced stalks of underbrush, he watched for any sign of movement. He expected to see a pair of combat boots, but a chill raked his spine when he saw the source of the noise.

CHAPTER 27

A mountain lion.

And a damned big one. Two hundred pounds of solid muscle, sharp claws, and yellow ivory was a mere twenty feet away.

Taking slow, deliberate steps, the animal slunk forward with its head low, its eyes searching for the source of blood it smelled. Had the rifle shots awakened it? Nathan knew mountain lions were mostly twilight predators. The rifle shots should've spooked it, made it haul ass out of here, but a fresh blood scent triggered a powerful instinct, especially if it was hungry.

When it reached the edge of the fallen log Nathan had traversed a minute earlier, it sniffed the ground and froze. Then it looked straight at him.

Go away, damn you. Go away!

Like something out of a developing nightmare, it took a step into the sun-bleached sand.

Moving as slowly as humanly possible, he eased his hand down to his gun belt and pulled his Sig Sauer. There was no way to unsling his rifle without significant body movement, which would certainly make the animal charge. It would be upon him in one bound. He searched his database of survival training on encounters with mountain lions. *Never run* was at the forefront of his memory.

Now less than two body lengths away, the animal kept coming. That he was concealed in his ghillie suit didn't matter. The cat's eyes weren't guiding it.

Something else shot through his mind. Movement. The cat was a damning source of movement, and movement is what catches the eye.

* * *

From deep shadow on the south rim of the canyon, Leonard followed the lion through his rifle scope and smiled. It seemed to be following an invisible scent. Quite possibly his opponent. He watched the animal pace the length of a fallen log and approach the edge of a dry streambed that fed the larger stream in the middle of the canyon. It froze for a few seconds before stepping out into the sand.

* * *

If Nathan were going to shoot this lion, he'd better do it within the next two seconds while he still had the angle to manage the shot from the hip. If he wasn't precise with his aim, he could easily blow a hole in his own foot. Damn it, he didn't want to kill such a magnificent predator. In many ways, they were just alike, but his own survival and that of Harv's took priority. He also knew as soon as he pulled the trigger his cover was blown, because if his first shot wasn't fatal or severely crippling, he'd have to shoot the animal a second time, and possibly a third. The first report would alert Leonard to his general location, but the second and third reports would pinpoint him. He might was well stand up and wave a flag.

Both his options were equally unpleasant.

He could lie here and be mauled to death, literally eaten alive or he could shoot the cat, and in turn be shot himself. All things being equal, he preferred the second option, but it had already expired. The animal was directly beside him now—he no longer had the angle to shoot it.

He heard the sound of its paws on the sand.

He buried his face in his shoulder and stopped breathing. If he played dead, maybe it would lose interest and move on. Deep down, he knew it was wishful thinking. A mountain lion will just as soon scavenge for food than hunt it.

The cat brought its face to within inches of Nathan's head.

Its hot breath penetrated the strips of his ghillie suit and brushed the skin on his neck.

It issued a low, growling murmur deep in its throat as it realized it had found the source of the fresh blood. An easy meal.

The cat issued a second, more forceful growl and jabbed Nathan's neck with a paw. It was funny what the human mind was capable of thinking at times like these. With bizarre detachment, Nathan thanked God it had missed his wounded arm, but that thought died when he felt cool air on his skin. The cat's jab had opened a hole in his ghillie suit.

The animal pushed again. Harder.

His lungs screaming for air, Nathan continued to play dead. If things kept going like this, he wouldn't have to play dead.

Go away!

When he felt the cat's sandpaper tongue lick the back of his exposed neck, he'd had enough.

With as much strength as he could muster, he simultaneously issued a war cry, the loudest, most fierce sound he could make. He snapped his body to the left and cracked the cat in the nose with the butt of his gun.

* * *

Leonard watched the animal traverse the sand and stop at some sort of low shrub. It lowered its head and sniffed. Had it lost the scent? If it had been following someone, where were the tracks? Looking for human footprints, he swung his scope back to the edge of the underbrush where the cat had emerged, cranked it to maximum zoom, but saw only the cat's footprints.

At the left edge of Leonard's magnified image, he caught sudden movement. He swung the rifle back. "What the fuck?" he said aloud. The mountain lion jumped six feet into the air.

When it landed, it bolted away from the shrub at a full gallop.

The shrub went vertical and began sprinting across the sand. Not a shrub, a ghillie suit, and a damned fine one at that. "Oh, you're good," Leonard said. He placed the crosshairs slightly ahead of the green mass.

And pulled the trigger.

* * *

Nathan's timing had to be perfect. He needed to vary his speed as he ran. Now! Five feet from the safety of cover, he hit the brakes and nearly skidded to a stop. A split second later, he heard the telltale crack of a supersonic arrival. Out in front to his right, the sand exploded from the impact. If he'd kept running at the same speed…Using his left hand, he pointed the Sig at the ground slightly left and ahead of his path and fired five shots. The sand burst into the air. It wasn't much cover, but it would have to do. He dived into the underbrush on the opposite side of the wash and scrambled behind the thick trunk of an oak. He pressed his back against its form as a second bullet tore past his position on the left.

* * *

Leonard missed. Before he could reacquire, the sand in front of his target erupted, obscuring his view. He heard five quick pops, like firecrackers going off, and knew his mark had fired a handgun into the sand to provide a smokelike screen. Clever move. In combination with his motion and the irregularly shaped ghillie suit, it worked. Estimating where he thought his target would be, Leonard sent another bullet before pulling back to relocate.

* * *

Harvey heard the report of the rifle roll down the canyon in a crackling reverberation that lasted for nearly five seconds. Then he heard five quick handgun shots. A few seconds later, he heard a second rifle shot. What the hell was going on?

The tiny speaker in his ear went off. *"Five-by-five, Harv. Stay down, he's on the south rim. I'm coming to you."*

"Copy."

* * *

As Nathan made his way upstream along the tree-covered bank toward Harv's position, the small speaker in his ear came to life. *"That was some trick with the mountain lion. How'd you manage it?"*

Nathan instantly knew who it was. "The money's not worth it. Walk away."

"Fat chance." A short pause, then, *"You leaving her there to die?"*

Nathan saw no point in responding to that.

"The shot isn't immediately fatal," said Leonard. *"But the longer she lies there...Well, you get the picture. I guess you have a decision to make, don't you?"*

Nathan clenched his teeth and felt rage begin to boil again. Leonard Bridgestone had purposely gut-shot Grangeland. He couldn't let Leonard know how much saving her life meant. He had to play it cool. If he showed even the slightest concern, it would both embolden and empower his enemy. Choosing his words carefully and grateful Grangeland no longer had her radio, he called Leonard's bluff.

"She's nothing to me. I'll sacrifice her before I let you walk."

"*Bullshit. She's a looker. I can't imagine you didn't notice that.*"

Nathan could feel the tension building. He had to turn it back on Leonard. "Speaking of sacrifices, why'd you serve Ernie up?"

"*What are you talking about?*"

"You know damned well what I'm talking about. You placed him where you knew I'd nail him."

Leonard didn't respond right away. "*Was it that obvious?*"

"He was your brother. How could you do it?"

"*He gave me up, I could never trust him again.*"

"He gave you up under torture. But that's not the real reason, is it?"

"*Do tell.*"

"Is your love of money so perverse that you'd feed your own brother to the wolves to keep it all yourself?"

"*The way I figure it, you did him a favor. Did the world a favor.*"

"What's the matter, Lenny, you don't have the balls to clean up your own mess?"

"*I used him rather than waste him. I might have found you from the shot you took. You got lucky, McBride.*"

"You'll never leave here with your money. I'll make sure it gets donated to charity. How about the Purple Heart Fund? You've got two of them, don't you?"

"*Cute, McBride.*"

"Give my regards to Ernie when you see him in hell." Nathan turned off his radio.

Fifty yards from Harv's position, Nathan issued his signature warbling whistle. Harv returned it, and he worked his way up to his partner's hiding place.

"Damn, it's good to see your sorry ass," Harv said as Nathan crouched down beside him.

"Sorry I'm late, I had an argument with a local."

"I heard your exchange with Leonard. A mountain lion?"

"Tell you about it later."

"Is Grangeland alive?" Harv asked.

"Yeah. I saw her moving. There's no way to know the extent of her wound."

"Shit."

"We can't let her die, Harv. Getting Leonard isn't worth her life."

"Yeah, but she might die anyway. Or he might go ahead and kill her. He served up his own brother on a silver platter."

"Here's the plan. I'll create a distraction down here and bring Leonard to my position while you work your way back to Grangeland and fly her out of here. He can't be in two places at once. If he's on this end of the canyon, he can't be watching the chopper."

"I can't leave you out here alone. And I've never flown that thing solo."

"Harv, I have to kill him. He's still got a lot of Semtex. We can't risk him coming after us, or worse, coming after your family. You know that. You've got dozens of takeoffs and landings under your belt. You're ready. Use the checklist for startup. Get her light on the skids before you lift off. You can do it."

"It feels like I'm abandoning you. You're bleeding bad."

"You're saving Grangeland's life. Leonard doesn't stand a chance against me. He has to die, Harv. For your family's sake."

"Promise me you won't follow me up that canyon and cover my ass at your own expense again."

"I promise."

"Here, take four of my Sig mags. I won't need them, and you just might."

Nathan stuffed them into his pockets. "Better give me the spool of fishing line from your backpack and your Predator knife too."

Harv turned around so Nathan could dig the spool out. Harv then bent down and removed his ankle sheath and handed it to Nathan. Nathan strapped it onto his good left ankle.

"How long do you need before I call in the cavalry?" Harv asked

"Give me two hours from the time you turn the ignition. Worry about Grangeland, not me."

"You won't last two hours. You're slowly bleeding out."

"I'll be fine. Get Grangeland to a hospital, Harv. Land directly on its helicopter pad."

"Shit."

"Go on. No long good-byes."

"Nathan, I—"

He smiled. "Get going. You'll hear me popping off shots to bring Leonard down here. Be careful traversing that sand wash."

"Nail his ass, Nate."

"You can count on it."

CHAPTER 28

Nathan turned his radio on and pressed the transmit button. Distraction time. "You copy, Bridgestone?"

"*Yeah, I'm here.*"

"You mad at me for the 'give my regards in hell' comment?"

"*Naw, it seemed appropriate at the time.*" Bridgestone stayed quiet for a moment. "*What's your story, McBride? Why do you give a shit? Why risk your life over this?*"

"Maybe it's the good-versus-evil thing. Maybe I'm curious to know if good truly is stronger than evil."

"*Who's who?*"

"Well, the last I checked, I didn't murder twenty-four innocent people sitting at their desks."

"*Point taken.*"

Nathan popped off two quick rounds at nothing. "Gotta go."

"*What's the matter, cat got your tongue?*"

"You've got a quick wit, better hope you're as fast with that rifle."

"*I am.*"

"You'd better be. We'll see you at your money stash." Nathan had purposely said *we'll*. He turned off the radio, popped off two more shots, and moved away downstream. So far, so good. If Leonard was on the move, he couldn't be stationary and actively looking for Harv. At best, all Leonard could do was stop every so often and make a quick sweep of the canyon. He'd never see Harv that way. Harv was too good.

Nathan took slow, deliberate steps through the underbrush, glancing over his shoulder for the cat. He knew the scent of his blood remained strong. Although he believed the animal to be long gone, he wasn't willing to bet his life on it.

He estimated another five hundred yards or so before he had any chance of seeing the rock spire at the money stash. Up ahead, he saw where the canyon made a horseshoe turn to the north and knew the spire was around that bend on the right side. If he were Leonard, he'd pick a spot within three hundred yards of the spire, probably on this side of it, set up shop, and wait for his opponent to come to him. One thing was certain: Leonard had the speed advantage, even if Nathan chose to throw caution to the wind. His calf was killing him, almost as painful as his arm, but it wasn't losing as much blood. The blood loss from his arm would soon become a concern.

Leonard had quickness on his side. In truth, he could run downstream along the southern rim of the canyon as long as he stayed back from the lip. Nathan wondered if Leonard would have time to retrieve the money before he even got there. Three million bucks in cash, just sitting out here, in the middle of nowhere. It seemed bizarre and hardly believable, but Leonard's presence confirmed it. He was here to collect his cash, his lifetime's worth of savings.

Nathan smiled, feeling a certain satisfaction at denying the murderer his money, but the smile vanished. *Keep focused*, he told himself. *Keep your head in the game.* As he dropped down to crawl through a section of low underbrush, he wondered how close Harv was to the chopper. They'd parted company...what? Twenty minutes ago? He should've looked at his watch. That omission had been careless. Maybe he was more injured than he cared to admit. He knew blood loss would soon take its toll in the form of shivers, nausea, and shock. He needed to end this battle. And end it soon. The early symptoms of shock were already evident. He had trouble concentrating and felt a little chilled. How long until his symptoms became crippling? Half an hour? Less? He doubted he'd last the two hours he'd asked for.

Approaching the horseshoe bend in the canyon, Nathan slowed his pace even more. He had to. The going was tough and he had to be careful not to disturb any of the tall stalks as he wove his way through. The good thing was that the growth was so dense here, he couldn't see the canyon's southern rim at all. Which meant he couldn't be seen either. Step after step, he moved with slow precision, always watching where he placed his boots. A snapped twig or a patch of quicksand could ruin his day. He hoped he wouldn't flush any birds either. Leonard could be twenty feet away and he wouldn't be able to see him, but he would be able to hear him.

But Leonard's presence wasn't what he heard right then.

What he heard warmed his soul—the distinctive whooping drone of a helicopter's blades biting into the afternoon air. Harv was flying Grangeland out of here. *Way to go, old friend.*

"McBride, you copy?"

He made Bridgestone wait.

"McBride, you there?"

A little longer...

"McBride?"

"I'm here. That's Harv, flying out of here with Grangeland. It's just you, me, and the mountain lion now."

"Good."

"Don't be so pleased. There's a catch, Bridgestone. You see, time is not on your side. In two hours, Harv is going to call in the cavalry and you can kiss your millions good-bye. You can't know how much that breaks my heart."

"Like you said, McBride, we've got a couple of hours to settle things."

Nathan yawned audibly. "I'm a little tired and I've lost a lot of blood. Maybe I'll take a little R and R. One eye on the money, of course."

"You former marine or army?"

"Marine."

"Sniper?"

"Sniper."

"How many?"

"Including your brothers, fifty-nine. Guess that makes you number sixty, a nice round number. Is the money really worth your life? Is flipping burgers or stuffing envelopes beneath you? Who says you can't start over and earn an honest living?"

"Not my style."

"Being dead is?"

"I'm not dead, McBride, far from it."

"Soon enough, Bridgestone, soon enough." He resumed his trek downstream to the east. After another hundred yards, the undergrowth thinned and Nathan could once again see the southern rim of the canyon. He figured he needed to advance another two or three hundred yards before looking for the right spot to set up.

It took fifteen minutes to cover the last leg. He'd seen the rock spire several times through openings in the underbrush. At one point, he had to divert away from the creek, nearly to the canyon's wall, to keep inside the cover of growth. Up ahead, a wide thumb of greenbelt would take him back to the sandy wash where a large copse of mature oaks and thick brush dominated the creek's bank for several hundred yards. Perfect. He knew he'd find what he was looking for out there. Crawling on his belly, he inched his way forward through the labyrinth of tree trunks, slowly closing the distance to the creek's bank. His arm stung like hell and he resisted the urge to look at the wound. No upside to doing that.

Up ahead at the creek's bank, the canopy of oak branches screened him from the canyon's rim, but gave him little cover from a lower perspective. He doubted Leonard would descend into the canyon and give up the high ground. Advancing toward the creek, he kept studying the canyon's southern rim, looking for potential shooting positions. From what he'd seen so far, there were at least half a dozen really good candidates up there.

He wondered how long Leonard would last before desperation set in. Would he risk his life and try to recover the cash as time ran out? He might as well commit suicide, because Nathan wasn't going to let him come within fifty yards of that rock spire without nailing him.

When he closed to within thirty yards of the creek, he spotted what he needed directly ahead, a huge fallen oak whose roots had been undermined by a flash flood. The exposed root ball was perfect. It towered over the sand in a chaotic tangle of wormlike tendrils, clods of earth, and river stones. The main structure of the tree fanned out toward Nathan's position at a 45-degree angle from the creek. Its trunk looked to be almost four feet in diameter, with large branches jutting out from its central structure.

As Nathan studied the tree, a plan came to him, fully formed.

He crawled to its prone form and shucked off his ghillie suit and backpack. The trees flanking the fallen oak gave him spotty cover at best, so he made slow, deliberate movements to avoid catching Leonard's eye. He shouldered his weapon and slowly swept the canyon's southern rim from west to east, ending at the rock spire. Nothing at all. No movement. Was Leonard up there? If so, where would he be? Would he pick the most obvious position, the deepest recess offering the darkest shadow? Probably not. A trained Army Ranger wouldn't choose a predictable location. He'd pick an unlikely spot, with marginal cover. But he *would* pick a location from which he could relocate after shooting.

Okay, Nathan thought, *let's assign names to the four most likely shooting positions up there.* He started with the closest place to the spire, a long bowl-shaped dip in the rim with a sandy surface flanked by low ledges of fallen limestone. He'd call that spot Ledges. The next place moving west was a shadowed crevice with a thirty-foot-long fallen slab of rock in front of it. That would be a good location because the slab of rock looked to be about three feet high, suitable for bench-resting a rifle. He called that location Bench. The next good candidate was a missing piece of striated limestone shaped like a coffee cup. He named it Coffee. The final location was a leaning chunk of limestone that formed a triangular opening with deep shadow. He'd call that spot Shadow.

Nathan didn't favor Shadow as much as the others because it didn't allow a large radius of fire. If Leonard chose Shadow, he'd have to sacrifice nearly half the canyon in order to stay concealed. It also didn't offer an easy way to relocate because it wasn't at the very top of the canyon's rim.

He studied each location through the rifle's scope again. Ledges. Bench. Coffee. Shadow. He favored Bench because along with its length of nearly thirty feet, it offered Leonard the easiest relocation capability. He put Ledges in second place, followed by Coffee. He thought the least likely spot would be Shadow.

He now had to find a position that could be seen from each of those four locations. He slithered along the fallen tree trunk and every five feet or so peered over the top, checking each shooting position up on the rim. Five minutes later, he found an ideal place near a main arterial branch. From this location, he could see all four of the potential shooting positions, and as a bonus, this spot also gave a view of a large section of the southern rim stretching toward the rock spire, in case Leonard wasn't occupying one of those four spots.

Perfect.

Ignoring his blood-soaked sleeve, he crawled back to his ghillie suit and backpack and removed the spool of fifty-pound fishing line. Dragging the pack and ghillie suit, he made his way back to the arterial branch and began looking for a piece of wood around three feet long and two inches in diameter. He found what he was looking for attached to the fallen oak's trunk. He removed Harv's Predator knife from the ankle sheath and began cutting the piece of wood free.

When the branch was detached, he cut a six-inch section off the end of it and notched the middle of it as if for building a log cabin. He did the same to the longer piece near one end. Using the fifty-pound fishing line, he secured the six-inch piece to the longer piece at the notches. When he finished, he'd ended up with a crude-looking crucifix of sorts.

Using loops of line around the butt of his Sig Sauer pistol, he attached the weapon to a branch extending out from the fallen tree trunk. He tied the handgun to a point on the branch where only the top of the gun could be seen from the other side. When the gun was tight and wouldn't budge, he cut the line and tied the loose end to the trigger.

He looked over his shoulder for a place to loop the fishing line around a branch or heavy rock. Shit. There was nothing. How could he have overlooked such an important detail? More to the point, what was he going to do now? He cursed himself for being so sloppy and ill-prepared. Damn, his arm hurt. His shirtsleeve was literally dripping wet with blood, and so was the upper half of his shirt. Worse, he was beginning to lose sensation in his right thumb. Nerve damage, he feared. Not to mention he couldn't remember the last time he'd slept.

Running on fumes, he considered kicking back and waiting for the cavalry to arrive. It didn't seem like such a bad idea right about now, but that might give Leonard a chance to escape. He thought about Grangeland and the cowardly bullet Leonard had fired. He thought about Harv's wife, Candace, and imagined Leonard shooting her through her kitchen window. Anger flared and he temporarily tapped it, then forced it aside. He studied his options again. Where would he loop the fishing line? *Think, damn it. Think.* He'd spent nearly twenty minutes setting up in this location. He didn't have time or energy to find a different location. His body was beginning to shut down.

An old hatred began to flood his soul. How could he have been so stupid and shortsighted? He was going to die in this remote Montana canyon, and Bridgestone would get away—*with* his money. A feeling of rage bored into his mind like an ice pick. He wanted to scream at the top of his lungs and beat his fist into the tree. He hated the idea of Bridgestone living a life of luxury, having never answered for burning James Ortega alive and killing all those FBI people. He squinted and balled his hands into fists. *Bridgestone, you lowlife piece of shit!*

He closed his eyes and concentrated. This meltdown served no useful purpose. He needed to suppress it. Nathan brought his mental image forward—his safety catch. He put himself under imaginary trees and let autumn-colored leaves flutter past his body. They brushed past his skin and tumbled along the ground. He slowed his breathing and relaxed his hands, then leaned his head back against the trunk and sighed. Falling leaves. Falling from where? From above. He opened his eyes and smiled. The solution had been right in front of him all along.

CHAPTER 29

Leonard hadn't heard any additional pistol shots for over half an hour. Maybe McBride had finally scared the cat off, or he'd bled to death. From his current position on the south rim, Leonard had a clear view of the canyon below, but he hadn't seen any movement at all, feline or human. Was McBride telling the truth? Were reinforcements arriving within the next hour? Maybe it was bullshit. Maybe McBride was just trying to force his hand, to flush him out. He wasn't sure. He knew nothing about McBride's past other than what he'd just learned. One thing was certain: the guy was a damned good shot. At the compound, he'd killed Sammy at a distance of six hundred yards. He didn't know how far away McBride had been when he'd nailed Ernie, but as with Sammy, it had been a single shot. One shot, one kill. The sniper's motto. If this guy truly had been a marine scout sniper, taking him out wasn't going to be easy.

Was the cash really worth it? Hell yes, it was. He'd spent ten long years amassing it, putting up with Ernie's short temper and endless baggage. Shit, he had three million dollars in cash no more than two hundred yards away—all he had to do was go dig it up. He knew McBride would be watching the spire, but from where?

He silently cursed Ernie for bringing McBride up here. Knowing he couldn't approach the money until McBride was dead, he had few options. Maybe he should try a different approach. What could it hurt at this point? Yeah, it might just work.

He pulled the radio and thumbed the transmit button. "McBride, you copy?"

Nothing, no response.

"McBride?"

"I'm a little busy right now."

"I'm willing to split the money. Fifty-fifty."

"Not interested."

"Come on, you can't use a million and a half in cash? Tax-free? Last chance. I'll split it with you. Right down the middle."

"Not interested."

"I'm sorry to hear that."

"No doubt you are."

"I'm going to enjoy killing you, McBride."

"Go ahead, give it your best shot. You've already missed twice. Why not go for the hat trick?"

"You're all talk." Leonard turned off the radio and clipped it to his belt.

Looking for anything out of place, he made a quick scan of his combat uniform. He found nothing dangling, out of place, or shiny. Satisfied, he began a slow scan of the creek's northern bank through his rifle scope. If McBride were down there, he'd be hidden in all that green undergrowth. The problem was, there was a ton of it and McBride's ghillie suit made him virtually invisible. If McBride were telling the truth, and he had no reason to assume otherwise, time was indeed running out. If he couldn't find McBride within the next twenty minutes or so, he'd have to abandon his cash and bug out. In that event, he vowed to kill McBride and his lousy partner. It might not happen two weeks from now, or two years from now, or even ten years from now, but McBride would die for denying him his money.

As Leonard swung his scope across a particularly dense area of brush, he heard two quick pops of a handgun. He focused on the general location where he'd heard the reports. "What's the matter, McBride?" he whispered. "Your furry friend come back?"

A few seconds later, he saw a bush move as though it had been bumped. There. Two more shots from deep within undergrowth, followed by the distinctive crackle of the shots echoing down the canyon. Handgun shots, not a rifle. He'd seen the actual muzzle flashes and had an exact location pinpointed.

"You're mine, McBride." He steadied his weapon and saw the top half of a handgun atop a fallen tree. As if seeing a gift from heaven, Leonard watched in stunned fascination as his enemy revealed himself. Slowly rising from behind the fallen trunk, the hood of a ghillie materialized like a ghost emerging from a grave. He caught the glint of a pair of field glasses inside the dark recess of the hood.

He added a click of elevation, took in a lungful of air, and blew half of it out. Placing the crosshairs directly between the lenses of the field glasses, Leonard smiled and pulled the trigger.

* * *

The supersonic crack announced the bullet's arrival. Nathan figured he had a good chance of actually seeing the muzzle flash. He'd been betting on Leonard being in the location he called Bench, but that was clearly wrong. He'd been watching the long slab of limestone nearly continuously. Nothing. No movement at all. No muzzle flash. If Leonard had been on that formation of flat rock, he would've seen the muzzle flash. He swung his rifle east toward the rock spire and looked at his second pick. Ledges.

Got you.

Near the left edge of the sandy bowl, half concealed by a small patch of brush, he saw Leonard working the bolt of his rifle, chambering another round. Only his head and shoulders could be seen. Nathan took one click off the elevation knob and steadied his rifle.

* * *

Sudden realization hit Leonard. Hit him hard. If McBride had been a marine scout sniper, there was no way in hell he'd be sloppy enough to reveal his position by bumping against a bush, firing handgun shots, and letting his field glasses show.

He chambered another round and scanned left and right for the real Nathan McBride.

Assuming McBride had fired the handgun at arm's length, he searched both sides of the fallen trunk but saw nothing until a very slow movement caught his eye on the left edge of his scope, farther and higher than he had imagined McBride could be.

He centered the crosshairs on the movement and felt a chill rake his body.

Impossible!

Well concealed near the top of an enormous root-ball, Nathan McBride was lined up on him.

Perfectly.

The movement he'd seen was McBride's left hand, waving good-bye.

In slow motion, he saw McBride's rifle wink.

Half a second after the muzzle flash burned his retina, he sensed an impact on his forehead.

* * *

Nathan's rifle bucked against his shoulder, but he hadn't antici-pated the level of agony it would cause. His vision grayed, then quit altogether. Blind and helpless, sudden dizziness and nausea ham-mered him. He remembered this sickening feeling well, recalled it with hideous clarity from his days spent in a Nicaraguan cage. He was seconds from passing out. How high was he perched in this root ball? Five or six feet? High enough to snap his neck on impact. As gravity pulled him headfirst toward the ground, his right leg slipped and hung up in the interior root tangle.

He felt and heard his shinbones snap.

Tib-fib. One-two. Oh man, that's a bad deal.

I'm so sorry, Harv. Sorry I let you down...

Just before his head struck the earth, Nathan Daniel McBride closed his eyes, and for the second time in his life, waited for the mercy of death to take him.

CHAPTER 30

"ETA one minute," General Mansfield said.

Flanked by two Black Hawks, Harvey flew Nathan's Bell 407 toward the canyon. Sitting next to him, Mansfield was coordinating the approach as the V-shaped formation of helicopters screamed over the town of Dupuyer. Harvey glanced at his watch, early by nearly twenty minutes. Nathan would just have to deal with it. No way in hell Harvey was waiting the entire two hours.

"We don't know what to expect up there," Harvey said. "We could take ground fire from Bridgestone. He could do some real damage with a sniper rifle."

"That's true, but if your partner is still alive, Bridgestone won't fire his weapon and give away his location. We don't have a lot of options at this point. I'm not willing to put men on the ground until we know what's going on."

"Agreed," Harvey said. "We'll be lucky to see anything at all. If they're engaged in a sniper fight, we won't see either of them."

"We should make a pass down the length of the canyon. Either McBride will signal us, or Bridgestone will shoot us. I hate to say this, but if Bridgestone managed to kill McBride, he might be long gone and it might be difficult to find your partner down there."

Harvey didn't want to think about that possibility. "Let's have your two birds fly the southern and northern rims of the canyon while we fly down the middle."

"Good plan." Mansfield passed the orders along.

The three helicopters cleared the canyon's rim and flew directly over the original landing zone where Nathan had set down. The Black Hawk on Harvey's right peeled off to fly the north rim of the canyon. The Black Hawk on the port side made a similar maneuver toward the south rim. Harvey slowed the Bell and expertly followed the canyon's streambed at thirty knots.

As he rounded the last horseshoe bend and had the rock spire in sight, the radio crackled to life. *"Civilian Delta, Rescue Alpha has a man down on the south rim. He looks dead."*

Before Mansfield could respond, Harvey pulled the transmit trigger. "Rescue Alpha, what is the downed man wearing?" Harvey looked up to his right, where the Black Hawk was orbiting in a tight circle above a bowl-shaped sandy formation on the rim.

"Can't say for sure, but I think it's digital desert."

Harvey felt relief wash over him. "Do you see anyone else? Our man is wearing woodland MARPAT under a ghillie suit."

"Negative, the casualty isn't wearing a ghillie suit."

"I'm going up there," Harvey said. He applied collective and climbed to the rim of the canyon. Fifty yards south of Leonard's body, he saw a sandy patch of clear ground surrounded by waist-high brush. He taxied over, made a landing, and throttled the RPM down. "I'll be right back. You've got her?"

"I've got her," Mansfield confirmed.

Harvey climbed out and sprinted across the rocky terrain, weaving his way through the brush and larger rocks littering the landscape. Overhead, the loud roar of the orbiting helicopter drowned out the Bell's engine noise.

Leonard Bridgestone lay facedown at the edge of the canyon's rim. The back of his head was gone. From the look of things, his rifle had been shouldered when Nate nailed him. Harvey stepped behind

Bridgestone and lined up on his position. Bone, scalp, and brain matter had been sprayed across the sand, and from the fan-shaped pattern, Harvey could approximate where the shot had come from. He sighted down Leonard's body and made a mental note of a huge downed oak near the streambed. Twenty seconds later, Harvey was strapped in and lifting off. When he descended into the canyon, there wasn't a good place to set her down except the wet sand of the stream-bed. In the center of the wash, nearly a foot of water still flowed.

"General, can one of your pilots test this LZ before I set her down? I don't have enough experience to try it."

"No problem." Mansfield called Rescue Bravo down to their location and ordered it to check the stability of the sand near the bank of the stream.

Harvey taxied Nathan's Bell away from the LZ so the Black Hawk could take his place. Thirty seconds later, the Air Force heli-copter was hovering over the moist sand. Its pilot carefully settled onto the wet surface, gradually putting more and more weight onto its skids until it was fully down. The skids sunk only a few inches into the wet sand before stopping.

The pilot radioed the results before lifting off again. "*You're good to go, Civilian Delta. Shouldn't be a problem lifting off again.*"

Mansfield cut in. "Rescue Bravo, set down and prepare for a medevac."

"*Copy.*"

Harvey hovered over, set the ship down, and started the shut-down procedure. Since General Mansfield was coming with him, he didn't want to risk the helicopter vibrating itself down into the moist sand by leaving its engine idling. It took an endless two and a half minutes before the engine was cool enough to cut its fuel for shutdown.

"Nice landing," Mansfield said. "Not bad for someone without a rating. Let's go find your friend."

With General Mansfield following, Harvey thrashed his way through the brush at the creek's northern bank and approached the fallen oak, but Nathan wasn't here. Panicked, he looked around. Nothing. But this had to be the place. Then he saw something, something out of place. Nathan's Predator knife, sticking straight up with its blade driven into a large branch attached to the fallen tree trunk. Harvey approached the knife and saw Nathan's Sig Sauer handgun tied to the top of the same branch. He frowned. A fishing line was attached to the trigger and looped around the butt of the knife. On the ground next to the branch lay Nathan's ghillie suit with a crude wooden cross inside. A broken pair of field glasses was attached to the crosspiece. A second fishing line, also attached to the crosspiece, was cleverly looped through a V-shaped area of one of the fallen oak's branches. Harvey now knew that Nathan had set up a dummy decoy, and from the look of the shattered binoculars, Leonard had taken the bait.

From over Harvey's shoulder, General Mansfield looked at the setup and whispered, "I'll be damned."

The two fishing lines were running out to the southeast, following the trunk of the fallen tree. Harvey worked his way along its length, maneuvering himself over and under dead branches until he saw a prone leg and combat boot screened by a boulder. He also saw blood, lots of it.

No. Dear God, no!

Harvey ran the remaining distance, thrashing through the underbrush.

His lifelong friend was lying at the base of a huge root-ball. Not moving. Two bloody spikes of bone were protruding through the material of his MARPAT just below his right knee. The fabric was soaked with blood, as was his right shirtsleeve and the upper half of his shirt.

"Aw shit, Nathan." He crouched down and held Nathan's head with his hands. "You can't be dead. You can't be."

Nathan spoke without opening his eyes. "Harv, what the hell are you doing? You're gonna give General Mansfield the wrong idea."

"Damn you, Nate, you scared the shit outta me."

"I feel terrible."

"You look terrible."

"Grangeland okay?"

"Yeah, she's gonna make it. You were right about her. She's tough as nails."

Nathan slowly brought his left arm up and looked at his watch, then let it fall. "You're early."

"So sue me."

"Did I get Leonard?"

"Yeah, you got him."

Nathan managed a smile. "It's over, then?"

"Yeah, it's over."

CHAPTER 31

Sharing a hospital room in Great Falls, Montana, Nathan McBride and Special Agent Grangeland were tired of watching the TV coverage.

Director Lansing got his headline, as promised. The two men at the top of his most-wanted list were dead, thanks to the highly trained professionals of the Federal Bureau of Investigation. In particular, to Special Agent Mary F. Grangeland, who was recovering from a gunshot wound received in the line of duty during the engagement against the Bridgestones in a remote area of western Montana. Every network covered the story. As a bonus, three million dollars in cash had been recovered from the scene, along with the balance of the missing Semtex.

Grangeland had insisted she be roomed with Nathan, even though such male-female room assignments were against hospital policy. She didn't care and wouldn't take no for an answer.

After being stabilized in the emergency room, Grangeland had undergone emergency surgery to remove a ruptured gallbladder and repair a torn liver. Even though much of its kinetic energy had been absorbed by the ballistic vest, Leonard's bullet had still passed through, missing her heart and lungs by less than two inches. Connected to machines monitoring every aspect of her bodily functions, Grangeland was outwardly in good spirits, but Nathan knew otherwise. This Ortega business had claimed another victim—alive, but another victim just the same.

Although Nathan's upper bicep injury wasn't serious enough to keep him in the hospital more than one night, the compound fractures of both his tibia and fibula were. Besides, he wasn't going anywhere until Grangeland got back on her feet.

"It's funny," Nathan said to her. "I never knew your first name until now."

"You never asked. I just thought of something horrible," she said.

"What?" asked Nathan.

"Did James Ortega know the truth going in, or did he find out under torture?"

Nathan looked at Harv. "I hope he knew going in. Try to imagine what learning the truth under those circumstances would've been like."

"It's hard to think about," she said.

Nathan spoke quietly. "I don't hate Frank Ortega for what he and Lansing did. And technically speaking, they didn't do anything illegal. Let's all keep that in mind."

Everyone fell silent for a moment.

"You know," Grangeland said, "you guys don't have to stay here and babysit me." She looked at Nathan. "The doctor gave you your walking papers yesterday."

"You trying to get rid of me?"

"I didn't say that."

"Good, 'cause I'm not going anywhere until Harv gets us that pizza he promised." Nathan felt a little better now. At least he had Grangeland and Harv smiling again.

"Then will you leave?" She gave him an innocent look.

"You know, Grangeland, making comments like that is what keeps our relationship healthy."

Nathan stayed with Grangeland for another day, grateful for the time off his feet. After Grangeland's near-constant reassurances that she was "going to live," he and Harv left Great Falls. Because Nathan's right leg was in a fiberglass cast from knee to ankle without a rubber walker on the bottom, Harv did all of the flying back to Sacramento. In another week, Nathan's cast would be replaced with a walking version. But for now, he had to avoid putting weight on it. On the flight south, he had to admit Harv seemed quite comfortable in the right seat. A few solo flights had done wonders to boost his friend's confidence. After landing at Sacramento Executive Airport, they rented a Taurus and Harv drove Nathan to Sutter Hospital under a deepening twilight sky. Harv dropped him off at the main entrance and said he'd be back in half an hour. Nathan used his aluminum crutches to maneuver himself through the automatic doors. Once inside, he diverted over to the gift shop for a quick purchase. It didn't feel right visiting Holly empty-handed.

As he hobbled his way toward Holly's room, his cell rang.

"Hello?"

"Nathan, it's your father."

"Hi, Dad, is everything okay?"

"I'm just leaving for a meeting with the president on this Bridgestone business."

"You're working late again."

"Damage control. I've only got a minute, but I wanted to talk with you first."

"Yeah, sure."

"I'm hoping to close the book on it."

"Fine by me," Nathan said. "Harv and I aren't planning to do anything, if that's what you mean."

"Not everyone would take that position. You were nearly killed."

"Because of my own mistakes on the ground. Believe me, Dad, we're willing to let it go."

"Are you sure?"

"I'm sure."

"You're far more forgiving than I'd be in your shoes. But I'm glad that's your decision. I don't want to see Director Lansing or former Director Ortega dragged through the dirt over this."

"I don't either."

"I'm going to let Lansing and the president know your position on this. It's not fair to let them twist in the wind."

"Yeah, I agree. What are you going to tell the president?"

"The truth."

"What will he do?"

"Lansing's his appointee, he doesn't want a scandal any more than I do."

Nathan stopped at Holly's door and lowered his voice. "I only have one request."

"Name it."

"Will you keep your eye on someone out here? Her career?"

"Sure, who is it?"

"The special agent in charge of the Sacramento field office. Her name is Holly Simpson."

"I'm writing it down. SAC Holly Simpson. Sacramento. I certainly will, to the extent I can. That's a promise."

"Thanks, Dad. I'd like to stay in touch more. Let's make the effort from now on."

"I'd like that."

"Me too. Take care, Dad.

"Take care, Nathan."

* * *

Nathan knocked softly on Holly Simpson's door.

"Come in."

Holding a dozen long-stemmed red roses, he hobbled into her hospital room. "Hello, Holly."

Her face brightened. "Hi, Nathan."

She was sitting up in the bed. Her hospital gown had been replaced with pajama-type garments with snaps holding them in place. The stainless-steel latticework supporting her legs was still there, but the colorful balloons and flowers were gone. He bent down and kissed her.

"How are you feeling?"

"Stir-crazy. I'm ready to get out of here."

"Where are your balloons?"

"I spread them around, we've got lots of wounded in here. How are *you* feeling?"

"Never better."

"Thank you for the flowers."

He set them down on a table and pulled up a chair. "We had a hell of a week, didn't we."

She took his hand. "Thank you for giving the reward money to the families. That was very generous of you and Harvey."

"We're glad to do it. You okay, really?"

"I'll never be able to pass through an airport metal detector again without setting it off. I've got more screws and plates than the Bionic Woman."

"Beats a wheelchair."

"Amen to that."

"How's Henning?"

"He's going to spend another week in a hospital bed. He's got all kinds of tubes and drains sticking out of him. He told me he looks like a Borg from a *Star Trek* episode, whatever that means."

"Are you and Director Lansing okay?" he asked.

"He knows I know about the Ortega-Bridgestone connection. I'm playing it cool, like it's no big deal."

"Good move. I'm sure he appreciates it. You've got a solid future in the FBI, Holly. You made some tough decisions, bent the rules. Very few people in your position have what it takes to make those kinds of choices."

She squeezed his hand and nodded. "The FBI's giving you and Harvey private awards for what you did."

They were both silent a moment.

"Are you heading back to San Diego?" she asked.

He nodded, didn't trust himself to say anything.

"I wish we'd met a long time ago."

"Me too."

"I can't help but wonder how different our lives would have been. You might be a father with six kids."

"Heaven help us."

"Don't sell yourself short, you'd be good at it."

"I appreciate you saying that."

"We shared something special. I know I've said this before, but I've never met anyone like you, and something tells me I never will again."

"I feel the same about you, Holly. Listen, I'm not very good at this. I'm not even sure I know how to say it…I'm not ready for this, for us right now. I'm not at a point in my life where I can make a solid commitment to you, and you deserve that. I'm not saying we can't still see each other. If we want to, it's just—"

"Nathan, it's okay. Let's just take things a day at a time and see what happens."

He bent down and kissed her on the lips. "I'll see you soon. I promise. But until then I'm really going to miss you."

She wiped her cheek. "Me too."

"I tell you what. I'll make a special trip up here, if you promise to go see *The Music Man* with me."

"Nathan McBride, it's a deal."

ACKNOWLEDGMENTS

I want to thank the following family and friends:

First and foremost to my wife, Carla. Simply stated, she's the most supportive and influential person in my life. Writing is a solitary endeavor and I couldn't have accomplished it without her patience and kindness.

And to my parents, Paul and Cindy, your love and support is not taken for granted.

To my brothers as well: Daniel, Matthew, and James. You guys are the best.

Next, to my freelance editors: Ed Stackler and Laura Taylor. You're more than my editors, you're my friends.

To my agent, Jake Elwell, of Harold Ober Associates. Thank you for representing me with class and excellence.

A warm thank you is owed to my editor, Alan Turkus, and rest of the Thomas & Mercer team. Amazon Publishing is an amazing company with talented and dedicated people.

Thank you to Ridley Pearson, David Dun, and Rebecca Cantrell for the outstanding cover blurbs.

Special thanks to Douglas Reavie, MD, FACS, for his generous help with the postbombing triage scene, and for allowing me to use him as a character in the book. Doug is not only the best plastic surgeon in San Diego, he's a kind and generous man who donates many of his hours to charity. It's an honor to consider him a friend.

And to Bill Thompson, who first believed in me as a novelist.

ABOUT THE AUTHOR

Photograph by Carla Martinez, 2010

A native of San Diego, Andrew Peterson won his first pellet-gun shooting competition at a young age, launching an award-winning competitive career in marksmanship and eventually earning the classification of Master in the NRA's High Power Rifle ranking system. A trained architect, he began writing fiction in 1990 and sold his first short story, "Mr. Haggarty's Stop," to *San Diego Writers Monthly* two years later. His debut novel, *First to Kill*, has allowed him the opportunity to visit veterans' hospitals around the country, and he has donated more than two thousand copies to wounded warriors and troops serving overseas. He and his wife, Carla, live in Monterey County, California

19277110R00216

Made in the USA
Lexington, KY
12 December 2012